Generation Dead

ALSO BY DANIEL WATERS

Break My Heart 1,000 Times

From OMZ Press:

Generation Dead
Generation Dead Book 2: Kiss of Life
Generation Dead Book 3: Passing Strange

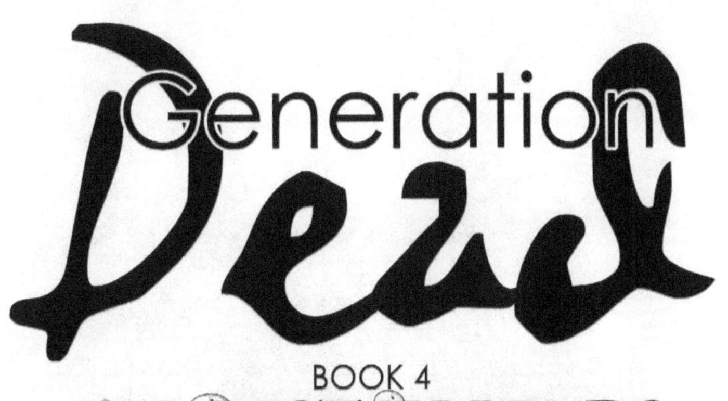

BOOK 4

MY BEST FRIENDS ARE DEAD

DANIEL WATERS

OMZ PRESS

Publication Credits

Published by OMZ Press in the United States

Cover art provided by:
Damonza.com

ISBN 978-0-9972942-6-2

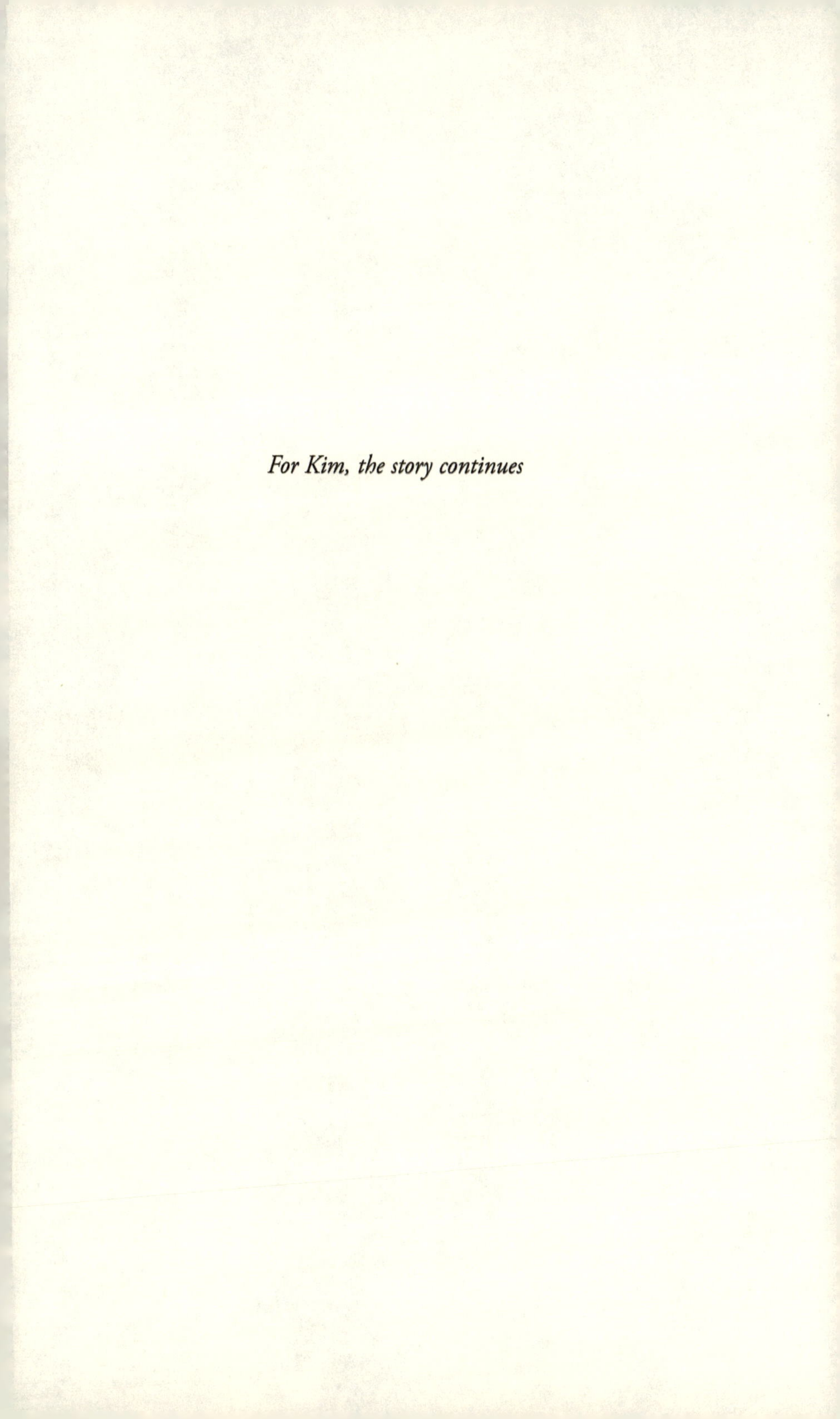

For Kim, the story continues

BOOK 4

MY BEST FRIENDS ARE DEAD

AUTHOR'S NOTE

Thank you for picking up *My Best Friends Are Dead*, the fourth book in the *Generation Dead* series. I'm happy to be repurposing the title, which I'd suggested early on as a marketing tagline for the first book (the "dead" was changed to "undead", which I thought much less provocative). The "friends" refers both to the characters in the books, many of whom are dead yet still walking around, and also to the stories themselves. *How's Life, Doll Parts,* and *Purpose Statement* first appeared as bonus stories, one each, in the electronic editions of the three novels, and they were collected with *My Dead Heart* and released as an "eBook exclusive" called *Generation Dead: Stitches. Still Small Voices, Melon Heads,* and *The Pain of Being Alive* are all original to this volume, as is *Passing Swiftly,* a *Break My Heart 1,000 Times* story. Readers of that novel know that ghosts appear with the same frequency as do zombies in the *Generation Dead* books, perhaps proving conclusively that, in fact, all of my best friends are dead. I'm thrilled that I get to resurrect all of these friends here in this book.

Also included are the collected entries from *My So-Called Undeath*, a blog I started writing prior to the publication of the first *Generation Dead* novel. There wasn't a lot of forethought put into the decision to do the blog; I loved the world I'd created and wanted to try out fictional material that didn't fit well in the novels. Tommy blogged within the pages of the novel and I thought it would be interesting and fun if his blog was also available to readers in the "real" world.

Most of the blog entries that follow were originally written and published over a couple of hours. I'd have an idea, write it in Blogger, read it through a couple times, run the spellchecker, and press the button to publish. Contrast that with the "traditional" publishing process, which for me involves multiple handwritten and typed drafts, rounds of vetting and editing, and publication dates set months in the future, and you have two distant poles of the publication spectrum.

The immediacy of publishing fiction through a blog was both thrilling and terrifying, especially as my "professional" publications at that point were minimal. What mitigated the terror and enhanced the thrill was the reader interaction. Readers would comment, sometimes as zombie characters, within minutes of Tommy posting a new entry. Tommy would answer back, a dialogue would ensue and often a new idea for a blog would spark. This interactivity was something entirely new to me in the experience of creating fiction, and I wondered if the buzz I got from eliciting and responding to the comments was similar to that of performing improv comedy or playing in a jam band, where the audience often becomes a critical part of the work. I cut Tommy's road trip from *Passing Strange*, so why not work some of it out in the blog, and get readers to suggest places for him to go? Colette and DeCayce have an intriguing relationship, but when was I going to get the chance to make them center stage in a book? Margi seemed to be a reader favorite but was never a primary POV character in the novels, doesn't she deserve a turn in the blog? Using the blog to provide fresh material to an enthusiastic audience, I felt, justified whatever weaknesses therein—Tommy was trying desperately to connect to his readership and draw attention to his cause; I was trying desperately to connect to a readership and draw attention to my work. Sooooooo cathartic!

Fun as it is, interactive art and entertainment isn't without its perils. Connectivity can become a drug which inhibits rather than enables an interior vision. As much as I enjoyed the collaborative nature of the blog, I was and remain fiercely resistant to the idea of the "main" storyline of *Generation Dead* being anything but my own. I've always known how the series will end. What I often said, truthfully, in interviews was that I wasn't certain how many books (or blogs, or stories, or multi-media performances) it would take me to get there. I still don't, but I feel like the horizon is drawing nearer.

I realized that whatever I wrote in the blogs needed to be *complimentary* to and not in *conflict* with the novels themselves—and so my hand needed to stay firmly on the narrative wheel if I wanted to reach that horizon. Mainly, that involved not disrupting the continuity of the novels, if I could avoid it—which I couldn't, really. The events depicted in *Generation Dead, Kiss of Life* and *Passing Strange* all occur within a single year despite being published over the course of three years, and I wrote the blog entries before, during and after those publications, trying to fill in gaps and enhance the readers' immersion and enjoyment of the world. Further complicating things (like Popeye in what might be my favorite single GD story, I can never seem to take the easier path), I was writing short stories that had very specific places in the continuity, some existing in the spaces between the published books and others occurring later and providing momentum for an additional novel. All of the material collected here from *Purpose Statement* onward occurs after the action of the first three novels. I've eliminated the posting dates and, sadly, the comments from the entries. I would have loved to include them here as part of the "story", but

I thought that another 200 pages of blog comments would tax the patience of even the most ardent GD readers (Erica & Yaz, I'm looking at you). Newlydeads are encouraged to seek them out at *MySoCalledUndeath.com,* which still inhabits a corner plot of the Internet cemetery.

Working in the *Generation Dead* world, no matter the medium, was nothing short of exhilarating for those years, even during the times I left the tenuous security of my high-wire and stepped out into open space. Every moment was fun, and when work and fun are one and the same, life is endlessly abundant.

Even creative work, though, can begin to feel like *work,* and the time comes to take a break. In my experience with writing it is best to do that before the fatigue begins to show up on the page. I'd been thinking about writing Karen's post-*Passing Strange* adventures on *MySoCalledUndeath.com*, but she and I had been through too much together for me to write with only half my heart in her story. I took a break, not from writing, but from writing *Generation Dead.*

We always return to the things we love, don't we? Sometimes we may wonder why we ever loved them in the first place, but usually our feelings return in a rush of passion and gratitude. My love for *Generation Dead* is so passionate and obsessive it borders on the pathological. I've begun work on a fifth book in the series, a novel. Provided that my (or Tommy's) previous readership finds this book, and that the series continues to find a *new* readership, I'll write and publish *Generation Dead* stories until I reach the horizon I've envisioned since writing that first scene of Karen walking across the Oakvale High cafeteria. Work and fun are once again united.

As always, I appreciate all that you do to support the differently biotic.

CONTENTS

MY SO-CALLED UNDEATH

MY LIFE AS A ZOMBIE

About Me

My name is Tommy Williams. I'm a junior at Oakvale High in Oakvale, Connecticut. I'm new to the area. I moved here with my Mom because she likes the school. We've got a cat named Gamera that hates me. We live in a trailer park near Lake Oxoboxo. Mom says it's temporary but I kind of like it.

My main hobby right now is writing, but I played football and baseball at my last school.

Oh yeah—I'm also a zombie.

Welcome

I'm Tommy Williams, thanks for stopping by MySoCalledUndeath.com. I'm currently a junior at Oakvale High School. I should be a senior but I stopped going to school for a while after I died.

I've been dead a little over a year now. My mother and I moved to Oakvale after she'd had a discussion with the principal, who told her that Oakvale High was not averse to admitting "living impaired" students. Their term, not mine. Zombie is just aces by me. Most of the other undead kids I've met prefer being called zombies, although there are plenty of other fun names to choose from.

Yes, I am being sarcastic.

There are quite a few of us zombies in Oakvale, and some attend school with me. The zombie kids with families are usually the ones that end up in school, I've noticed. The ones who were abandoned, or worse, driven from their homes by violent means are the ones that have the most trouble.

I'm going to be writing for those kids in this blog because they have zero voice in society. No one has figured out why so many American teens are coming back from the dead, but trying to figure out why it is happening is not going to be the main thrust of this blog, unless it is to comment on some of the more absurd theories out there as to why we exist. I'm sure I'll write about my good pal "Reverend" Nathan Mather, who believes that we zombies are demons, the harbingers of an impending apocalypse. I've read his cheery books—he's got a few out on us—and they sell really well despite being long, hateful tracts filled with speculation, lies and brimstone. Lots and lots of brimstone.

Enough of him for now. There are other people out there that want to help us, and I'll write about them, too.

But mostly I'll write about what "life" is like as a zombie. High school was hard enough when all we had to worry about was homework or the condition of our skin. Trying to get along when everyone else is alive and you're not is just murder sometimes.

Stupid Theory of the Day

Ok, I'm sorry to break the narrative thread here, but I just had to comment on the newest Zombie Creation Theory. Granted, the "scientific" community has already forwarded a number of wonderful theories for our existence, such as:

* mold spores
* hormones and food additives
* heaven being full (okay, that one wasn't cooked up by a scientist)
* first person shooter games
* syzygy (the straight-line alignment of three or more celestial bodies in a gravitational system) Apparently the Earth, moon, Pluto and of course the sun were all in alignment a week before Dallas Jones went undead. I actually like this theory
* global warming
* subliminal messages in downloadable mp3s (what?)
* Apocalypse (Not from a scientist either, although the Rev. Nathan Mather sometimes adds "PHD" to his by-line).
* childhood inoculations
* Halle-Bopp

And the latest and greatest:

Microwaved food

Yes, friends, I walk the earth because of generations of Williamses before me eating microwaved food. According to Dr. Andrew Coti, the microwave alters foods' DNA, which in turn altered my grandparents' DNA, then my parents, then mine, and the cumulative effect of all this DNA altering is that me and my dead pals get to live after death.

You know, it isn't even that I find this theory implausible (though I do) it's just that I'm so sick of every lab jockey with a test tube rushing to judgment about us after a half-baked (or half 'waved', I guess) experiment. Rather than rushing to market with your latest, mostly theoretical science project, why don't you spend some actual time and brain power trying to figure out what really makes us tick?

I wonder what would happen if we *ate* microwaved brains?

What are some of the zombie creation theories that you have heard?

Dead Man's Best Friend?

I read an article online today about zombie dogs. Seriously. If you Google "zombie dogs" you'll probably find it; scientists are trying to bring dead dogs back from doggie heaven. Glad to see the scientific community actually working on something useful. I can assure you all, however, that this is not how we were created.

I'm really hoping that Mom will let me get a zombie puppy to replace my cat Gamera, who hates me. I think she is prejudiced against undead people. Gamera, that is, not my mom.

Names Will Never Hurt Us

Don't know what to call your undead neighbor? Not satisfied with any of the following charming and colorful terms: deadhead, corpsicle, worm burger, worm bait, shambler, ole stinky, smelly, hellspawn, pokey, rotter, deadsy, Mr. Squishy, old meat, cold meat, maggot brain, oozer, Scary Mary, Raggy Annie, flaky, Rigor Morty, Frankenstein, stiff, graymeat, carcass, necro, necrophiliac, ubergoth, graver, deader, decomposer?

None of those suit you? Well, how about *Cadaver Vivens*, which is the suggested new genus/species name for zombiekind. Translated literally, it means "living corpse".

Yay.

Would anyone else like to contribute a suggestion? Or is everyone happy with "zombie"?

Dead Get to Vote, Living Dead Get Nothing

I saw an article in my home state about how lots of truly dead people are apparently voting each election. Apparently this is something that happens with some regularity in political elections, where some unethical soul rigs things so that lots and lots of dead folk "vote" for the unethical person's candidate of choice.

Meanwhile, I'm legally prohibited from getting my drivers' license. I can't open a bank account. Most lawmakers and educators outside the Oakvale school district are unclear if I should be allowed to attend classes. I can't even get a library card.

Ok, technically I'm not of legal voting age anyway but this kind of thing really makes me paranoid. I sense the dark hand of conspiracy in this one—for "thousands" of dead people to be voting, there has to be some sort of organized effort to make it happen. I picture a parade of white vans rolling up to the polling booths.

Wouldn't it be ironic if all those dead voters who were the ones keeping the anti-zombie politicians in office?

My Cat Hates Me

I really think my cat Gamera hates me. He rushes out the room whenever I enter, he makes a point of tossing kitty litter all over the floor when he knows I'm the only one home, and he chewed a big hole in one of my favorite basketball sneakers. You can tell me that he is just exhibiting normal feline behavior, by I think the truth is that he is prejudiced against dead people.

Then again, he wasn't overly fond of me when I was alive, either.

Pardonnez-Moi

A few weeks ago in my blog about zombie creation theory (*Stupid Theory of the Day*) I made a comment about eating microwaved brains. Based on the amount of email I received, and the amount of hassle I received from friend and foe alike, I thought I should write.

I apologize if the "brains" comment offended you. It was just a joke. Yes, I realize that it could be interpreted as perpetuating a negative zombie stereotype. Oh excuuuuse me, a negative living impaired stereotype. I did not mean to offend anyone, least of all my fellow undead brothers and sisters. Well, maybe I did mean to offend someone, namely the "scientists" that seem to be more interested in getting money and publicity than they do in actually helping undead Americans.

But really, people—I think we need to work on developing our sense of humor as much as we work on trying to learn how to talk and walk again. I know what we all go through on a daily basis just trying to exist in a country that for the most part wishes we would just stay dead. I fear that if we lose our sense of humor about our condition, it is only a matter of time before the rest of the country gets their wish.

Cat-tastic

I received an email from Lissa T., a zombie from Cincinnati, Ohio. Lissa wanted to let me know that since she died her only friend other than her little sister Tracy is her cat Gumball. After she died Lissa was no longer allowed to stay in her family's house, but her parents let her stay in a sheet metal tool shed at the edge of their property. Apparently Gumball likes to visit Lissa on the nights he gets locked outside. She said that in January and February Gumball liked to be wrapped in a blanket and sleep in her lap, but now that it is getting warmer she'd rather play.

So it appears that cats are not inherently prejudiced against zombies. It may well be that Gamera is just a jerk.

All the names in this post are changed except for Gamera's, because "Tracy" would be in major trouble if her parents knew that she was letting "Lissa" in the house to watch TV, use the computer, play Wii, etc. with her when they weren't home.

Gumball was the best I could come up with, sorry.

Does anyone else have any zombie-loving (or hating) animal stories?

Not Another Cat-Related Post

Today was the first day in three that it wasn't raining, so I went for a walk in the woods behind the trailer park. I don't know how long I was walking; time doesn't mean quite the same thing when you are dead, and we don't fatigue. Eventually I ended up at a lake. I sat down on a fallen tree on the shore and watched the water glitter.

After sitting awhile—it could have been minutes, it could have been hours—a butterfly alighted on my hand, and then I had two things to watch: the glittering water, and the butterfly poised upon my hand, slowly opening and closing bright wings as though stretching in anticipation of a long journey. The butterfly remained on my hand for a few minutes—or it could have been hours—and then fluttered away out over the lake.

It was a start, I thought.

Happy Mother's Day

Today I just want to take a moment to say thank you to my mother, Faith Williams, for everything she does to support me. I am so, so fortunate to have a mother like Faith, who has stood by me through my death and everything else.

I'm especially thankful because many zombies are disowned by their parents, not allowed to return to their homes or, worse, driven from them. If anything, my death and the death of my father has brought us closer together. Faith is always there for me and I know she always will be.

I love you, Mom.
T

I Miss Sleep

Also cheeseburgers, driving, the feel of sunshine on my face, team sports. Among other things.

For the zombies—what do you miss the most about being alive?

For the living—what do you think you would miss the most if you were a zombie?

I Don't Miss Mosquitoes

Or colds, stubbed toes, shaving, or having to get up in the middle of the night to go to the bathroom.

How about you? What don't you/wouldn't you miss?

Lame Joke of the Day

What do you call three zombies in a hot tub?

Lame Joke of a Brand New Day

The answer to the lame joke from the last blog: *stew*

This one isn't quite as offensive as the last.

What does a vegetarian zombie eat?

That Voodoo That You Do

The answer to the lame joke from the last blog: *Graaaiiiiins*

LATEST ZOMBIE CREATION THEORY: Our country has fallen victim to a voodoo curse placed upon it by a disgruntled witch doctor. Why the witch doctor was disgruntled at us, or how we could go about gruntling him/her and get the curse lifted is unclear.

I swear, people aren't even *trying* to come up with a realistic explanation any more. It seems more and more the "theories" offered are subtle attempts to demonize us—if we are the result of a voodoo curse, we must be evil. If we are harbingers of the end times, we must be evil, etc.

I was talking to Karen the other day and she said we should just come up with equally crazy theories that make happy fluffy associations in people's minds, instead of the dark/monstrous associations that are being made. As an example, she said that we were created when bee pollen fell onto our bodies from honeybees on their way to pretty flowers. This doesn't make any more or less sense than any of the other wacky ideas out there.

BTW, "gruntling" isn't a word, but I wish it was.

White Vans

I've seen a white van parked at the edge of the trailer park twice now. The second time I went outside to go take a look at the driver but I was still coming down the steps when it started up and drove away. I didn't see the driver or the plates. The white paint gleamed in the sunlight, making the vehicle look new or at least recently washed. There weren't any windows in the back, and the ones at the front were tinted. I've seen a similar van—or the same one—parked across the street from my school. I've never seen anyone get in or out of the vehicle.

I'm sure there are hundreds of thousands of white vans driving the roads of America, so I'm sure that my writing about them just makes me seem like a paranoid dead teen. But I do think that it is odd that out of the dozen or so articles I've found on the web regarding zombie abductions, two of them mention a white van as possibly being involved in the abduction. The detail stands out to me, mainly because such articles rarely have any detail at all beyond "a living impaired youth was reported taken"—half the time that's all you get, as though we don't have names.

Most zombie abductions—and reterminations—go unreported

by traditional news sources, the stories surviving only as oral histories passed on among undead teens. Almost every zombie I know has known another that has been taken or reterminated. Even prior to starting this website and getting word of similar stories from around the country I personally knew three zombies that aren't to be found anymore. What happened to one of the three was a deciding fact in my mother's decision to move us to Oakvale.

So maybe I'm a paranoid maniac. Or maybe you ought to watch yourselves when you see shiny new white cargo vans parked and running on the shoulder of the road.

White Vans, Part II

I'm sorry I haven't posted for a few days. Some days I'm just dead on my feet.

Sorry, just a little zombie humor, there. So yesterday I looked out the window and thought I saw a white van pull into the driveway of the trailer next to ours. I couldn't see it once it was parked, though, because the drive is on the other side of the trailer.

I went outside to investigate. I know I was being stupid, because Mom was at the hospital ministering the sick. So just Gamera and I were at home, and Gamera would probably love it if someone wrapped me in an old rug and threw me in the back of a van. But it was a bright sunny afternoon, so I didn't think they'd try anything. One of my neighbors was out working on his car, also. Besides, I'm the only dead person in the park, so if they had any business here at all, it was with me.

I went down the steps and crossed the space between our yards, trying not to drag-step too much. It's something I've been working on and have been mostly successful, but it is one of those things, like a nervous twitch or expression that I'm sometimes not even aware I'm doing it. But I got to the edge of the trailer and started to peer around the corner when the van kicked into gear and started roaring back down the driveway in reverse.

I got a really good look at the van and the driver. I got a totally clear look at the huge Fed Ex logo on the side. The driveway, when she saw me peeking at her like a moron, even smiled and waved at me.

How embarrassing.

A Thought for Summertime

It's getting hot outside. Don't forget to wear sunscreen.

I do. It works really, really well.

The Voice of Generation Dead

I was at the Haunted House the other day with Karen. We were looking at the "Wall of the Dead", where we post up all of the photos of zombies that we've taken or that people have sent us, and I commented that there were about twice as many as there were just a couple months ago.

Takayuki was playing cards on the floor with Tayshawn and this new kid everyone calls Popeye. Popeye is kind of weird—he never takes his sunglasses off, for starters, and he thinks he's an artist or something. Anyhow, he hears me make this comment and says "And we owe it all to you, Tommy Williams—the voice of Generation Dead." Imagine your most sarcastic friend using his/her most sarcastic tone, with a few speech pauses, and you'll be pretty close to how Popeye sounded.

Tak told him to shut up and play. Tak and I don't see eye to eye on a lot of things, but there's a grudging respect between us, I guess. Popeye did like he was told but his words got me thinking. I was standing there, looking at all these zombie kids, most of them lost or forgotten or abandoned, and his words rang in my ear. I almost felt dizzy.

"Don't be mad, Tommy," Karen said, like she could sense what I was feeling. She's got a habit of knowing my thoughts. "Even though he was being a jerk, he's right. And it's a good thing."

I hope she's right. About me being the voice, and about it being a good thing, because I'm not so sure.

There's more kids on that wall every day.

The Zombie Meme

Phoebe wrote this, and thought it would be a fun thing to do on the site. The first person she gave it to was Jacinta, a newlydead at the Haunted House. Phoebe's plan is to have as many zombies as possible fill it out, so feel free to cut and paste an answer.

Why she wants to do this, I have no idea. She also says that if you have any other good questions to post them.

The Zombie Meme

1. How did you die?
2. How long have you been gone?
3. Death age/true age?
4. What do you miss most about being alive?
5. What, if anything, is cool about being a zombie?
6. How did your family react to you coming back?
7. Most humiliating moment as a zombie?
8. Visible signs of zombiism?
9. Goals/ambition?
10. "If I were alive today, I would…"

Jacinta's Meme

1. **How did you die?** I can't tell you, it's way too pathetic and embarrassing. Let's call it "Death by Misadventure"

2. **How long have you been gone?** 3 months, 7 days, six hours.
3. **Death age/true age?** 14/14. I would have turned fifteen in October.
4. **What do you miss most about being alive**? My friend Cassandra. Her mother won't let her speak to me.
5. **What, if anything, is cool about being a zombie?** Not having to go to bed.
6. **How did your family react to you coming back?** With surprise! But my parents were actually really happy. My little brother gets mad because he says I get all the attention now.
7. **Most humiliating moment as a zombie?** Being pelted with rocks by kids I used to babysit for.
8. **Visible signs of zombiism?** I have a really, really bad scar that I keep covered at all times. I'm very, very slow, too.
9. **Goals/ambition?** To live again!
10. **"If I were alive today, I would…"** listen to my parents more. OMG did I just type that????

Colette's Meme

1. **How did you die?** I drowned in Lake Oxoboxo
2. **How long have you been gone?** About nine months
3. **Death age/true age?** 16/16
4. **What do you miss most about being alive?** Hanging out with my friends
5. **What, if anything, is cool about being a zombie?** Nothing
6. **How did your family react to you coming back?** My father chased me off our lawn when I came back, and then my parents moved away without telling me where they were going.

7. **Most humiliating moment as a zombie?** See #6
8. **Visible signs of zombiism?** I'm very pale and very slow.
9. **Goals/ambition?** To find my older brother—I want to know what my parents told him about me.
10. **"If I were alive today, I would..."** Talk to my parents about zombies and encourage them to be more understanding.

Mal's Meme

The following meme is from Mal, the largest zombie I know. Mal doesn't talk a whole lot, but he's sweet on Karen (who isn't) and he gave it to her. She and Phoebe are really into this meme thing for some reason.

1. **How did you die?** Shot in the back
2. **How long have you been gone?** two and a half years
3. **Death age/true age?** 18/20
4. **What do you miss most about being alive?** My grandmother's cooking, working out, my little boy. Not in that order.
5. **What, if anything, is cool about being a zombie?** No more pain. Physical pain.
6. **How did your family react to you coming back?** My ex-girlfriend won't see me and she won't let me see my son. I still visit my grandma, though it is hard for her.
7. **Most humiliating moment as a zombie?** Not seeing my son since I died
8. **Visible signs of zombiism?** Bullet holes in my back. Slow as molasses.
9. **Goals/ambition?** See my son one last time, even if he doesn't see me.
10. **"If I were alive today, I would..."** Be something I never tried to be... a father.

We Are Now Experiencing Technical Difficulties

If you tried to post this week, you might have noticed that your posts did not take right away. I think that anti-zombie hackers are responsible.

Some of the posts that you made appear under my name because that was the only way I could rescue them from the hackers. Sorry for any convenience.

Mal and Colette, BTW, thank you all for the outpouring of support. Your posts have caused a number of the Haunted House crew to do memes which Phoebe and Karen will get to me for posting in the near future.

Plus, it is great so many of you from around the country are contributing your stories as well.

Popeye's Meme

I don't know how Karen got Popeye to do this—must be the sweet talk.

Be advised, his relationship with the truth (and reality) is somewhat tenuous. I think they decided to "just be friends".

1. **How did you die?** I was struck by lightning
2. **How long have you been gone?** Three years
3. **Death age/true age?** Eighteen/Twenty-one
4. **What do you miss most about being alive?** Nothing
5. **What, if anything, is cool about being a zombie?** Everything about being a zombie is cool, especially the reduced ticket prices at the theater. Tak and I went to see Frozen this weekend.
6. **How did your family react to you coming back?** They were so jealous of me they threw me out of the house.
7. **Most humiliating moment as a zombie?** When other zombies don't understand my art.

8. **Visible signs of zombiism**? I am an artist, and my art is performing Bodifications, which are even more radical than piercings or tattoos. I did ones on my left rib cage, left calf, and left shoulder. Plus, there's the reason for my nickname.
9. **Goals/ambition?** To be the greatest zombie artist—and therefore the greatest artist, period—ever
10. **"If I were alive today, I would…"** Pray for the day I could become a zombie.

Zombie-sploitation

I've been approached by Skip Slydell, owner, CEO and mail clerk of Slydellco for a possible business venture. Slydellco, you may be aware, are distributors of such fine products as the *Z* and *Lady Z* lines of cosmetics and personal hygiene products, not to mention a whole line of what my trad friends like to call "inactive wear"—t-shirts with pro-zombie slogans like "Some of My Best Friends are Dead" and "Open Graves, Open Minds".

Skip wants to pay for me to put banner ads for his products on the site. I've purposefully tried to shy away from any corporate sponsorship, but there are some zombies in the Haunted House that think we could put the money to some good uses. Others, of course, are totally opposed. I asked Tak and his reply was "I don't even know why you would talk to a beating heart." Real helpful, that guy.

I'm torn. While I've written before about how cheesy I think Skip's profiteering is, he *does* use a percentage of his profits for pro-zombie causes. And despite their sometimes goofy message, I do think his products end up increasing awareness for our plight. To be totally forthcoming, I myself wear *Z* occasionally and am told it smells nice.

But straight-out corporate sponsorship? I don't know. I think I'd feel kind of icky.

What do you think?

Get Animated!

With the recent debate about whether or not I should accept corporate funding from Skip Slydell, and with an election coming, I've been trying to think of creative ways to advance the cause of getting rights for the differently biotic. Many of us have been dead long enough to be legal voting age—if in fact our citizenship hadn't expired when we did—but until Proposition 77 passes, and anti-zombie legislation like the Undead Citizens Act defeated, we don't really have any legal recourse.

I've been corresponding with a zombie in Ohio named Buttercup (she insists that is her real name, and she claims to be a third generation hippie) who has given me some good ideas, and after talking with the Haunted House crew we decided we would start brainstorming some ideas to affect positive social change—primarily for zombies, but in a way that would be good traditionally biotic people as well.

We're calling it the "Get Animated!" campaign (Get it? "Animated" as in "excited", and also "animated corpse". I thought it was a clever joke. Guess who thought of it?).

What are some of your ideas on how we can work together to make the world a better place for zombie and trad alike?

Karen's Meme

1. **How did you die?** I'd rather not say
2. **How long have you been gone?** 2 years
3. **Death age/true age?** 16/18
4. **What do you miss most about being alive?** Sensation

and unconditional love. I also wish my sister Caitlyn had been born when I was still alive so that I'd know what it really felt like to hold her.

5. **What, if anything, is cool about being a zombie?** Don't have to sleep, don't have to diet.
6. **How did your family react to you coming back?** They didn't kick me out, which is something. I think they were more hurt about the way I died than me coming back. My father seems to be "coming around" a bit more than Mom and treats me as though I were human. Almost. Caitlyn was born about nine months after I died. I suppose that is a reaction, of sorts!
7. **Most humiliating moment as a zombie?** See above. Also I have to live in the basement even though there is an extra bedroom upstairs. Oh well, at least the basement is furnished!
8. **Visible signs of zombiism?** My skeery skeery eyes, which I'm told look like diamonds, and my pale skin and bleach blonde hair.
9. **Goals/ambition?** To live—*really* live—again!
10. **"If I were alive today, I would..."** Not do what I did.

Clean Up Your Mess

I got a hate mail post the other day, but unlike most of the hate mail posts we get here at MySoCalledUndeath.com, this one actually made me think.

Basically, the poster's point was that we should think about what kind of world and culture we leave for future generations. Unfortunately, the poster (anonymous, of course)could not seem to make his or her point without cursing, and he/she went on to say that I am polluting the minds of children by writing about zombie-based concerns. I supposes s/he feels that I am also polluting the planet just by walking around, so what can you do. If it wasn't for the language (well, and the re-death threat) I would have liked to publish the post because I think it would have made for an interesting discussion.

But even a dark cloud can produce a flash of light. What kind of world and culture *are* we leaving for future generations? Or creating for ourselves, for that matter.

Faith, my Mom, has a tendency to divide the people of the world in two basic camps: Givers and Takers. She doesn't think it matters what race, gender, nationality, preference, or age you are, whether you are the president of a major world power or a walking mushroom, you are either a giver or a taker. Givers, she'll explain (but you have to ask) are defined as people who "leave things better than how they found them", and takers "subtract—they ruin things for everyone."

It's easy to be a taker. Being a giver is much harder, because quite often in "giving", you might inadvertently "take away" from someone else. Not to beat my own drum, but I thought I was being a "giver" when I went out for the football team. Certain people—teammates, coaches, and people in the community—obviously felt that I was "taking".

It's something to think about.

Tayshawn's Meme

1. **How did you die?** Acute asthma attack on the baseball field
2. **How long have you been gone?** About six months
3. **Death age/true age?** 16/16
4. **What do you miss most about being alive?** Sports
5. **What, if anything, is cool about being a zombie?** Nothing

6. **How did your family react to you coming back?** Not so great
7. **Most humiliating moment as a zombie?** Being so slow
8. **Visible signs of zombiism?** My skin is now ash gray
9. **Goals/ambition?** None
10. **"If I were alive today, I would…"** Make sure I've got my inhaler

Tak's Meme

Hi, sweeties! Karen DeSonne, girl reporter here! I wanted to bring you Tak's Meme today, and I thought he'd play nice because his "old school" bff's Popeye and Tayshawn gave theirs. Here is a fairly accurate transcript of my interview with him, which I conducted on the rotting porch of the Haunted House.

Karen: "Hi, Tak!"

Tak: (Stares, half his face hidden by his beautiful long black hair)

Karen: "Do you mind answering a few questions for the zombie meme? We just put Tayshawn's up at mysocalledundeath."

Tak: (Stares some more, cracks knuckles)

Karen: "Okay, then. Let's get started, shall we? Question number one: How did you die?

Tak: (Flips hair back, revealing hole in cheek, molars) "I was… never… alive."

Karen: (Taps pen, tilts chin, smiles prettily) "Now, be nice, Takky. I happen to know that you were killed riding your motorcycle on the Garden State Parkway. You told me yourself in an unguarded moment!"

Tak: (Turns away, makes noise like piece of paper caught in electric fan)

Karen: (Flutters long lashes) "Okay, let's try this one: How long have you been a zombie?"

Tak: (Hides scars with hair-flip, looks away)

Karen: (Sparkly eyes narrowing) "Let me try that again. How… long… have… you been… a… zombie?"

Tak: "Why are you… pandering… to the… beating hearts, anyway?"

Karen: "We aren't 'pandering' to anyone, we're trying to raise consciousness and…"

Tak: (Gives dismissive wave, jumps off porch, walks towards woods)

Karen: (Shouting) "So I guess the interview is over, then?"

There it is, kiddies! The deepest, darkest secrets of that cutie, our very own teen heartthrob, Takayuki!

(P.S.: Sarcasm aside, Tak really isn't such a bad guy once you get to know him. He'll never win a merit badge in Plays Well With Others, tho. Bye!)

Missing Zombie

Has anyone seen or heard from Bobby Hoffman? He's a newlydead that came to the Haunted House at the beginning of the summer. No one here has heard from him in a week.

It doesn't seem likely that he would take off without letting any of his friends know what he was doing.

If you have any info, please post.

Change the Season Change Your Reason

Is it just me, or is it getting colder outside?

That's just a little joke. I don't really feel changes in temperature like that. But school has started, so I guess that would be an indicator.

Still no sign of Bobby.

Secret Mission?

So Tak, who hasn't been around much since he ditched Karen's attempt to get his meme, asks for "a meeting" at the Haunted House. For some reason he and I never just talk, we always have to have a "meeting". He tells me not to worry about Bobby because he sent him on, and I quote, a "secret mission". I couldn't get him to elaborate any further.

I don't know what scares me more, white vans or the idea of Tak sending people on secret missions.

But I thanked him anyway, and I let him know that the Hunter Foundation was still looking for people who wanted to participate in the Undead Studies class.

You should have seen his expression.

Respect My Authoritah

Just a quick note on Haunted House politics—a few of you have mentioned that I/we should have forbade Tak to let Bobby go on this "secret mission". Well, I just wanted to let you all know that no one here really has any authority to prevent someone from doing something. Everyone is here by choice (or at least, they are here because they don't have the choice of going home) and we try to keep things as democratic as possible. Tak and anybody else can come and go as they choose, and they don't really have to answer to anyone. I'd like to think that people would keep each other informed—but there aren't any "laws" that say they have to.

Bobby Update

Bobby came back last night like nothing had changed, apparently having completed his mission. I don't know what it was, and I don't really care. I'm just glad he's relatively safe.

Stranger Than Fiction

You know what one of the Top Ten things that many zombies list as being one of the things they miss most about life? Right after family, friends, pets, food, sleep or their favorite hobby?

School.

Karen and I are two of the lucky ones who have parents that insist we keep going to school. Many zombies that don't have a parent or legal guardian either can't get to school or aren't allowed to attend, and many school systems across the country don't allow *any* zombie students.

Of course, I wasn't feeling like one of the lucky ones yesterday after someone put a sign on my back. Instead of the traditional "Kick Me" it said "Kill Me". And instead of the traditional tape, whoever hung the sign used a thumbtack. I didn't feel it.

Mrs. Rodriguez was kind enough to remove the tack for me.

Don't get me wrong, though. Overall, I like school.

Virtual Wall of the Dead

We have a wall in the Haunted House where we've put up pictures of all the zombies we know in person or through the Internet. With some of the new Blogger features, we can do the same thing here on mysocalledundeath. Click the link under "The Wall" if you'd like to post your picture. Zombies and beating hearts alike are welcome.

Also, if you want to subscribe to the posts and/or the comments, click the links beneath the one for the wall.

Old School

No tacks were inserted into my body today, which is cool. There was a petition going around the school to ban zombies from the cafeteria, because apparently the very sight of us makes some students nauseous. There are a few zombies that have the same lunch period as I do—Colette Beauvoir and Kevin Zumbrowski, but I don't have any classes with either one of them. Most of the zombies, regardless of what age they are, are in a remedial-type classes, not necessarily because of any real learning disabilities or deficiencies, but more because they can't express themselves quickly enough. Karen (who seems to be the only other zombie in ""mainstream" classes" calls their condition "reverse A.D.D." Attention Surplus Disorder? Maybe someone can invent a zombie Ritalin which will get us to move faster. The school doesn't really seem to know what to do with us, but then again I'm not sure that schools knew how to deal with ADD kids back in the day, either.

I've got a couple classes with Thornton Harrowwood, a traditionally biotic boy who is unlike most of his trad peers in that he doesn't seem to notice I'm dead. Most people call him "Thorny". He'll ask me questions about it sometimes—what is it like being dead, do you ever sneeze, etc.—but just from being curious, not like he's trying to start something.

He's a pretty cool kid. I hope he doesn't take any heat for talking to me.

The Wall

Pretty impressive—since inviting people to send pics to the Wall of the Dead, we've had 41 people, zombies and trads alike, join. And what a good looking group we have.

You know what makes me happy? The fact that Rae, my bus driver, seems to not care that she has zombies on her bus. I wish that all of my teachers were the same way—they don't do anything really overt, but you can tell the ones who wish we'd just lie down already.

Sorry, folks. Not going to happen.

Gamera's Revenge

Proof Positive that my cat, Gamera, hates me: I came back from the Haunted House Sunday night to discover that he had shredded my History notebook, and I have a test this week. Such a dear, sweet kitty.

We Don't Need No Thought Control

Another twenty people—some zombies—have posted on The Wall. Very, very cool.

I think I'm ready for the History test. I've been studying with Phoebe, Margi, and Thornton J. Harrowwood, who prefers for some off reason to be called "Thorny". We usually go to Phoebe's or Margi's, because my mom's trailer isn't big enough and Mr. Harrowwood doesn't allow "corpses" in the house.

Thorny is a pretty competitive guy. He proposed that whoever got the lowest grade on the history test has to buy the others a milkshake at the Honeybee Diary. Margi smacked him, and it took him a minute to realize that I don't drink milkshakes anymore.

I told him he can buy me the new issue of *Batman* when he loses.

Detained!

Hello! Karen DeSonne, intrepid undead girl blogger here!

Tommy is letting me take the blog today. He's off studying (and for those that care, he got a 97 on the History test that Gamera tried to help him fail). He's such a smartie—I can't say that all the extra time I get with not sleeping has improved my study habits at all. I'm B minus all the way.

I manage to keep things interesting, though. On Friday on was given a detention by Principal Kim because the length of my skirt violated some arcane dress code policy. I tried to point out that my skirt was no shorter than those worn by the Oakvale High cheerleading squad, but that didn't get me anywhere. Then I told the principal that I was proud of her for not going easy on me because I was a zombie, that her universal and non-prejudicial application of stupid, outdated rules was to be commended.

She told me I better zip my lip and get to my next class if I didn't want her to double the detention.

Oh well. Time, I've got.

History Test

The final results:

Tommy: 97
Phoebe: 97
Margi:91
Thorny: 91

Margi and Thorny have to split the milkshake bill and my comic book. Thorny lost most of his points on the multiple choice questions, Margi got all of those but got marked off for her essay.

Thorny asked me if I wanted to go double or nothing on the quiz we have coming up: not above trash talking, I told him he might as well buy me a subscription now and end the suspense.

Kevin's Meme

Kevin Zumbrowski's meme, as collected by Karen and posted by me:

1. **How did you die?** An illness that I don't want to talk about. Even though I'm dead I still have nightmares about it.
2. **How long have you been gone?** A year
3. **Death age/true age?** 15/16
4. **What do you miss most about being alive?** I had a great collection of action figures.
5. **What, if anything, is cool about being a zombie?** Nothing
6. **How did your family react to you coming back?** My parents thought I was a monster and wouldn't let me come home. My uncle drove me all the way from New Hampshire to drop me off at the Hunter Foundation.
7. **Most humiliating moment as a zombie?** Not being able to speak quickly so everyone thinks I'm dumber than I really am.
8. **Visible signs of zombiism?** I'm slow, pale, and not growing.
9. **Goals/ambition?** I'd like to have another family someday
10. **"If I were alive today, I would..."** Be happy with what I have.

All in All

Sweet—we now have over a hundred people—zombies/beating hearts/trads/differently biotic and maybe even some vampires (they aren't real, are they?).

Congrats to Erin!Mal for being #100. You will be given a hall pass when the inevitable zombie invasion occurs.

I'm just kidding.

About the hall pass.

I mean the zombie invasion.

Seriously.

Anyhow, if each of you were to recruit one more person, we'd have 200 people "on the wall". Two hundred and two, actually, thanks to our one hundred and first member, TheRealDeal04_Vamp.

Costumes

Hello!

Karen here, with a quick Halloween update. We've decided to have the first annual Haunted House Haunted House party this Halloween, in lieu of the treats that most of us have no use for (we're going to avoid tricks for the time being also, actually). I've done a quick poll of some of our friends to see what they are planning on going as, and here's what they told me, along with my own editorial comments:

Phoebe: A flapper (ooooh, pretty, I bet!)
Margi: Countess Bathory (Huh?)
Tommy: A zombie (jerk!)
Colette: "Evil Tinkerbell" (huh?)
Kevin: Rorschach (some sort of superhero, I guess)
Tak: (Stares sullenly, doesn't answer question)
Popeye: Pinhead (I won't tell you how he's making his "costume")
Tayshawn: Indiana Jones (Good for you!)
Adam: A zombie (big jerk!)
Sylvia: Hannah Montana
Melissa: Clown (Scary!)
Jacinta: "The Green Woman" (Not sure what this means, but apparently it involves wearing shrubbery)
Mal: Dumbledore (I can't wait!)

I was going to go as a "Traditionally Biotic Person" and dress in a way that I imagined would be incredibly ironic and funny, but

A). I started to think it was a lame idea when Adam and Tommy shared their "ideas", and B). I kind of dress that way all the time, anyway.

So I need your help: What should my costume be?

What are you going as?

Ideas, people! (And please—don't tell me I should be a cheerleader!)

Bye sweeties!

Halloween Recap

I just have to say that Karen was an exceptional Jeannie. And Phoebe was stunning as a flapper. I wanted to reread *The Great Gatsby* while listening to the Squirrel Nut Zippers after seeing her.

I didn't dress up, but I did hand out two Snickers bars to kids that trick or treated at the trailer park where I live. They're nice kids.

We had a little gathering at the Haunted House—we didn't get any Trick or Treaters, but Margi and Phoebe stopped by after driving Kevin and Karen around to look at the little kids going around Oakvale Manor.

Did I mention that Margi has her drivers' license? There, I just told you a horror story. Who says I don't have any Halloween spirit?

T.

The Creepiest Thing

Today my Mom was driving us down to the beach (I know, it's a little cold but it is nice to walk along the boardwalk when no one else is around). We saw three identical white vans in a row, maintaining distance and driving the same speed. Not like soccer-mom minivans either, but the larger cargo vans with no windows except in the cab and small ones on the back doors.

She made me get down in my seat when she passed them. She said she couldn't see much, except that each van had a male driver and passenger wearing what looked like dark blue jackets and blue ball caps. Every one she could see was wearing sunglasses as well, even though it was kind of a gray day.

She said the driver of the lead car is the only one that looked over at her. She wasn't sure, but she thought he might have given her a little nod.

She didn't want to go to the beach after that, but I insisted. We actually had a pretty good time. The seagulls don't care that I'm dead.

Haunted House

I went to the Haunted House today after school. As usual, people were fighting over what to listen to. As much as everyone fights about it, though, music seems to be the quickest way to find common ground when people are in the right mood. We ended up listening to some industrial noise band that Popeye likes. Not my kind of thing, but Kevin, who is kind of a classic rock guy, and Jacinta, who is pop all the way, said that they liked it. Kind of hard to dance to, though.

What's on your iPod right now?

The Zombie Horde Grows

Wow-we've got over 200 people on the wall! I feel so happy that there are so many people out here supporting the differently biotic I almost feel… alive. Thank you all so much.

Plus, I've always secretly harbored a desire to be part of a horde.

Giving Thanks

I'm very thankful for all of you, my friends, zombie and trad alike.

And I'm very thankful just to be here.

I really, really, really wish that I could have some turnip tomorrow

Our Thanksgiving

I watched Faith eat part of a turkey pot pie (one of the big square ones) with slices of canned cranberry sauce on the side. She even fed Gamera some pieces of the crust from the table.

Afterwards we drove over to the Haunted House where she gave all my dead friends hugs in lieu of pie. I miss pumpkin pie almost as much as turnip; I must have had a thing for round, orange foods. Like oranges. We stayed there until late at night, when the cold that none of us but her could feel started seeping through her coat. The kids were sad to see her go, but they were the happiest I've seen them since before Karen and I and a few of the others went back to school.

Thanks, Mom.

Zombies in the Mall

Went to the mall this weekend with Margi and Phoebe to do some holiday shopping. I wore a heavy coat, big scarf and big ski hat so that no one would see I was a zombie, not because I'm ashamed of who I am but because I really didn't anyone hassling the girls. I picked up a few presents for my Mom.

As we were walking around, Phoebe had the great idea of having a bunch of us chip in on little presents for the Haunted House gang, but we really didn't see anything that jumped out (we did see some plastic glow in the dark zombies, but they were really zombified, old school zombies and I don't think most of the kids would appreciate the irony).

We need some ideas. We're thinking small and relatively inexpensive. Can any of you help?

The Spirit

Great, great news on the Zombie present drive. Three amazing things—

A. Everyone who is participating in the work study at the Hunter Foundation has offered to donate one weeks' pay to "the cause".

B. The Hunter Foundation is donating a Wii along with a few games—Rock Band, Tennis, and Bowling. There's some stuff they are asking us to do—they want us to keep track of progress in the games to see if playing has any effect on zombie motor control. I didn't have the heart to tell them we don't have a television at the Haunted House; maybe one will turn up.

C. I emailed Skip Slydell about what we were trying to do and he sent along (overnight!) a generous assortment of Slydellco. samples and products, including

Z, *the body spray for the active Undead Male*
Lady Z, (which, although there's no tag line, is presumably for the Active Undead Female)
Kiss of Life lip gloss
Arise! Invigorating Facial Cleanser (Invigorating?)

...and various shampoos, conditioners, and skin creams "specially formulated for active undead teens". There were also a few shirts and hats in the big box with some of his new designs. The one I liked most was a black shirt that says *I Wasn't Finished* in an elegant white Gothic script.

(All products trademarked by Slydellco.)

Things are shaping up for a festive holiday season at the HH. Let's hope nothing happens to wreck it all.

The Gift List

This is what we've been able to buy for the Haunted House zombies thus far:

4 sets of magic markers
2 boxes of blue pens
1 box of black pens
1 package of pencils
1 huge box of copier paper
8 wire bound notebooks
two pencil sharpeners, a stapler, three pairs of scissors, one of them left handed
17 books
A four person hovercraft
Various balls, Nerf and otherwise
Two baseball gloves and a bat
14 assorted stuffed animals of various sizes
2 decks of cards
The game of Life
The Dungeons and Dragons core rulebook set, with two sets of dice
A lava lamp
A huge pile of clothes from Goodwill.

Many thanks to Phoebe and Margi for picking all this stuff up. We've still got some money left and the consensus seems to be more art supplies.

PS I was just kidding about the hovercraft

Holiday Report

Faith and I went to the Haunted House on Christmas morning after exchanging presents. She bought me a nice pair of hiking boots and some other hiking gear and clothes; I went with an "all living" Christmas theme this year, giving her two potted plants, a cactus, and a hermit crab in a tank. Have you ever tried to wrap a cactus?

Karen and Margi made it over to the HH, but neither Adam nor any of our other beating heart friends were able to come, which is too bad because we had a blast. The zombies had decorated a tree outside because they didn't want to cut one down for the inside. There were some decorations inside, and even Popeye got into the spirit by walking around wearing some ornaments. I won't tell you what he did with the hooks, though. Mal played Santa, wearing a hat and beard that Karen had picked up for him. Pretty much everyone from the HH community was there except for Tak.

The kids were pretty enthused about the gifts (no hovercraft as I mentioned, and we decided against the television and video games in the end), especially the art supplies. But you know what ended up being the hit gift of the whole event? Something that Karen (who swears she doesn't have a creative bone in her body) picked up: a spice rack.

Yes, a spice rack. The idea, she said, was that we could all use it to "practice" our sense of smell. How we're supposed to practice a sense I don't quite understand, but it was pretty interesting to everyone to discover that *almost* everyone could recognize cinnamon. I ended up being able to identify six of the seven spices on the rack, losing only to Karen, who edged me out of first place by correctly identifying turmeric. Turmeric? I don't think I could get that one right if I was alive, even.

"The sense of smell is our sense most connected with memory," Karen told everyone. This led to a number of people sharing cinnamon-infused memories of holiday's past, back when they were with their families, back when they were alive. It was a little nostalgic, a little sad, a little hilarious and mostly happy and heart-warming, the way all the best recollections are.

I thought I saw Tak drifting through the woods like a shadow when Faith and I were headed to the car to leave, but if it was him, he didn't answer when I called.

Helping the Horde Get Animated!

There are now more than three hundred people on the Wall, zombie and trad alike. I had no idea that we would get so much support in such a short time.

I've been thinking about how I want to make Get Animated! more impactful this year; I think it will involve more than playing school sports and going to school dances. I want to initiate real change.

Can you tell I've been emailing Skip? That's why sort-of words like "impactful" start showing up in my vocabulary.

TV with Margi V

Margi here. Thanks Tommy for letting me take over not that u could stop me mwah hah hah haaa. Watching television the other day with Colette because we are mad for Christmas specials. Rudolph, Frosty, Mr. Heat Miser, Abominable, and all of the other horrific Yuletide creatures. We were watching some festive show or other when, during a commercial break, we saw an advertisement for a video game filled with murder and face punching. Maybe there was a little mayhem, too. I don't really remember. Then there was another commercial for yet another video game.

This one was called Zombie Summer Camp.

The basic premise, or so I gathered, was that you are a ten year old kid named Jimmy who is sent away to Camp Attawaugan for summer vacation, and sometime during your first night away from home zombies invade the camp and start eating all the kids, some of whom return from the dead and try to eat you.

Onscreen we watched as Little Jimmy rammed a skewer with a flaming marshmallow on the end through the chest of an attacking zombie, driving the rotter back into the campfire.

I was about to make comment condemning the game when I realized that Colette was making that snorty snuffling noise that meant she was laughing.

"You think this is *funny*?

On screen, Jimmy was fending off three zombie cub scouts with a canoe paddle.

"Yes," she said. "I… do."

In the last sequence, Jimmy whipped a live squirrel at a dead camp counselor. We both started laughing then.

"Popeye… loves… this game," she said.

"Get out."

"Seriously. His favorite… weapon… is the… tent… spikes."

"He kills zombies? In the game?"

"He says it… is… cathartic."

I giggled some more.

"That Popeye is a weird kid," I said.

Anyway, I thought those were strange commercials to run during children's holiday shows.

"I wonder… what's on… ABC Family?" Colette said.

I changed the channel.

All Colette Wants for Christmas is…

Merry merry merry Christmas, everyone! Margi here. I found Colette's very zombie Christmas list! It's pretty weird. She's been naughty all year so I don't think Santa will be delivering:

* A set of electric traaaaains
* Bread made of whole graaaaains
* A pair of Great Daaaaaaaanes
* A box of candy caaaaaanes
* An umbrella to stay dry when it raaaaaains
* Aspirin to cure all her paaaaains
* Oxiclean to remove stubborn staaaaaains
* Drano to clear clogged draaaaains
* And of course, the thing a zombie like her needs the most,

braaaaaaaains! **Braaaaaaaains!**

Hee Hee! She hates when I do that. Actually she wasn't naughty at all and so I bought her a scarf. A pink scarf and maybe she will let me borrow it.

And what did *You* get from the jolly old elf this year?

A Word About Adam

A number of you have asked via blog commentary how Adam was doing, something that I'm sure he and all of us here at the Haunted House greatly appreciate.

I'm not going to lie to you. Things are really, really difficult right now. I've been asked to respect his family's privacy so I won't go into any further detail.

But we all remain hopeful. The ability to hope is perhaps the most powerful ability that humanity, living or dead, has, after our ability to love. Exercise both abilities frequently.

HOW'S LIFE?

"SO... HOW'S... LIFE?"

Margi looked at her friend. Colette was smiling, as much as she could smile. The left side of her face still didn't work very well; her lips curled upward on the right side of her mouth, but on the left they were still a thin, tight line. Still, Margi thought, even this was a remarkable improvement. A month before, Colette hadn't been able to move any of her facial muscles at all.

"Funny you should ask," Margi said. "Right now, it is actually kind of suckish."

"Still... beats... the alternative."

"Tell it to Adam," Margi said, looking out the window, out into the woods where Adam lost his life just a few weeks ago. Margi was on edge; she'd been putting this day off as long as she could, but now it was here. She and Colette were in the Haunted House, an old abandoned farmhouse on the edge of the Oxoboxo woods, where the differently biotic of Oakvale congregated. They were alone in what had at one time been the living room. Margi could hear low voices and shuffling from upstairs, but as yet she hadn't seen any of the other zombies who stayed at the house besides Karen, who'd traveled over in the van with them from the Hunter Foundation.

Colette hesitated before responding, and Margi felt ashamed for adding to her already considerable misery. Then again, Colette always hesitated before responding.

"Phoebe... looks... pale."

Margi had to stifle a giddy laugh that was fluttering around in her chest. But that's the way life, or "life," was for her and her friends lately, a constant stream of moments where you weren't certain if you should laugh or cry. Colette commenting on anyone's lack of pigmentation just added to the absurdity.

She, Colette, and Karen had taken the blue van back to the Haunted House after another depressing Undead Studies class. Phoebe was normally one of the most enthusiastic contributors to the class, but since Adam's death, she had sat in silence except when called upon. The class itself was down more than a few members, with Tayshawn having quit and Evan being reterminated, and newlydead Adam not having made an appearance since the tragic event. The class—and life in general—was suckish, just like she'd said.

"Phoebe spends all of her time with Adam now," Margi said. "Not that I blame her, or anything. But it has been a couple of weeks since he died, and he can't really talk or walk yet. That's got to be awful for her. For both of them."

Karen walked into the room, bearing a large stack of blankets. "These are for you, sweetie," she said to Margi, dropping the stack on the edge of the sofa. "In case you get cold."

Margi thanked her. Karen's smile, unlike Colette's, was natural in form. Her lips were a shade too pale and her eyes were like diamonds, but Margi thought she was the most beautiful girl she knew. She was wearing a light white blouse, short plaid skirt, stockings, and patent leathers. If anyone needed some blankets against the cold it should have been her, but zombies didn't feel the cold.

Karen's smile fluctuated a fraction, became a shade less warm and happy, as though she could sense that the bond between Margi and Colette was of a sort that excluded her, but Margi allowed that she may have imagined it, because surely the dead girl couldn't have that kind of precise control over her expressions.

"Well, then," Karen said after a moment. "I'll just leave you two… alone. Ta! I'm off… to see Mal."

"See you," Margi said. When Karen left, Colette told Margi that since Adam's death Mal spent most of his time perched outside on a large flat rock overlooking the lake, staring into the sky. Day and night he sat there, looking at clouds and stars, so motionless that birds would alight on him.

"Does he ever say anything?" Margi asked. "Or does he just sit there?"

"Just… sits. Karen… claims… to have conversations… with him. But I… think… she is the… only one… talking."

"Wow," Margi said. She pushed her hand into the stack of blankets. The temperature was cold inside the Haunted House, nearly as cold as outside but without the added wind chill. The zombies "living" there had no need to run the heat, if in fact it even worked any longer. She'd worn her favorite puffy black jacket and her matching pink hat and mittens, though, and was warm enough.

"Are you cold, Colette?" she said. "I mean, it really is kind of cold in here."

"I'm not… cold. Thanks… for asking."

"Sure," Margi said, but was doubtful. She knew the dead weren't able to register sensation like the living, but how could she not feel cold in this gray, bare room?

"Well," Colette said, the half-smile returning to her face. "Shall… we?"

"We shall," Margi said. "But, um, first—does the plumbing work? I have to pee."

The right side of Colette's mouth ticked up. "You… wouldn't… rather go… outside?"

Margi made a goofy face at her. "Har har."

"It... works. At least... the shower... does. We don't need... the toilet."

"'Kay. Thanks." Margi went down the hall and found the bathroom, which seemed about ten degrees colder than the rest of the house. When she was done she flushed and then washed her hands, and although the water was ice cold, at least everything worked the way it was supposed to. She opened the door.

"Hey, Colette," she called. "Aren't you guys afraid the pipes..."

She cried out. Standing in front of her was a tall, gaunt zombie with madly staring eyes. He was wearing an open leather jacket, with nothing underneath, and she couldn't help but notice that there were patches along his ribs and abdomen where his skin had been removed. His lips curled back from his teeth, which had been filed to points, in a disgusted grimace.

"Ugh," he said. "Who let the... beating heart... in here?"

She realized that his mad stare was a permanent one, because he had no eyelids.

He was looming in the doorway, blocking much of the light from the hall. Margi wasn't tall, but she could see another figure just beyond his shoulder. The first one turned so that she could get a better look.

The second zombie didn't look like any of the ones she knew; it looked more like the ones from the old George Romero movies she used to watch with Colette and Phoebe. His face was a ruin, pitted and scarred, permanently frozen in a look of shock and surprise. His nose was missing. His matted gray-brown hair stood up in tufts from his skull. He wore a tattered brown corduroy shirt, and she thought that she could see bone and torn flesh through its many holes. His eyes conveyed no spark of life or intelligence; they were the eyes of an animal lying dead on the side of the road.

Margi didn't realize that she'd been backing up until her hip struck the edge of the sink.

"What's… the matter… bleeder?" the first one said. "Scared?"

She was, but she didn't like to be intimidated, either. Knowing that they were *trying* to scare her made her more angry than frightened.

"Um, excuse me," she said, moving off the sink, seeking to thread her way through them.

The bald, lidless one pushed her back, leaving his hand on her shoulder. "What? Just because… we're dead… we can't… use the bathroom?"

"Use it all you want," Margi replied, her anger piercing through the hazy wall of her fear. She hoped he couldn't feel her trembling through the padding of her jacket. "Just get your hand off of me."

He ignored the request. "Maybe… I want… to look in… the mirror," he said. "I… bet you spend… lots of time… looking… in the mirror." Most zombies had to work hard to convey emotions via their expressions, but this one had no problem radiating his hatred. The one behind him was completely devoid of expression, which Margi found much more frightening.

"You don't know anything about me."

"Oh, I… don't?" he said. "Miss… pink hair. Miss black clothes and… bangles. Your favorite… possession… on earth… is a… mirror."

"Whatever. Let me go."

He squeezed instead. The points of his nails, which were sharpened into claws, popped through the fabric of her coat.

"You think… because… I'm like… this… I'm afraid… of mirrors."

"I would be, if I were you," she said, the holes in her jacket pushing her over the edge of irritation. "You're one ugly so-and-so. Your pal with the clown wig back there is a real cutie, too."

He straightened, smiling with his pointy teeth as though her words were compliments rather than insults.

"Bioist," he said. "I like… the way… I look. I… made myself… this way."

"Goody for you," she said. "You've quite a fashion sense. Now get your hand off of me before I make you wish that you were dead."

After saying this, she widened her eyes with mock innocence, half covering her mouth with her hand.

"Oops," she said.

"Bioist filth," he said, hissing the epithet.

Margi was angry enough to smack his hand away.

"I'm not a bioist!" she yelled. "All of my friends are dead!"

He laughed then, and unlike his evil, sharp-toothed smile, it took real effort. The result wasn't like real laughter at all but a harsh hacking sound, like someone in the final throes of choking to death.

"They just… wish… they were," he said.

Margi pushed past them, rejoining Colette in the living room. Colette had gone into Margi's backpack and fished out her iPod and had the earbuds pressed into her ears. She was trying, and failing, to snap her fingers. Colette, turning, saw the look on her friend's face and pulled one of the buds from her ear.

"I'm… sorry," she said. "I didn't… think… you'd mind."

"I don't," Margi said, although the idea of other people—living or dead—using her earbuds always skeeved her out. "Who are the new meat? A couple of real friendly guys."

"Who?"

"Popeye and the son of Romero back there. What jerks! They called me a bioist!"

"George called… you… a bioist? He… actually… spoke?"

"Is George the guy with the eyeballs? He did all the talking."

"No. I don't… know… his name. He never… gave it. The quiet one… we call… George. He's… nice."

"Oh yeah, real nice. If cornering living girls in the bathroom passes for nice around here. Went to the Takayuki School of Charm and Etiquette, did they? Nice."

"They are… Tak's friends."

"Figures."

Colette removed the other earbud. "Let's go… outside," she said. "I think… it is… cooler… outside."

Still fuming, Margi slipped and nearly fell on the concrete steps leading from the kitchen to the backyard. She kicked at a little hillock of snow, booting it high into the air.

"Haven't you guys ever heard of deicer? Would it really be so difficult to spread a little rock salt around to keep your living friends from breaking their necks? Or is there a recruitment drive going on?"

"Sorry," Colette replied. "It makes us… melt. Like the… Wicked… Witch."

Margi stopped. "Really?"

Colette gave a slow nod. "That's how… Tak… got the skin… on his hand… burned off. Reaching… into a bag of… rock salt."

"Seriously?"

Colette's expression never changed.

"No."

Margi debated bouncing a snowball off her dead friend's head, but she realized that Colette was only trying to distract her to snap her out of her foul mood.

"Let's walk to the lake," Colette said.

No speech pauses at all, Margi noticed, like she'd been waiting this whole time to blurt out that one phrase.

"I don't know, Colette," Margi said. She wasn't scared of the zombies that confronted her, but she was more than a little frightened of going to the lake.

Colette took Margi's mittened hand in her own; Margi could feel how cold she was even through the thick fabric.

"Come on, it will… be fine," Colette said, giving her hand a short squeeze.

Margi forced a smile, wondering if her difficulty in doing so was what it was like for Colette every time she tried to smile.

"Okay," she said. "Let's go."

Let's go, she thought. Let's go to the Oxoboxo, back where I let you die.

That's why she was here for after all, wasn't it? She was there to discuss Colette's death, and Margi's role in causing that death. She shivered.

They walked straight back through the woods, the snow-dusted leaves crunching underfoot.

"You could have worn a coat or something," Margi said. Colette was wearing a thin Rosedale's T-shirt. "You know, as solidarity with your bioist friends. I'm cold just looking at you."

"Not… true," Colette replied. "You are… always… warm."

They were still holding hands. Margi wondered if Colette could actually feel her warmth the way she could feel how cold Colette was.

"I guess that's true. I'm sort of like a human internal combustion engine. A furnace. Even when the heat is down I end up kicking all the blankets off my bed."

"You… always… did," Colette said. "Remember when… we three… went camping? You slept… on top… of your… sleeping bag."

This time it was Margi who gave Colette's hand a squeeze. Every reminder of their past and how much of their lives they had shared was also a reminder of the great barrier that Margi had allowed to come between them—namely, Colette's death.

She was about to reply when they entered a small clearing.

"That's where it happened," Margi said. "That's where Adam died."

They stood at the edge of the clearing. A blue jay lit upon the branch of a thin birch tree, looked at them askance, and then flew away.

"He died saving her," she said. "He gave up his life so that she could live."

She was talking about Adam, but she was talking about other things as well. Her and Colette. She sniffed, rubbing her eye with the back of her free hand. She'd felt like crying ever since Colette mentioned the lake, and she wished that she had done more in preparation for this day, other than merely dread its inevitable arrival.

"Let's… keep going," Colette said.

Lake Oxoboxo was where she drowned. Margi remembered everything about that pretty summer day so well, like she'd relived it each day since it happened. She even remembered shopping for the suits that they'd worn that day. They got them on a Weird Sisters' outing—she, Colette, and Phoebe all had matching bathing suits that they had bought at the mall.

"Good thing we're all different sizes," Margi remembered saying. "Otherwise I'd have to kill ya. That's how much I like this suit." The suits were one piece, black, and were cut low in the back. Margi was short and buxom, Colette a little on the skinny side, and Phoebe "just right"—perfectly proportioned for the suit. She stepped out of the dressing room looking like she'd just walked out of the pages of the swimsuit catalogue.

"We look like Goth Baywatch," Margi said as they stood in front of the dressing room mirrors. Phoebe made a comment about their having moon tans.

Phoebe was on vacation with her folks when the drowning occurred.

Margi realized that she'd never worn the suit since. She'd never even been swimming since.

She allowed Colette to lead her across the clearing. They left footprints where Adam's body had lain.

"In fact," Margi said, as though Colette had been able to hear the rest of her thoughts, "I've only been back to the lake once. With him—Adam, I mean."

Colette managed to raise a curious eyebrow. It looked, to Margi, like it took considerable effort.

"No, it wasn't like that, pervert," Margi said. "I wish. Adam's hot. Was hot. Is. Whatever. But we just talked. Phoebe was out with Tommy or something and Adam and I were having a pity party."

"What did you… talk… about?"

"You, I guess," she answered. "Mostly about how scared I was, and how guilty, and… and weak."

Colette didn't answer right away.

"Do you know what happened?" Margi said. "Do you know what I was doing while you were busy dying? I never told anyone this."

Colette turned her head from side to side. Margi was about to tell her when she heard Karen's voice winding through the trees.

"Hello, sweeties!"

Margi looked ahead and to the left, and she could see Mal on his rock and Karen sitting on a much smaller rock in front of him. She was so white, and her blouse so especially white, that Margi almost didn't notice her against the snow. Mal's skin was grayish, similar to the slab of granite he was sitting on. Margi felt her bracelets sliding down her wrist under her coat sleeve as she lifted her arm to wave.

"Nice day for a walk," Karen said. Mal didn't even turn.

"It sure is!" Margi called. And then, for Colette's ears only, "Doesn't she know you can totally see her bra through her shirt in this light?"

"I think… she knows," Colette said.

On cue, Karen lifted her hands to her temples and waggled her fingers at them, sticking her tongue out and crossing her diamond eyes.

Margi was shocked. "You don't think she… ?"

"Best not… to think… about it."

They walked up a little hill, leaving Karen and Mal behind, and at its crest the Oxoboxo was visible through a thick copse of trees about fifty yards downhill. The surface of the lake was covered with snow broken up by patches of dark ice like freckles on an immense oval face.

Margi decided she was going to try not to be frightened. She tried to skid down the hill on the heels of her boots, pulling Colette along with her. They didn't get very far before Colette tripped over a root and dragged Margi tumbling down with her for the next ten or twelve feet.

Margi got a face full of snow, but was laughing as she came up for air. She rolled onto her back for a moment, breathless and giggling, her head pointed at the bottom of the hill.

Colette was leaning against a tree, watching her. "What were you… trying… to say… to me? Before, I… mean?"

"Huh?"

"You were telling… me… what… you were doing… that day."

"Peeing," Margi said. "I was *peeing*."

She laughed until tears came to her eyes, and then it wasn't really laughter anymore.

"Peeing," Colette said. "OMZ! What is… with you… and your… bodily… functions, anyway?"

"When you gotta go, you gotta go," Margi said, taking off her mittens so she wouldn't rub snow in her eyes. Realizing the multiple meanings of what she'd just said, she sat up and looked at her friend. "Oh, Colette, I'm so sorry."

Colette waved her apology away. "Tell me. Tell me… what happened."

"Do you remember? You were already splashing around like a porpoise, and then I walked in up to my knees. The water was a little cool. Cold, actually."

"So that's what… triggered… the pee… reflex."

"Or as I call it, the peeflex. Yes. It was the really chilly water that you were splashing all around in, and I said I gotta go."

"I guess… I remember… that," Colette said, standing up.

"I went out, and it took me like forever to find a spot where I could go. This one had poison ivy, that one had too many pricker bushes, this one was exposed to the free world, that one was all mushroomy."

"Mush… roomy?" Colette stood still as Margi brushed all the snow off her butt and back.

They resumed walking toward the lake. "You get the idea. So then when I finally found a spot where I could go, it took forever and a day to actually go."

"The peeflex… had deserted you."

"Totally. But finally, finally my business was done, and then I realized that when I'd gone into the water before I still had all my bracelets on."

"Your… metal… bracelets."

"Exactly. I didn't want them to rust, so I had to take them all off."

"And that took… twenty… minutes."

"Har har. But it did take a while. I do have a lot of them."

"I've noticed."

They reached the shore of the lake. Margi placed an exploratory boot toe onto the ice and pressed down.

"When I finally came back, you were gone."

She put her boot down flat on the ice and then tested her weight on it by bouncing up and down. Satisfied that it would hold her weight, she moved a few steps out onto the ice.

"You think this will hold me?" she said. "This will hold me, right?"

Colette shrugged. Margi stomped as hard as she could with her heel, twice. The dark ice barely looked dented. Stepping gingerly, she walked out a few more feet, imagining herself light as a feather. She felt good to be out on the ice, crazy good, like she knew that she was taking a risk but that it was a risk worth taking. Wet feet wouldn't kill her, anyway.

"Maybe… you shouldn't," Colette said. She was still standing on the shore.

"It's okay. The ice is pretty thick. Want to join me?"

Colette shook her head, holding her left elbow to her body with her cupped right hand. Margi realized that her friend might be as scared as she was.

"Okay. So I was looking for you, and I was starting to get frightened. But not frightened for you! Oh no! It was Pinky McKnockers I was scared for," she said. "I was afraid that you used my bathroom break to find a good hiding place to jump out and scare me and give me heart failure. That's what *I* was worried about."

Colette stepped out onto the ice. Her expression was completely unreadable, even to Margi, who considered herself to be Colette's best friend on earth, and if anyone should be able to read Colette's expression, it was Margi. But she couldn't, and that made her a little nervous.

When Margi was nervous, she talked. She talked at an increasingly rapid pace.

"Then I saw something," she said, walking ahead another three steps, forcing her movements to seem casual and nonchalant. What was she going to do, run across the lake, away from her friend?

"Right about here," she said, pointing down. "A wide web of floating black hair, like in all of those J-horror movies we used to watch all the time. The *Grudge*s and the *Ringu*s and all of those. I started moving into the water then because I knew. I knew immediately what it was that I was seeing, and I knew that you weren't going to come leaping out of a bush at me. I got in up to my knees, no farther than I had before, and then I got scared and went back out. I was too scared, Colette. I was too scared to even check if you were still alive."

The last part of what she said came out of her mouth no more than a soft whisper.

Colette was half the distance from the shore to her, her thin T-shirt flapping in the chill wind that was kicking up. Her arms were at her sides, and Margi could feel the fear welling up within her again. She took a couple of steps backward, not even aware that she was doing so.

"I understand," Colette said, moving toward her. "There was… nothing… you could… have done."

"I let you die," Margi said, whispering, but her whispers seemed to echo and amplify across the lake. "You must hate me."

Colette turned her head from side to side, her movements looking to Margi even slower than they were before.

"There was… nothing… you… could have… done, Margi. It wasn't… your… fault."

"I might as well have killed you. And then… and then when your parents rejected you, I didn't do anything! I didn't do anything at all."

"Margi…"

"I could have done… done… something! I let you die, and then I left you alone, and then…"

"Margi," Colette said, lifting her arms. "Listen… to me. I had… a weak… heart. Something… brushed… against my leg. A turtle or… a snake. Something… big."

Margi took another step backward. Colette's tone was meant to be reassuring, but her expression was still blank.

"I thought it was… a crocodile… or something. Margi, please… don't go out… any farther. Please. Come… here."

Margi shook her head with the same slow movement that her dead friend had made a moment before, not even knowing if the gesture was meant to convey agreement or denial.

Colette held out her hand. She was still ten feet away.

"I… panicked. I got caught… on the branches… of that tree limb and I… thought… it was some… creature… dragging me… down. I think I had… a heart attack."

She took another step, and then they heard the sickening sound of cracking ice.

"Margi," Colette said, almost sounding panicked. "Please. Come here. Get off… the ice."

Margi looked at her friend, her friend that she had let die. How Colette must hate her. She was vaguely aware that she was still moving her head back and forth like a child lost in darkness, wishing the monsters away.

There was another sound like the cracking of wet bones. Margi couldn't see them beneath the covering of snow, but she imagined an elaborate webbing of white cracks spreading out across the black ice beneath her feet.

"Margi, please!"

Margi looked at the hand her dead friend was offering her. She hadn't been there to take it on the day Colette died. Fear had kept her away.

There were more cracking sounds, and this time Margi could see a thick white crack appear in a patch of ice a few feet away. She felt too frightened to move. She held out her hand, but the distance between them was too great.

Colette smiled with the half of her face that worked.

Then there was a loud roar, a bellow, and then something—some*things*—burst from behind the trees and brush near the shoreline, moving toward them. Margi, catching sight of stiff limbs and jerky movements, was startled. She moved too quickly, and both boots slid from under her at once so that she landed hard on her backside, the force of the impact driving all the air from her lungs. Which was not a good thing at all, because when she landed, she didn't just crack the ice, she shattered it, plunging through to the water below. She heard Colette shriek her name.

Cold enclosed her like a fist. Dimly, she felt her body rising corklike toward the surface, but then her progress was halted by the ice shelf—somehow she'd drifted beyond the hole that her body had made, slipping under the hardened ceiling of the lake. She pressed her palms flat against the shelf, but the solid ice ceiling did not budge. She looked up, the freezing water stinging her eyes, and saw a blurry dark image directly above her, realizing that it was Colette peering down. Their faces were less than a foot apart, but separated by the thickness of the ice. Colette's mouth was opening and closing, but the ice filtered out the words' meaning. She may have been screaming or she may have been laughing, Margi couldn't tell.

Margi felt like her heart was seizing up in her chest, and she wondered if that was what it had been like for Colette. She had no breath left in her body; her nice puffy jacket was waterlogged and like a suit of armor, pulling her down. The freezing water had most likely put her into shock.

If you can't beat them, join them, she thought. She'd considered her own mortality many times since Colette had drowned. She wasn't nearly as frightened as she should have been.

Except… there was no guarantee that she *would* join them, was there? Not every teen who died came back. What if she ended up truly dead instead of newlydead?

She had the sensation of drifting down, down, sinking into a cold dark sea. She was peripherally aware of being pulled, and whatever was doing the pulling seemed to be below her. She opened her eyes and saw that she was being tugged toward a light; she wasn't sure if the sensation was one felt by her body or by her consciousness. She wasn't certain if the light she saw represented the gap in the ice or something else entirely.

Don't go into the light, she thought, but the tugging, though gentle, was insistent, and then she was in the light, and where there was light, there was air. Her mouth yawned open as she broke through the surface, and she took a gasping breath. The hands were trying to push her out onto the ice, but the weight of her body cracked through, and then she was submerged in the water again.

I'm like one of those beached whales people try pushing out to sea, she thought. But like in reverse. She was aware that there were more bodies in the water beside hers and Colette's. The cold had drained her of energy and her blood; she couldn't seem to move any of her extremities and so wasn't able to help when the hands took her again and lifted her above the water.

Something was smashing at the ice with heavy blows. Margi opened her eyes—her lids crackled like cellophane wrapping as they parted—and she saw Mal and the zomboid zombie she'd seen leaving the bathroom, George, whacking away at the ice with their fists and a tree limb, hacking out a path to shore for whoever was holding her up out of the water. She could feel hands in her back and others on the seat of her jeans.

"You are such… an ass… Popeye!" she heard Colette say from right beneath her.

"We just… wanted… to scare… you!" he replied.

Margi, still not certain if she was in shock, smiled despite the dull ache she felt throughout her body. Popeye's hand was pressing right on her tailbone where it had made abrupt contact with the ice, but the pain seemed to help clarify her thoughts, cutting through the numbness the way the zombies were cutting through the ice. She hoped that the name she'd christened him with, and that Colette had just invoked, stuck—although the jerk probably would think the name was cool.

"You could… have… killed her," Colette said. She had her under the arms now, and Popeye her legs. A moment later strong arms—Mal's, no doubt—took her from both of them.

"She might… still die," another voice said over Popeye's apologies and excuse-making. Tak's, Margi thought. At some point on her trip back to shore her eyes had closed again, and she lacked the effort and the will to force them back open. He'd made the observation with no emotion whatsoever, like he was telling them that the pizza was burned.

"You too, Tak?" Colette said, her words coming out at a rapid clip. "Don't you… know better… than these idiots?"

Popeye was saying that Tak had nothing to do with their prank, and that George had only come along because Popeye had told him to, running his mouth very similarly to the way Margi ran her own mouth when she was nervous. As Mal laid her down on the snowy shore, Margi thought she heard Colette slapping Popeye, but then she could hear her friend's voice at her ear.

"OMZ, her lips… are blue."

"Hypothermia," Tak said. "Does anyone… know… CPR?"

Margi was a million miles away. Or a few feet away; she had the very odd sensation of standing outside her own body, looking down at herself, the center of a ring of dead kids. She hoped that Tak wouldn't be the one to try, but then realized that he probably couldn't, not with half his left cheek missing. His were about the last set of lips she wanted on hers.

How could any of them give her mouth-to-mouth anyway, when they didn't even breathe?

"I'll… try," Colette said, and before Margi could summon the energy to protest, she felt cold lips—cold, but still warmer than her own—pressing down on her mouth. She was back inside her own body the moment their lips touched, but Margi wasn't sure if her return was a causal effect of the touch of Colette's lips or of the rather painful way Colette was pinching her nose closed. Margi felt Colette force three exhalations into her body. When she pulled up and began counting, Margi shoved her as hard as she could. Colette barely even moved.

"What are you… trying… to do?" Margi said. "Finish… the job?"

"Margi!" Colette said, grabbing her by her shoulders, causing her jacket to shed water like a squeezed sponge. "You're… alive!" Then, "You are… alive… aren't you?"

"No thanks… to you," Margi said. She hadn't been certain at first, but then a moment later she could feel her pulse throbbing through her body like a raging river. The pauses in her speech were a result of her extreme cold, not undeath.

She tried to smile, hoping to reassure Colette, who looked stricken, but her face was numb.

"She needs… to get warm," Tak said. "And out of… her wet… clothing."

Margi looked up at them then. The wind was whipping Tak's long hair over his shoulder, and despite his words she could see no sympathy in his eyes. The bare skin on Popeye's chest looked like it was coated with a thin sheet of ice, and frost had gathered in the places where he'd removed his skin. Mal and George seemed rooted to the earth, like statues. There were icicles threaded in Colette's hair.

The many faces of death, Margi thought. She realized that she wasn't afraid anymore.

As though summoned by her thoughts, Karen arrived, looking as beautiful—more beautiful—than ever.

"I went and got the blankets," she said, holding the large stack of them in her outstretched arms.

Colette and Karen helped her get out of her wet things, while Tak, the only other zombie besides Karen who hadn't gone into the water, stood at a respectful distance holding the blankets. Mal waited with him, while Popeye and George shuffled away into the woods.

"Tak wants you to wear his coat," Karen said once Margi was free from her soaked clothing. "It's leather; it will help keep the heat in."

"I didn't… know he… cared," Margi said, her teeth chattering.

"He feels responsible," Karen explained. "Some of the newer zombies look up to him, some to Tommy. Chad and George are more… like Tak."

Margi pulled the jacket on, expecting it to smell like rot and grave dirt, but instead it smelled like leather with a hint of motor oil.

Karen and Colette wrapped her up like a mummy from head to ankle, and when she was all cocooned, Mal came and hefted her up in his arms, and then they wrapped up her feet as well.

"I'll go… ahead… and build… a fire," Tak said. Before moving, though, he took a look back at the Oxoboxo, as though it held new secrets and possibilities for him.

"I'll help you," Karen said. She placed her hand, a decidedly warm hand, on Margi's cheek before skipping ahead to join her coatless friend.

"I feel like… an idiot," Margi said. Colette had used one of the blankets to towel her off, and the friction seemed to have restored some life and feeling, but she was still shivering.

"Don't," Colette told her. "We all… make… mistakes."

"Mal sure… is strong, isn't he? Hey… Mal. Who would win… in a fight? You or… Adam?"

Colette laughed. "Mal's… pretty strong. Are you… warm enough?"

"No, but I'm… much better. Are they… really going… to build a fire?"

"They will… try. I have some… dry clothes… at the house that you… can wear."

"Me," Mal said. Margi realized that he was answering the question she'd posed a few moments before. She looked at Colette, and they both laughed.

"Sorry, Mal," Margi said. "You *are* awfully strong, though."

"I'd have thought… that water… would be… deeper," Colette said. "It was only… six or seven feet… deep."

"It was plenty deep. I'm only five feet one."

"There's… that," Colette said. "Hey, we should… call your… Dad. Your cell phone…"

"Was in my jacket pocket."

"Ouch."

"Yeah."

Margi could smell smoke, and she saw a great billowing puff rise up into the air ahead of them.

"Wow, he got a fire going."

"Tak is… very… resourceful."

"Thank… you," Mal said.

Colette stayed with Margi as she warmed herself in front of the fire Tak had constructed in the remnants of a stone fire pit at the edge of the Haunted House's yard. The others were gone when they arrived, and Mal wandered off, probably to return to his rock. They were alone.

The warmth from the fire seeped into Margi's skin, replacing and erasing the cold of the lake. Soon she began to sweat.

"Can you feel that at all?" she said. "The warmth? I can't tell you how good it feels right now."

"A… little," Colette said, the dancing flames reflected in her eyes.

When Margi was sufficiently thawed, they went inside to change. Colette exchanged her wet Rosedale's shirt for one with the Skeleton Crew logo; to Margi she gave basic black.

"It's a little tight," Margi said. "And these jeans. OMZ, I can't even snap them."

"You've got blankets."

"My dad is going to kill me."

"Maybe… you'll… be lucky," Colette said. "And come back… as a… zombie."

Margi giggled, then laughed out loud, then grew serious.

"Colette, you saved my life," she said.

Colette turned away to look out the window, perhaps at the flames that by now must be dwindling down.

"You really did, Colette," Margi continued. "I couldn't save you, but you saved me."

Colette lifted her head, and Margi could see her reflection in the cracked window pane.

"That's what… friends do… when they… can, Margi," she said. "Save each… other's… lives. That's what friends do… every… single day."

Her father didn't kill her, not even when Margi finished her story and made her request. Margi watched a thousand thoughts and emotions swimming across his face as she was talking to him, but to his credit he managed to quell all the recriminations and admonishments that he surely wanted to say to her, and in a very loud voice. But when she was finished all he did was embrace her. Margi was aware of Colette watching from the rickety porch of the Haunted House as they spoke outside her father's warm car. Finally released from her father's embrace, Margi walked back to the porch.

"See you… tomorrow," Colette said, the half-smile back on her face.

"No," Margi said, shaking her head, her expression grave.

"No?" She looked confused, which cheered Margi considerably. The more expressiveness that returned to her friend's face, the better.

"No," Margi said. "Go get your things. You're coming to live with us."

"Really?"

Margi nodded, watching as Colette's half smile became complete.

"I'll… I'll go get my things."

Margi watched her go back into the house, moving as hastily as a zombie could move.

"That's what friends do," Margi whispered as she waited for her friend to return. "Every single day."

MY SO-CALLED UNDEATH

MY LIFE AS A ZOMBIE

Attack of the Yeti

Global warming seems to have given Oakvale a hall pass because we've had three solid days of snow. What, you might ask, is the favorite pastime of differently biotic youth when it is snowing outside? Making snow zombies? Cross-country skiing?

Nope. Snowball fight.

Snowball fights are pretty fun when you A). Don't get tired B). Don't get hurt and C). Don't get cold. We had pretty much the whole Haunted House crew out in the Oxoboxo woods bombarding each other. Tayshawn is pretty darn good with a snowball; he must have pasted me a dozen or so times.

The fight lasted for hours. One of the funniest things I think I've ever seen is when Kevin and I took refuge behind a snow bank to ambush Popeye and Tayshawn, only it wasn't a snow bank—it was Mal. He'd must have been hiding there for hours waiting for someone to come by, and when he rose up out of the snow, frost and ice clinging to him like a second skin, we were so startled we kind of just both flopped on our backs. Kevin had just enough time to scream "Yeti!" before Mal dropped boulder-sized snowballs on us. Mal paid the price later, because he's so huge all you have to do is throw a snowball in the same zip code where he's standing to hit him.

I guess it is supposed to stop snowing sometime later today, just in time to get the roads cleared so those of us that go to school can get there. Joy.

Sticks and Stones

A comment Annette (and why aren't you on the Wall with the 352 other zombies and friends of zombies, Annette? Join us… join us…) made the other day on the yeti blog reminded me of a blog topic I wanted to write about.

Why is it whenever there is a story about zombies on a television news show, that the newscaster always wants to make some smarmy joke at the end of the story? I realize that they have to put a bow-tie on their stories (how else would we have closure?) but do they have to be so condescending and insulting?

Here are a few I've written down in the past few weeks You can imagine the air quotes over the appropriate words:

After a story about a zombie-fronted punk band: "Well, Jane, I guess I'm surprised they are such fans of live music."

After a story a group of teens who cast a zombie in their YouTube video serial: "That won't be making the jump to the Lifetime network."

After a story a group of teens who created Zombie Zine, a magazine about zombie culture: "Would you call that a *life*style magazine, Marianne?"

Look, I like a good joke or pun as much as the next dead guy. If Karen or Phoebe or someone said one of these, I'd probably laugh. I just can't stand these fake plastic people, most of whom probably couldn't stand to be in the same room as a zombie.

And then there's this comment, the absolute worst, that ran on a local news station after a story about two zombies hunted down and reterminated in Pennsylvania (their murderers have yet to be identified): "That's life!"

As a great man once said, common sense isn't so common.

Dead in the Family

Another fifty people have joined the Wall in the past week… we've got enough for a zombie walk!

Did anyone catch the program *Dead in the Family* that ran on one of the news networks the other night? It was a profile of three families with who have dealt with the death and return of a child. Two of the families did not take their zombie child back while the third did. The program was fairly well done, and I think there was a lot to be learned from one the people profiled had to say, no matter which side of the issue you come down on.

I'm going to transcribe excerpts from the interviews over the next few days.

Dead in the Family, Excerpt One

The first excerpt was conducted with the "Joneses", "Steve" and "Erin" (not their real name), from Verona, Wisconsin. The Joneses look to be in their early forties, moderately well off (He has an IT job in Madison, she has a local state job). Their sixteen year old son "Rick" was killed in a car crash and returned as a zombie the next day. The interview is conducted in their house, which looks to be a comfortable upper middle class suburban home. They have another boy, "Steven Jr.", age 13. The camera occasionally pans to show him tossing a ball with a large golden retriever in the back yard. The woman conducting the interview is never shown and the camera remains fixed on the couple except for these few shots of the boy and his dog.

How did your son die?

Steve: Rick was killed in a car accident, along with two other boys, his best friends. They were on their way to a party. (Pauses) Alcohol was involved.

Was Rick driving?

Steve: No, one of the other boys was. Josh. All three were drinking, though. (Pauses) He and Rick were co-captains of the school's wrestling team.

(His wife, Erin has begun to cry)

When did Rick come back?

Steve:(With irritation) That's the wrong term. I hate it when people use that term.

I'm sorry. What term do you mean?

Steve: "Come back." Rick didn't "come back". Rick left the moment he and his friends hit the parked car.

I'm not sure I understand.

Steve: Look, there's no such thing as "coming back". When someone dies, they die. Whatever those… those… *zombies* are, it isn't someone's deceased child returning from the dead. It is something else entirely. I think you people have to stop planting this false hope in people's minds.

Something else? What?

Steve: (Folds arms. Erin is drying her eyes with tissues) I've got no idea. All I know is that it isn't our children. And when you say "coming back", it makes us out to be the monsters, like we abandoned our children or something. But that thing was not our son.

Erin: We knew as soon as we saw him.

Could you tell us about the first time you saw him after the car crash?

Steve: It was the day after the crash. The call we'd been dreading came from the hospital the day after the crash, and the woman that called us said the same thing you said; "Your son has come back". Like we were supposed to be happy about it, or something. They told us to come down to get him. So we…

Excuse me. We?

Steve: Yes. Erin and I.

You didn't bring your other son. Steven Jr.?

Steve: No. Why would we?

Erin: He… the body had been damaged in the accident.

Steve: We didn't want our son to have nightmares for the rest of his life. Which he'll probably have, anyway. When we got to the hospital they brought us to this room in the basement. The zombie was there. They'd put a hospital gown on it.

Erin: His arm was broken. And his face…

Steve: They'd cleaned the body up some, but not entirely. (Pauses) I think it is disgraceful, what these people put us through. Bad enough that we have to live through the trauma of our son's death—now they want us to have to see that… that *mockery* of him? And they barely even clean it up first? It isn't right. It isn't right at all. (Pauses) They're lucky we don't sue them. I'm thinking that we should.

What went through your mind when you saw the zombie?

Steve: That it wasn't my son. That it wasn't my son at all.

I'll post the second part of the excerpt with "The Jones" in a few days.

Dead in the Family, Part 2

Here is the second part of the *Dead in the Family* transcripts.

What do you mean when you say he wasn't your son?

Steve: Just that. It was his body, but it wasn't him.

Erin: We could tell.

Steve: His eyes. They were flat, like there wasn't any intelligence behind them at all. There was nothing there at all.

Erin: He'd been such a funny boy. A happy boy.

Steve: The zombie was moving the way they do, staggering, like—and he reached for me. I thought he was going for my throat. (Pauses). It wasn't him.

Do you consider yourselves to be religious people?

Steve: I know my son is in heaven, if that is what you are asking. But I don't know if that thing has anything to do with religion.

Many people believe…

Steve: That they are demons, signs of the apocalypse or whatever. I know. I don't know anything about that.

What happened after you saw your son? The zombie?

Steve: We told the hospital that he wasn't our son, and we left.

Have you had any contact with the zombie afterwards?

Steve: No.

Erin: He was staying with one of the other families that lost a boy in the crash.

They took in their son? And yours?

Steve:(angry) They took in zombies.

The interview was terminated almost immediately after this comment. The film crew leaves the camera on as they exit the house, and the cameraman turns towards the boy playing with his dog in the backyard. One gets the impression that the boy desperately wants to say something, but in the end he turns away.

In a few days I'll post excerpts from interview #2

Dead in the Family, Part 3

This continues my excerpting a program that ran a few weeks ago on television entitled *Dead in the Family*, where parents from three families were interviewed about their zombie children.

The following interview was with "Mrs. Smith". I'll warn you that this is perhaps the most shocking and horrifying of the three interviews, so please if you are sensitive or susceptible to nightmares you might want to skip this one and wait for the interview with the Utleys later in the week.

Mrs. Smith is seated on a bright couch with a floral pattern. She is a husky woman with soft features, except for her lips, which are compressed as though she is perpetually holding back something she wants to say. She looks to be in her early fifties, and we are told that Mr. Smith died soon after her only daughter Amber was born. Her hair is short and the lenses of her glasses often reflect the light and hide her eyes from view. She has made tea for herself and the interviewer. Vapor rises from the china pot.

How did you daughter die?

Mrs. Smith: Amber had fallen in with the wrong sort of people. Her death was not an accident.

How, then, did she die?

Mrs. Smith: I prefer not to go into the details. They are both embarrassing and painful for me.

I can understand that. Can you talk about when your daughter returned?

Mrs. Smith: My daughter never returned.

What do you mean?

Mrs. Smith: It was a demon wearing my daughter's flesh.

A demon?

Mrs. Smith: (pouring tea) Yes. Reverend Mathers is quite clear, and correct, on the subject. You are familiar with Reverend Mathers and One Life ministries?

I…

Mrs. Smith: If not, you should read his book *And the Graves Gave Up Their Dead*. He illustrates the situation in an easily understandable way, even for more, shall we say, secular people.

By demon, do you mean…

Mrs. Smith: My personal belief is that my daughter let the demon inside of her heart when she was still alive. When she died, it was already there. The Reverend writes that the climate of the times is such that even the righteous may have their bodies usurped, but I am not so sure. I am beginning to think that all of the things that you call zombies were teens who allowed demons inside of them while they were still alive. (Smiles) You haven't touched your tea!

What... what did you do when you saw your... when you saw the demon?

Mrs. Smith: Did you see my gardens outside?

Excuse me?

Mrs. Smith: Please tell me saw my gardens! I spend so much time on them. The flowers along the walkway. I know your cameraman saw them; he was very careful when I asked him to mind my flowers.

I saw them. They are very nice. *(Pauses)* When the demon...

Mrs. Smith: Sometimes the blossoms on the flowers fade and die. I'm very careful to attend to my flowers when the blossoms die, because if left unattended the flowers would begin self-seeding. And they look terrible! I have garden snips that I sometimes use for deadheading. That's what you call it when you remove a spent blossom. "Deadheading." Sometimes I don't use the snips. I often just pinch the dead blooms between my thumb and forefinger. My hands are quite strong, you know, from all the years of gardening. When Paul died I really threw myself into my gardening. But sometimes I work with plants where my hands or the snips are not sufficient. I have many tools in my little shed. Did you see it? Gardening shears, an electric hedge trimmer. A spade and a trowel for digging out stubborn roots.

(sips tea)

Gardening has been such a comfort to me. I think it says a lot about a person, how they maintain their garden.

Are you… are you saying…

Mrs. Smith: Your tea is getting cold. (Pauses). I think that this interview is over, don't you?

Horde-ing Friends

450 people up on the wall, some living, some zombies. Thank you for your support.

I'll post the third and final interview transcript from *Dead in the Family* in a couple days. I promise you a more positive experience than the previous excerpts.

Dead in the Family, Part 4

Today's excerpt from the *Dead in the Family* features an interview with the "Utleys" (not their real name) Jeff and Rachael. Unlike the parents interviewed in the previous segments, the Utleys have taken their zombie son Joshua back in. They have two older boys, Albert and Paul.

How did your son die?

Jeff: Joshua died in an accident at summer camp. He died in a fall from a tree.

Did he become a zombie immediately?

Jeff: He came back a little over two days after his death.

That must have been difficult, waiting to see if he would return.

Rachael: It was awful. They wouldn't release his body from the hospital.

Jeff: Five days. They will wait five days now. The longest until rising is five days.

How did they notify you?

Rachael: A doctor came to the waiting room to tell me.

You were at the hospital?

Rachael: One of us was there the entire time they held him there. Jeff had just left to check on the boys.

What was going through your mind when the doctor told you? Were you happy?

Rachael: Overjoyed!

Really?

Rachael: Of course I was.

What did you think when you saw him?

Rachael: (tearing) All I could think was how lucky I was that I was able to tell my son how much I loved him again, so that was what I did.

Did he look any differently to you?

Jeff: (handing tissues to his wife, keeping one for himself) Of course he did. He couldn't talk, and he could barely walk. It was like the left side of his body had been paralyzed at first. He didn't blink. And he had terrible wounds on his chest and abdomen. (Smiles). But who cares how he looked? Or that he was slow? He was back, that was all that mattered.

Rachael: He was smiling again in two months.

Jeff: Two months! Some differently biotic kids are lucky if they are expressing themselves within a year after their deaths.

So you didn't have any reservations about taking Joshua back in? No question about whether he was really your son?

Jeff: (waves hand) None whatsoever. Look, I'm not going to say it wasn't difficult. But the difficulties we had to deal with were societal—many of our neighbors were not thrilled about Joshua coming home. As though we were supposed to turn him out of our home just because he was different!

Rachael: It was hard seeing him that way. It was hard knowing that he was going to have a much different… time with things now that he was dead. He would get frustrated. He missed his friends, many of whom were forbidden to play with him now. And I'd watch him as he watched his brothers playing basketball in the driveway. They would include him, but it wasn't the same. He used to be quite the player.

Jeff: But to answer your initial question—what I think you were questioning, anyhow—there was no question that he was our son. I've read everything that's come out on the topic and I really have to wonder what is going on in the heads of parents who deny their children when they become differently biotic. It really makes me wonder about people in general.

I'll post more of the interview with the Utleys in a few days.

Death in the Family, Part 5

The final installment of the Dead in the Family transcripts, which features the second half of the interview with the "Utleys".

What was the hardest part about your son becoming a zombie?

Jeff: Everything about it was hard. Everything.

Rachael: It was difficult in so many ways.

Jeff: He wasn't allowed to attend school. We had friends—ha! "Friends" who ceased all contact with us immediately.

Rachael: It was painful, watching him struggle.

Jeff: I was harassed at work. "Presents" left on my desk. A dead squirrel draped on the hood of my car.

Rachael: (Looks at Jeff) I think the hardest thing of all was that his brothers were scared of him, at first.

They were scared of their brother?

Rachael: (Nods) And it hurt him, I know it did, even though he didn't show it. They were cruel about the way they treated him, not intentionally, but I knew they were avoiding him.

How did you help them get over their fear? Or could you?

Rachael: We were patient and didn't try to force acceptance. We tried to make it safe for them to talk about their feelings, while at the same time including Joshua in everything we did as a family. The interaction was helping Joshua regain some control, and as he "returned" in some ways, the boys were more comfortable being with him.

Jeff: The process fed itself.

Rachael: The boys had long talks with our rabbi as well, and that helped greatly. He has been incredibly supportive. It meant so much when others were turning us away.

Jeff: It's strange. Many people ran away, couldn't get away from us fast enough, but others stepped up. Neighbors. There was a petition to the school board to allow Joshua to attend school. And we won.

So Joshua is going back to school?

Rachael: We prefer to home school right now. (Looks at Jeff). We're considering moving to Connecticut.

Jeff: There's a program there with the Hunter Institute which fosters inclusion of differently biotic kids in public schools. We're considering it.

Do you have any advice for other families with differently biotic children?

Jeff: Read everything you can on the subject. The bad and the good. Skip Slydell's books are great. (Laughs) But get the bad stuff at the library; don't give any of those jerks money.

Rachael: Forming a support group with other families with differently biotic children can be very powerful. We have two other families that we meet with on a regular basis in each other's homes, and we correspond with many others on the Internet.

Jeff: (Looks at Rachael, smiles) Rachael contributes to a parenting blogring where she writes about raising a differently biotic kid.

Rachael: I think the most important thing is to love your child. Never stop loving your child. No matter what he or she does, no matter what happens, he or she is still your child. They need your love and approval. Never forget that.

Zombie Social Networking

I just wanted to make everyone aware that a virtual Haunted House was created by a friendly zombie/trad coalition. If you ever want to hang out and discuss all things zombie on the web, it is a great place to be. They discuss books there as well so if you like to read, check it out. Zombies, living people, and yetis are all welcome.

Click the link and register today: The Haunted House

The Horde Grows

We now have five hundred people on the Wall.

I'm amazed and humbled. When I first started this blog, I did so really for my own sanity. If it weren't for a few people close to me in Oakvale when I started, I don't know that I would have continued. I had no idea there were that many of us; no idea that people would come once I started writing and posting.

The idea that my words have may have helped give zombies hope, and maybe helped them survive, as well as helping traditionally biotic people understand us a little more and have a little more compassion, truly astonishes me. I'm so grateful for all of you.

Thank you all so much.

But I feel like there's so much more to do, and so many of us out there, lost and without friends…

The Care And Feeding of Your Undead Friend

I'm not really going to be writing about feeding zombies—we don't eat. Although some people speculate that we "feed" off of ultraviolet radiation, and others think that we actually absorb moisture and toxins from the air, sort of like undead air filters. I've got a friend who is testing the UV theory, using one of those lights that people use to grow plants.

But in terms of "caring"—I've had some discussions with folks at the Haunted House about a number of topics regarding zombie/trad relations, the difficulties and barriers that exist. One of the first—and biggest of these barriers is the difficulty most zombies have with *expression.* Our post death-bodies, for whatever reason, don't lend themselves well to expression, so if you have an undead friend, you are unlikely to be greeted with the smiles, lightening and softening of the eyes, and rosy-cheeked expressions you get from your trad friends, unless that undead person is trying really, really hard to be expressive. And we are well aware that the results of our attempts at expression are sometimes, well, grisly. Picture an eyebrow frozen in a permanent arch, a smile that reaches only one side of the face and shows too many teeth, an eye made permanently lazy. Most children learn expressiveness from their parents beaming down at them in their cribs; all of that needs to be re-learned, and the unwilling muscles retrained after death.

Undead people are frequently frustrated by the attempt to show expression. Karen, who is particularly good and "natural" at it, actually works pretty hard at making her facial expressions seem effortless, but for other kids it can take months.

Positive feedback, works. Saying something like, "Hey, Kev! You've been working on your smile, haven't you? Looks great!" can go a long way towards making a dead kid feel good about the effort they are making, whereas framing your comments in a negative manner, like "Yo, Sylvia, only half of your lip is working" is a guaranteed buzzkill. Never, never, never suggest to an undead person that they "turn that frown upside down". We can't be held responsible for the consequences.

And for zombies, I'd suggest that you stay patient with your trad friends who might be having a difficult time understanding you. A great deal of communication between people is exchanged non verbally; living people send out hundreds of different signals and cues from posture, expression, gesture, etc., so it can be very difficult trying to "decode" a person who doesn't exhibit any of those behaviors. Think of how easy it is to send mixed signals to people, even ones you know really well. Think of all the times you accidentally hurt someone's feelings when you were trying to do the opposite.

The key, for both living and dead, is patience. Ask questions, communicate often, don't be afraid. I think everyone will find it is well worth the effort.

Horde-O-Rama

In less than two weeks another fifty people, living and dead, have added themselves to the Wall.

Dead Men Tell Slow Tales

In addition to the "expressiveness" difficulties with communication, zombies and traditionally biotic folks have the hurdle of our slower rate of speech to contend with. Most… of… us… speak… very… slowly. Please note, however, that most of us hear just fine, so shouting at the top of your lungs isn't going to speed the conversation up any faster than it would with, say, someone who only speaks Norwegian. Conversely, volume is a problem for us as well; many zombies can make their voices raise above a whisper only with great effort.

I'm afraid that our inability to speak at a normal speed causes many of us to not speak at all, unfortunately. To be dead in public is almost the very definition of being self-conscious, where the dead person is well aware that all the eyes of the living are upon them. Add to that the idea of speaking in public when you can't quite get the words out fast enough and you have many kids that would rather say nothing at all.

This doesn't mean we don't have anything to say.

The fact that typical communication happens at a much faster rate, perhaps, than ever before in human history only compounds the matter. ZOMG! Lol, srsly. We understand that it is difficult to go from speed-of-thought texting and near-telepathic communications with living friends to the slow, drawn out dialogue you may have with a zombie, trust me. It wasn't all that long ago when we were doing the same things as you were.

I have a friend, a zombie, named Melissa who lost the ability to speak in a fire. For the record, the fire that injured her in this way was not what killed her; she was hurt in a fire that was meant to destroy her and a group of zombies she lived with. A fire that was mostly successful—only she and a boy escaped a blaze that left many others reterminated.

Melissa communicates now with a whiteboard and marker. She can't write very fast, or very neatly, and it sometimes takes her longer to write what she wants to say than it does even the slowest zombie to speak. Communicating with Melissa, then, is an act of patience even for a zombie. But, like most acts of patience, it is always well worth the effort. Despite all of the pain and heartache she has gone through (or maybe because of it), the things that she writes are inevitably profound. I've talked to her a few times since she began taking classes at the Hunter Foundation, and she has often provided me the necessary insight to solve an issue that I or one of our zombie friends is dealing with.

I guess what I'm saying is, just like in my post regarding expression, patience is the key. I've come to the realization that, between two people, the listener has the primary responsibility in communication. The best, most erudite speaker in the world is going to have a hard time getting through to someone who isn't paying any attention, whereas a good listener—one who is patient, open, and making an honest effort to understand—can often hear even the things that the shy, still voice *isn't* saying.

Srsly.

Thinking Out Loud

I'm thinking that this might be a good time for a change…

March of the Newlydeads

Margi here; I'm taking over cuz Tommy says he's got some deep thinkin' to do. Busy week here at Oakvale High. We have like seventeen feet of snow on the ground (Okay, that's an exaggeration. A slight one) and we had two snow days and two delays this week. Plus, various sporting events and after school activities were cancelled. And everyone is in just a rotten mood. Rotten, rotten, rotten. I don't think anyone likes the snow except for maybe T.C., and the only reason that T.C. likes it is because there was a group of differently biotic kids coming up the icy concrete steps, and the maintenance staff hadn't done a very good job of sanding… and let's just say the results were not pretty. Unless you were T.C., who was standing on the sidewalk and pointing and laughing like that bully kid on the Simpsons. And so I whipped out my mad ninja skillz and totally ginsued him with my flying fists of fury, and then I reduced him to a fine red mist with some Norrisian roundhouse kicks.

Except I don't really have mad ninja skillz. I do have mad notebook-decorating skillz, and crazy mad fashion skillz, but neither of those superhero-quality abilities seemed of use at the moment. So I just stuck my tongue out at him.

But not all of the week was bad. There are five, count them, five new newlydeads coming to school next week. Five! Omz! And guess who was appointed by Principal Kim to be the special Orientation Ambassador for these lucky, lucky students? That's right, yours truly. I'll get to show the new kids around the school and hang out and help them get acclimated and all that fun stuff. It should be fun, fun, fun!

Classes sure are getting crowded, though.

Happy Valentine's Day

Tomorrow is Valentine's Day, so I thought I would wish you all, zombie and trad alike, a happy one. I hope that you have a happy one filled with mushy cards, flowers, and free candy. Especially free candy. Last year some trad kid gave Karen a box of candy for Christmas, which I guess was really sweet of him but, guess what? Zombies don't eat, brainiac! Karen did eat one, though, before giving me the rest of the box which I very greedily devoured barely sharing any because I can be that way sometimes. I did ask Karen the next day if she wanted another one (I had a few left, and I suspected that they were pretty much all those chewy chocolate covered caramel ones, yuck) but she declined and then did some Jedi mind trick where she told me exactly how many I ate and what order I ate them in. Spoooky! But we miss yoooouuuu, Karen! Where are you? When ya coming home? Anyhow, she didn't have any more of the chocolates and I wondered if giving a zombie a chocolate was like giving a dog a chocolate but that really isn't a good thing to speculate about, omz!

I do not have a special sweetie (sob) but that does not mean my heart is not filled with love. Some of the nastier, meaner zombies (yes, I'm talking to you, Popeye) call us beating hearts as some sort of insult, but I actually think it is kind of a nice thing to be called. They like being called zombies, so go figure.

Anyhow, a certain zombie believes that love is the answer to making dead hearts beat again. I look forward to the day when that happens, for everyone. Maybe tomorrow!

A Mystery...

So I ended up getting a valentine after all. It was a day late, but who's complaining? The valentine came in a little red envelope and had a pastel drawing of two kittens, the boy kitten (you could tell it was the boy kitten because it had a blue bow, and the girl kitten had a pink bow and long eyelashes) with his tiny forepaws clutched over his heart, and he was beseeching his sweetie to "Be my Valentine?". It looked like the sort of card you'd get by the bagful when you were in kindergarten or first grade and then, sadly, never get again in your life. And the card was signed… well, that's the mystery. It wasn't signed. It had been pushed through the gap in my locker until just the corner of it was sticking out.

I have three suspects—I mentioned a little while ago that I would be chaperoning a group of newlydead kids around the school? Three of them are boys, and I am pretty certain that the Valentine came from one of them. Which is very flattering at all but I assure you that I was very professional in my chaperoning and not flirtatious at all so I hope none of them got the wrong idea.

Meet the suspects—

Eric

Eric is very quiet and shy but he did tell me that he died because of a long illness. He didn't tell me what the illness was but I get the idea that he was bedridden or hospitalized for a long time; he is very frail and his skin tone is a shade paler than most zombies, even. He has very wide blue eyes that almost look too big for his face, but he doesn't let you look at them very long. We didn't get the chance to talk much but I know he really likes cartoons. I think he said *Invader Zim* was his favorite.

Travis

Travis is almost the polar opposite of Eric; he's one of the most outgoing zombies I've ever met. He apparently died as a result of a Jackass-style stunt he tried to do involving a dirt bike, a long ramp, and a woodpile. He said that he was impaled on a tree branch during the stunt and died, and then he asked me if I wanted to see the scar. Omz, no! He bla bla bla'd the whole time I spent walking him around—he talks so fast that he nearly sounds trad, and all of his stories involved some extreme activity he'd done—rock climbing in

Utah, white water rafting in Colorado, shark hunting off the coast of Florida. His parents are "rich and still love him even though he's dead" and I wasn't sure which fact was more important that I understand.

I guess I'm kind of painting him out to be a blowhard but actually he was kind of funny once he settled down a bit. And although it sounds grisly and sick, he had a whole table of us—trad and zombie alike—laughing at the story of his death. Not many zombies have a sense of humor about that stuff so that at least was refreshing.

Luis

He's the mystery within the mystery, because he shared almost nothing with me. Eric was shy but he'd at least answer a question when you asked it; and unlike Eric, Luis would maintain eye contact an uncomfortably long time. Zombies do that, especially newlydeads who haven't regained much of their functionality, so I don't think he was being intentionally creepy. Plus he has really nice dark eyes and I bet it if he were still alive he'd be really good looking. That sounds really shallow and judgmental—he's still kind of good looking, but if he was alive he'd look even better. You get the idea. But I got almost nothing from Luis at all about his background. About the only thing that he said to me unprompted was "I like... your... bracelets... and your... hair," which was very sweet and nice of him and probably the only remotely flirty thing any of the three said to me the first week I was showing them around. But the Kitten Kard? Doesn't seem like his style, somehow.

So those are our suspects. What do you think? Who slipped the valentine into my locker? Eric? Travis? Luis? Or... someone else?

I'll share more clues as I discover them...

Mysteries Among Mysteries

Okay, so my "Secret Admirer" wasn't Luis.

How do I know? you may well ask. Well, I used all of my considerable powers of deduction, espionage, observation, and detection. And plus I asked him why he put the card with the kitties on it in my locker.

"What… card?" he said.

The problem with differently biotic people—okay, problem is the wrong word, if Phoebe bothered to edit my entries any more she'd slap my wrist for suggesting that *anything* about the poor dead dears was problematical—what I meant to say was *one of the many unique and endearing distinguishing characteristics of* differently biotic people is that it is nearly impossible to tell when they are lying. They don't blush. Their eyes don't twitch up and to the left, they don't shake, and you can't tell if there is an additional quaver in their voice. All of which adds up to me not really being able to tell when they are lying. And they *do* lie. Colette Marie Beauvoir especially is always telling lies. I know you stole my pink socks, Colette! Confess! Confess!

But Luis wasn't lying. I didn't need telepathetic powers to tell me that.

"With… kitties?" he said.

"Never mind," I said.

So now my attention turns to the other new kids, Travis and Eric. This time I will need to be more cunning, more subtle. A direct question wouldn't work with Eric or Travis; Eric would get scared, Travis would make jokes. I'll have to bide my time…

But what if it isn't one of them, as I originally thought? What if the card is a joke, as some of you suggested, or what if it isn't from a secret admirer at all but a secret *creeper*? Brrrr.

By the way, it isn't from Norm. Don't ask me how I know. I just do.

BTW and OMZ, after I asked about the card, Luis said he "liked me". Bells rang. School bells, not wedding bells of course, so he didn't really have time to elaborate.

Another Newlydead Suspect Eliminated

It wasn't Travis, either.

Turns out he has a girlfriend back in his hometown somewhere in Long Island. I guess the schools aren't as welcoming to the undead there or something. Colette, who is Watson to my Sherlock, Robin to my Batman, Kato to my Clouseau (although her kung fu is weak!) overheard him bragging to his friends about his "wicked hot trad girlfriend" back on "the Island". She couldn't get close enough to see, but apparently he backed up his claims with some Facebook-ish type evidence.

"Yeah, right," says I. "The old 'girlfriend back at home' ploy. I ain't buyin' that snake oil, sistah!"

Sometimes, when I have a mystery to solve, I find that it helps to wear a fedora and talk tough like a 1940's L.A. gumshoe. I didn't have a fedora, though, just this really cute black with pink polka dots headband. Colette just looked at me like I was crazy.

"He had messages from her," she said. "And pictures."

"Right," I said. I decided that confrontation was the key.

"Hey, Trav," I said when we were walking to his next class, on what was supposed to be the last day of me chaperoning him, "I need to ask you…"

"Look," he said. "Before you hit on me, you should know I have a wicked hot girlfriend on the Island."

"What?" I said, and then he proceeded to tell me how he'd been seeing her for three years, they are in love, they will be together as soon as super-science finds a cure for zombiism, etc. etc. etc.

"Really, Travis? OMZ!"

"Look, Margi," he said. "Don't be sad. You are cute and all, but Bree and me… it's really love."

Grr. I wasn't hitting on him, for the record.

And now, to talk to Eric and find out what this kitty obsession is all about!

Mystery Solved

So then Colette asks me if I liked the valentine she gave me.

"What valentine?" I ask.

"You know," she says. "The one with the kitties."

This after I have already embarrassed myself with all three of my suspects. This after have already called the girl Watson to my Holmes.

"Colette," I say. "Do you mean the valentine that I have spent the past two weeks trying to discover who it came from? That one?"

Colette looked confused. "You didn't know that was from me? I thought you'd gotten a mystery valentine and that's what we were trying to find. I thought you recognized the kitty one."

"Recognize it?" I said. "what do you mean recognize it? That wasn't your handwriting."

"I know," she says. "It's yours."

"What?

"You gave me that card when we were in first grade."

I took the card out of my bag. Yes I have been carrying it around all the time so shut up. The written words were wobbly but I guess that could have been my handwriting back then. And the "Margi" I guess could have been a signature rather than a greeting. And I guess I have always liked kitties.

But then I reverted quickly to Sherlock Vachon mode, all suspicious-like.

"Wait just a minute," I said. "How did you get this, then?"

See, when Colette died and came back her parents literally chased her off of her front lawn with garden implements and wouldn't let her return. And then they moved away and didn't tell her where they were going.

"My brother," she said, and she was smiling. "He's back from the war. He found some of my things in the basement of my parents' new home and sent them to me."

"Your brother? How did he find you?"

"He saw my photo on the Virtual Wall of the Dead," she said. He never believed them when they told him I didn't come back." She sort of laughed. "Margi, he's going to come see me."

I shrieked right there in the hallway and hugged her because I was so happy for her. And because her brother is kind of hot, at let he was a few years ago when he left for his service. I was so happy I didn't even mind that I didn't really have a secret admirer and that nobody loves me and I am destined to die a lonely old spinster with a dozen cats.

Ok maybe I was a little disappointed. But mostly I was just happy for my friend.

The Zombie Meme Replay

We have lots of new zom—I'm sorry, *differently biotic* kids here in town, so Phoebe thought that it might be nice if I reposted The Zom—I mean, *differently b*—no, I don't. I mean the Zombie Meme. Here it is, my Zombie Meme:

1. **How did you die?** Um, I didn't. Yet.
2. **How long have you been gone?** I'm still here but I haven't blogged in a while!
3. **Death age/true age?** Sweet sixteen!
4. **What do you miss most about being alive?** I think I would miss ice cream

5. **What, if anything, is cool about being a zombie?** The inability to feel pain would be sort of cool
6. **How did your family react to you coming back?** My family would be mostly OK with me being a zombie. I think. They let Colette move in, and she's *creepy*.
7. **Most humiliating moment as a zombie?** I can't imagine anything more humiliating than my last blogs
8. **Visible signs of zombiism?** There would be none—I am an artiste with makeup
9. **Goals/ambition?** Sigh. First kiss. A *real* first kiss. Hopefully while I'm still alive!
10. **"If I were alive today, I would…"** Be very, very thankful.

See ya!
Margi

Zombies Are Good at Stuff

Zombies really don't get the credit that they deserve, I have noticed. In fact, I would go so far as to say that there are many, many, many things that zombies do than he differently biotic. When I was helping the newlydead students get used to going to our school, I was often impressed at their hidden undead skill sets. Here is a short (and partial) list of things that I noticed that zombies are way better than us at:

* Sitting still (very, very still)
* Looking like they are paying attention
* Not talking in class
* Not taking unnecessary bathroom breaks
* Waiting patiently in line
* Keeping their hands to themselves

* Not running in the hallways

That's all for me right now. Can you think of any other ways that zombies distinguish themselves at your school? If so, post a comment! And don't forget to sign up on the Wall!

Bye!
Margi

A Message to the Horde

Tommy here—thanks Margi for the fill-in.

We are now six hundred strong—and so now it is time to strike! Arise! Arise, my undead brothers and sisters! Arise and FEAST on the FLESH of the LIVING! AH HA HA HA HAR ARGH NOM NOM NOM NOM NOM…

Just kidding. Honestly, after dying even having a hamburger sounds kind of gross, never mind "the flesh of the living". Yuck. I don't even know why I wrote that, I'm in a very strange mood lately. You know when you feel as though everything has changed, and yet, nothing has? Me, neither. I don't know what I'm talking about right now. I apologize in advance to all the trad folk on the Wall and here as visitors. I didn't mean to scare you or freak you out. Just having a little fun.

But, on a serious note—six hundred! And it isn't just The Wall that is growing—we've had more permanent guests here at the Haunted House in the past week than we had in the first few months after we moved to Oakvale. The "official reports" say that there are less than two thousand of us, but I think those numbers might be considerably off.

Like I wrote the other day… I'm feeling that it is time for a change. Many changes, even.

A Numbers Game

I think it is very strange that we can't seem to get even a semi-accurate count of how many undead Americans there are. In the past three months I've seen two news articles that mentioned the zombie population, one of which estimated that there "may be as many as two thousand" zombies in the U.S.", and another which said that the figure was likely to be near *ten thousand*!

Quite a difference. What I'm wondering is, why such a discrepancy? Obviously, there are some factors that make an accurate count difficult—one being that in many states being undead is criminalized to the point where zombies need to go into hiding, and another would be that zombies are quite often destroyed within days after returning.

I'm wondering if this lack of accuracy with regards to a zombie census is a way for certain interests to keep the zombie community destabilized.

What do you think?

Location, Location, Location

How hostile to the undead is your hometown? Oakvale is almost schizophrenic; on the one hand we have the Hunter Foundation and Oakvale School, two pro-zombie (at least, they seem pro-zombie) institutions, but on the other hand we've got a very strong undercurrent of bioist bias here.

In your town, is the "zombie phenomenon" well known, or (pardon the pun) underground?

Are people generally supportive of the undead, or hostile?

Are the undead generally permitted to be in public places (the mall, the library, the local bowling alley)?

Are the undead allowed to attend school?

I'm interested for a number of reasons. First, to be able to compile a list of areas that are not hospitable to zombies and steer them away from those areas, and second, to have a similar list for zombies needed to relocate.

Ultimately, it would be great to figure out *why* the pro-zombie areas are that way.

Any ideas or comments, please send them our way.

Strength in Numbers

Six hundred and fifty people on the wall…

I received a post to this blog from "anonymous" that suggested that I was basically undermining zombie/trad relations with how I presented information in my blog. Here's a quote:

"By hinting that every mention of zombies in the national media is another example of an anti-zombie conspiracy, and by constantly referring to so-called 'white van abductions'—no proof of which exists—you are actually doing more than just about anyone else to ensure that the living and the dead will not be able to coexist without fear and suspicion."

I get the sense that this post was from a basically well-meaning living person, but one who is truly ignorant as to the amount of very real ("alleged" white van incidents notwithstanding) violence done to nonliving persons daily. I don't have to look any further than my own town for concrete examples of such violence. Even so, I think there is a valuable point here—the line between "raising awareness" and "creating paranoia" may be a thin one.

What do you think?

A Little Help Here

Um, could one of you get one of your friends to join the Wall? Right now we have a number that Reverend Mathers would have an apocalyptic field day with. Iron Maiden sings about this number.

What do you suppose the events would be if there really was an apocalyptic field day? 100 Yard Flaming Dash? High Jump into the Pit? Nine-legged race? Javelin catch?

Sorry. Please get someone to join.

Membership Drive—Successful

Thanks to those of you who encouraged friends to join the Wall, which now has over seven hundred members.

You know what I don't miss at all? Allergies. Poor Margi has been sneezing up a storm.

Can I Visit Your Hometown?

A few weeks ago I asked readers of this blog about how friendly/unfriendly your town is to the differently biotic. Now I have a new question to ask you, if you could help me out.

I'm starting to plan a trip across, and I'm looking for places to visit, the idea being that I would write about the places I visit and then post the writings on the blog. I'm looking to visit two kinds of places specifically:

1. Places that are very hospitable to zombies
2. Places that are very hostile to zombies.

If you would like me to visit your town, please post a comment to this blog with the following:

A. Your town and state
B. Whether your town is friendly or hostile to zombies
C. Why you think your town is friendly/hostile to zombies

I'd appreciate it. Phoebe and Karen are bugging me to do this as a contest or something, so if your town is picked for a visit we may end up sending you something for your trouble.

Can I Visit Your Hometown II?

I've decided on two stops of my tour, which I'm calling Zombies Across America.

New Orleans, Louisiana
Memphis, Tennessee

Many thanks to Gabrielle and Fantastic Book Review for the suggestions. If you are either Gabrielle or Fantastic Book Review and would send me an email with an address I can send you a gift—a wristband that shows your support of the undead—I'll get it in the mail right away. My email addy is

TommyWilliams17 at aol.com

I've still got eight more stops to locate, so please keep the selections coming. I haven't been through all of the posts yet, so if you've already posted your suggestion you still have a chance.

Housekeeping

We've had a number of new people put themselves on the Wall—the horde is 750 strong! —so I thought I'd do a little updating for the newbies and newlydeads.

I'm Tommy Williams, this is my blog. I try to write about things that are happening in the zombie community. You can click onto the wall in the link at the right and join the virtual Wall, which is open to traditionally biotic and differently biotic people alike.

Every so often either Phoebe or Karen will write a guest blog. Come to think of it, neither has written here for a while so I'll bug them.

I'm going to be taking a trip across America soon, and am looking for place to visit—if you think that your town would be a good place to check out, either because it is hospitable or hostile to zombies, let me know. Post to the blog and let me know where, and whether you think the town is pro or con zombie. Pro con zombie is not a delicious dip that tastes great with tortilla chips; that would be chili con carne.

Thanks to Lily B for suggesting a visit to Charleston, S.C. She, like the other nine people whose towns are chosen, will be sent a wristband from the Skip Slydell collection. So far I'll be going to Charleston, New Orleans and Memphis.

Stay whole,
T.

Zombies Across America

I'll be making a stop in Netcong, NJ. Thanks to SNZA for the suggestion. SNZA, let me know where I can send your wristband.

That's four stops locked up—I need six more. Please keep your suggestions coming.

Z.A.A. + The Growing Horde

800 people on the Wall! How did that happen?

A few more people will be sent wristbands if they email me at TommyWilliams17 at aol.com:

CrazedKittyCat for suggesting Pekin, Illinois.

YourDeadFriendBee for suggesting Los Angeles, California.

Axel, for suggesting Marietta, Georgia.

On my swing into Georgia I might visit Montgomery County. I read a story recently about Montgomery County High School that disturbed me—the high school holds two proms, which are referred two by many students as "the white folks prom" and "the black folks prom". I have to admit that I was amazed that there would be racially segregated events in any high school today; if America cannot clear these existing hurdles, I can't imagine that we'll ever see the day were zombies are fully included with living society.

I've got three more stops to select for Zombies Across America—keep those suggestions coming!

Itinerary Completed

Thank you, everyone who sent in suggestions telling me where to go (everyone, that is, except poster "RevMathers"—you can guess where he told me to go.

Here are the final official stops for the Zombies Across America Tour:

Denver, Colorado
Cleveland, Ohio
Omaha, Nebraska

Kelsey, MaliceinWonderland, Werewolf Moon and Sonakaru should all send me an email with an address I can send a Generation Dead wristband to them.

In other news, we somehow had another **72** people post their names to the Wall in the past 8 days. Maybe we could get 1000 by the end of the month?

Rumor has it that I am not the only one taking a trip, btw. The word on the street is that Pete Martinsburg is also going to be leaving Oakvale for an undisclosed amount of time. Does anyone have any information on that?

1000

One thousand people, zombie and otherwise, have now joined the wall. I can't wait to meet some of you out on the road.

Phoebe promises me that she will write an installment of "Words from a Beating Heart" for the blog by the end of the week.

Stay tuned…

Words From A Beating Heart

Every decision we make in life has some element of risk. Faced with two choices, each contains risk, even if one path appears to be the safer of the two. What might seem the secure choice in the short term might end up being the one most fraught with danger down the road.

Tommy Williams is the first zombie that I became friends with. I suppose it goes without saying that this was a risky proposition for both of us, although it was far more dangerous for him than it was for me. Laws are in place to give me some protection, whereas for Tommy and other zombies, their very existence is considered to be an unlawful act by some. If I'm being honest, though, which is something I always try to be, our becoming friends didn't feel like a risky or radical act. It just seemed the right thing to do. I have many, many friends who are zombies now, and Tommy has friends and admirers among us "traditionally biotic" people.

But now Tommy is taking another risk. He is going to travel, alone, around the country. There's many reasons why he is doing this, and he has many goals, some of which he's talked about and some he keeps to himself. He's leaving a community where, although these sentiments are not universal, he is respected and loved by many people. He's leaving this environment to visit places in our country where he will not be welcomed. He's travelling to places where, if the reports are true, zombies are routinely destroyed or "reterminated" by people who have no interest in understanding "differently biotic" people.

So Tommy is taking a trip with great risk. But knowing him as I do, he doesn't consider the risk. All he considers is that it is the right thing to do.

I'm worried about him, of course, but I wouldn't try to stop him or convince him to do anything other than what he's doing. But in writing this, I'm hoping that I can convince others to help remove some of the risk from his journey. If you see Tommy "on the road", say hello. I think he lives a lonelier life than any living, breathing person can imagine. If you see him, let him know where he needs to be careful and where he might be in danger. Let him know also where he would be accepted, because I think that will help him on his way.

Karen and I will be moderating mysocalledundeath for the time that Tommy is on the road, and we hope to soon have some of his correspondence to post before too long—he's leaving tomorrow. We'll also be writing a few posts of our own to fill the time in between—but don't be surprised if the blog is "silent" for a while—there's a lot going on here in Oakvale.

Thanks for reading,

Phoebe

PS: We're having a little trouble with the site, so comments might not be posted for a while.

Words From A Beating Heart—Tommy's Travels, Adam's Observations

Hello—

I just wanted to give you a quick update on Tommy. He's safe with friends in Pennsylvania right now, and he's going to be sending road reports pretty soon. For reasons known only to him, he was lucky enough to have caught a ride from a sympathetic truck driver he met at a service center on the highway. He said that so far just about everyone he's met along the road has been very kind and helpful to him which has been great. But he also said he's seen some horrific evidence of crimes against the undead. Please keep him in your thoughts and prayers.

Speaking of thoughts and prayers, Adam wanted me to thank everyone who has posted on mysocalledundeath for all of the kind thoughts you've sent his way. We both really appreciate it, and I really think it helps Adam as he tries to deal with things now that he's on the other side of life. The thing that amazes me the most about Adam in this difficult time is how he's kept his sense of humor. It shows up at really strange times in really strange ways. Like we were watching a basketball game (ok, he was watching a basketball game and I was trying to read) a few weeks ago and every so often he'd make a comment. He doesn't speak all that much right now—it still takes him a great effort—but during the game he was practically chatty.

The first time it happened I was right in the middle of a really good paragraph so I hadn't really caught on to what he said, just that he'd spoken.

"What?" I said, looking up.

He nodded at the screen, where a tall man in green was trying to in-bounds the ball.

"Dead... ball," he said, not looking at me.

A few minutes later he spoke again.

"Watch," he said. I looked up at the screen as another player in green was jumping and sort of falling back as he shot the ball from far away from the basket.

"Dead… eye," Adam said as the ball left the player's fingers. It sailed in a perfect arc into the hoop.

The other team called time out, and after some milling around the station cut to a commercial, and there was a three second gap between the broadcast and the advertisement.

"Dead… air," Adam said. I made a funny face at him, but when he turned towards me he was completely free from expression.

"I'm trying… to… wink," he said.

He's a funny one, when he wants to be.

Road Journal

Death On Two Legs

Okay, I am perfectly willing to admit that that is a stupid title for my journal. How about this, we'll have a contest where whoever sends in the best title will get a free Zombie-riffic T-Shirt sent to them, courtesy of the good folks at mysocalledundeath.com. It's death-tastic! Get those entries in!

Just kidding.

I've walked now for hours and hours. My app tells me that New Haven is 50.46 miles away from my starting point, most of which is on Rte. 95. I'm actually far past that now, nearly in New York. I stopped at a rest stop on the highway for awhile to type some notes and charge my batteries (literally charge my batteries, the cell phone and the computer). Most of the folks that drifted into the rest stop were there to either use the bathroom or to get something to eat from one of the two fast food options inside, so I got a number of strange looks during my stay there, presumably because I don't have to engage in either of those bodily functions anymore. At least one person saw me and decided to leave without buying any food. I wasn't insulted, I was happy to think that my death might have contributed to at least one person living a little longer. Some scientists believe that certain fast foods are what cause American teens to rise from the dead, but I suspect this is a rumor circulated by the companies themselves. Yes, they are that insidious.

I spent some time just people watching, but, being dead, I needed to be careful that it wasn't people-staring. Trads can get freaked out by that sort of thing. But there was this one guy who sat at a table not too far from me, and he had two Filet-O-Fish sandwiches. I have to confess I watched very intently as he unwrapped one from the crinkly blue paper. I really liked Filet-O-Fish sandwiches when I was alive. I could smell it from where I sat and I think if he offered me one I would have taken a bite. I can honestly say that I have never felt like taking a bite out of anything since I returned to life. I have a dead friend who has eaten and drank a few things since coming back and she says there haven't been any ill effects but I just don't know.

Anyhow, I must have been really staring because the man was talking to me and I wasn't even aware of it.

"You dead?" he said.

"Excuse me?" I replied, trying to sound as trad as I could. The man was pretty big, he was wearing a cap that advertised some brand of heavy machinery above the brim and he wore a large army jacket, stained like he'd worn it as he crawled under leaky vehicles. He looked like he was in his early sixties or so, but if he was he was a rugged, healthy sixty, overweight but with muscle underneath the extra padding. He had a round face that he shaved clean like a lot of rumpled looking but neat guys that worked with their hands. The Filet-O-Fish, which he hadn't bitten yet, was almost invisible in his hand, like a baseball deep in the pocket of a center fielders' glove.

He took a bite then, and chewed thoughtfully, "I said, are you dead?"

I said that I was. He nodded, and washed down his swallow with a big gulp of Sprite, just like I would have done.

"Thought so," he said. "Got a nephew who's dead. Stupid idiot brother-in-law wouldn't let him in the house so my sister had to move out with him. She lives with my parents now. They're in their eighties, still kicking as high as you please."

"No kidding," I said. "Whereabouts?"

"PA," he said, pronouncing it "Pee-Ay". "Scranton, to be exact. Terrible place for one of you to be living. Bunch of ignorant so-and-so's out there."

"Really," I said. "Where were they from originally? Around here?"

He nodded. "Lived over in Groton with my dumb ass brother in law. She wanted to send him over to that school in Oakvale, the one where a bunch of you go."

"No kidding," I said. "That's where I went. It's a great school."

Somehow he'd finished his first sandwich even though I'd only seen him take two bites.

"You don't go there any more?" he asked me. I told him I didn't and I tried to explain to him what I was going to try and do. When he was finished he scratched his jaw and squinted at me.

"No joke?" he said. "You've got some guts. There's a lot of ignorant bastards out there. Especially down south. You're going to have to watch yourself, you know?"

"I'll be careful," I told him.

And then the second sandwich was gone, and he was down to the ice in his soda.

"I gotta go jump a vehicle in Bridgeport," he said, rising. "My name is Al Johanssen. You want a lift?"

I told him that would be great, and I started packing my stuff up.

He owned his own towing business, and he worked mainly taking calls for Triple A, jump starting and towing cars. He did most of the talking as we cruised on down the highway, which was weird because I got the sense that he wasn't somebody who talked much. He told me that the tow truck business was a second career for him, that he used to have a pretty big heavy equipment and hauling business but he sold it all when his wife of thirty years "caught the cancer".

"She's been gone five years now," he said, "That was the worst thing. The worst thing ever until Joe, that's my nephew, got killed in a car wreck. He and a few of his buddies were goofin' off and drinkin' and they got in a car and that was that. Joey was the only one that didn't walk away."

He sighed heavily. "The only one that didn't walk away alive, that is."

I know this doesn't really happen any longer, but I thought I could feel the hair on my neck standing up. Most of you that read this column know that I was killed in a car wreck along with my father. I heard later the guy that hit us was drunk. I don't remember what it was like being dead, at least before I returned, but I can remember the impact of when that car hit us, and I remember the car spinning around in a circle that almost seemed lazy to me. I remember a lot about dying.

"We never had kids," Al told me. "Always wanted 'em, just couldn't have 'em. I guess Jeanie's plumbing was screwed up all along. Anyhow, we really spent a lot of time with Joey. Watching him for my sister whenever she wanted. I'd take him fishing. He loved fishing."

By this time I wasn't saying anything, I was just sitting and letting him talk. He was driving with a heavy hand slumped over the wheel. His eyes were focused on the road ahead but I could tell it was really the past he was looking into. I watched him swallow hard, and then he took a sip of the large Sprite he'd refilled on our way out.

"I really miss that kid," he said. "He was a real comfort to me when Jeannie died."

There was a lot he wasn't saying, too. I could feel the weight of his silence hovering in the space between us like family ghosts.

He drove to a Wal-Mart parking lot where some harried mommy had left her lights on while getting the shopping done. I saw her waving to us frantically from the center of the lot, breathless as she waited for Al to arrive with the big engine and the jumper cables. I pointed her out and Al nodded, but he drove over to the far edge of the lot and parked.

"I'm going to let you off here," he said. "No offence."

He didn't want the harried mommy to get spooked. I couldn't blame him.

"None taken," I said. "Thanks for the ride." I pulled my backpack from behind the seat where his tools were.

"You be careful," he said. "Like I said there's a lot of ignorant bastards out there."

I told him I'd be careful. I had almost shut the door when for some reason, I stopped.

I don't know why I stopped. I don't know how the synapses in our undead brains still seem to fire and spark even though the blood and oxygen doesn't flow. I don't know what possessed me to say what I said, just like I don't know why the Universe or the Fates or God or whatever force it is that came upon me when I died still allows me to talk and walk two years after my death.

"Hey Al," I said. "You know that people in Scranton need their cars towed, too."

And then Al looked at me, really looked at me and saw me, as though for the first time. I could tell. It was sort of like watching someone walking up. I could see something in his expression change, something beyond the smile that crossed his round, clean-shaven face as he held out his massive hand for me to shake.

"Stay safe, son," he said.

"Thanks again, Al," I replied, and then I started loping back towards the highway, thinking about how the dead could still influence the living, and the living still love the dead.

DOLL PARTS

SYLVIA LOOKED ACROSS the room at the long stainless steel table where her liver and another grayish, shriveled squiggle of an organ—her pancreas, maybe?—were floating in wide glass jars. The liver was in murky pinkish solution that two dangling pieces of plastic tubing brought in and out of the jar through a circuit powered by a whirring compressor on the floor beside the table. The jar with the squiggle also had lengths of tubing, and a wire that delivered an electric charge every thirty-seven seconds. Sylvia had counted, many times.

Sylvia felt fortunate that she had conscious control of her eyes. In the first few days since the scientists at the Hunter Foundation had begun what they referred to as her "augmentation," she'd only been able to stare straight ahead. The scientists, perhaps as a final indignity and torture, had placed a television directly across from where her body—where she—lay strapped, propped at a hundred-degree angle on some sort of medical table. The television was tuned to CNN the entire week that she couldn't move her eyes, and except for the couple of hours a day that the doctor worked their procedures on her, she received a steady diet of all the horrors of the world. Every day there were new stories about violence against her kind, but these stories appeared and burst like the clear bubbles rising from the fluid surrounding her pancreas, crowded out by more newsworthy topics like the world's many wars, the terrible earthquakes in China, or the marital problems of a dozen or so famous actors and pop stars. In those first seven days she couldn't even blink, and even if she could have, there was no way to shut off her ears.

Maybe that's why I'm insane, she thought. Maybe it was the television and not the sight of me scattered in pieces around the room.

But even as she thought it, her eyes flicking from some athlete denying he ever used performance-enhancing substances to the vat in the corner where she thought her digestive system was being stored, coiled like a long gray python, she knew it wasn't the television that had made her insane. The constant flood of input and sound bytes and information was maddening to be sure, but it was nothing compared to the complete absence of data. There was a time between when she accompanied old Alish Hunter to the laboratory and when her eyes opened in front of the television that was just *gone*, a time when there was just… nothing. When she died, it hadn't been like that. She'd been aware of herself, as a consciousness if not a body, during the hours she'd spent between her physical death and before her return as a zombie; but after Alish and one of the other doctors had helped her onto a gurney and then given her a shot of a neon blue substance, there was nothing. She'd overheard the doctors talking about the time she'd lost a few days ago. "Taking her off line" is how one doctor, the one she'd dubbed Dr. C, had put it.

Doctor C walked into the room as though her thoughts had summoned him. The "C" was for Cadaver, because that word described both his work and his appearance. He was balding, skeletally thin, with thick glasses and skin the color of wet parchment. Sylvia knew personally many zombies that looked far healthier than Dr. C.

He gave her a wide smile upon entering, his perfectly square white teeth a strange contrast to the rest of his appearance. He was one of the two doctors who visited her with the most frequency, the other being a heavyset man with a crew cut, whom she'd heard Dr. C call Beck. Beck liked to switch the channel of her television to ESPN and would check on all of her parts and the levels of juice in which they floated, the sports programs playing at an elevated volume in the background. Beck never spoke to her the way Dr. C always did—he never even looked at her, actually. Not the *real* her; he'd scrutinize the aquarium tank with her lungs, or take a sample of the liquid circulating around her liver, but he'd never make eye contact with her. This allowed her to observe him closely as he made his rounds (unlike Dr. C, who, when he caught her peeking, would shield her from his tasks with his body, saying "You shouldn't watch, my dear, as this might be very upsetting to you," as though spending the day in clear view of her internal organs—and the television—wasn't horror enough), although sometimes she did watch the athletes on the screen instead, their long, muscular bodies sailing through the air, through space, and through time.

"And how are you today, my dear?" Dr. C said. His grin conveyed just how happy he was to see her and to have another chance to muck about with her guts. He always called her "my dear" and never Sylvia. She doubted that he was an actual doctor, at least one that had any sort of medical degree.

He walked straight to her, invading her space until their noses were just a few inches apart, and he shined a penlight into her left eye, his free hand moving along her neck as though feeling for a pulse or for swollen glands. He was close enough that she'd be able to smell his breath, but that sense had not yet reliably returned to her. She'd get flashes of scents, but she thought they were probably memories and not actual smells. Yesterday she'd thought that she could smell an overabundance of peppermint, but there hadn't been anyone in the lab then, and she didn't think any of the vats and jars containing her parts were emanating such pleasing aromas. Moments later, the smell disappeared and did not return. She missed it.

His smile, impossibly, widened.

"You are doing fine, just fine," he said. "Is there anything we can do to make you more comfortable? Anything at all? Anything to enhance the augmentation process?"

Yes, she thought, wondering why Dr. C always used "we" when speaking to her. *You can make me thin. And pretty. And cure my asthma, and give me diamond eyes like Karen and make my hair blond not brown.*

And wings, she thought. *Give me wings.*

Inside, she was smiling. Dr. C, in one of his many monologues directed in her general direction, had mentioned that her mouth was usually opening and closing as if she were trying to speak, or take in a gulp of air, but she knew these movements were involuntary. She remembered that Dr. Chad frowned when he'd given her this information, which made her think such movement was not an expected or a good thing.

"No? Nothing?" he said.

Yes. Put me together, please. Please put me back together.

"Very well then, my dear. Let's check on how the rest of you is doing, shall we?"

He made kind eyes at her, but she wasn't fooled. He wasn't at all kind, and she hated it when he pretended to be. She watched him move to the large vat—it looked like the tub of an ancient washing machine—where some or all of her digestive system was being stored. A clipboard hung from a nail in the wall beside the vat. Dr. C took the clipboard off the hook, feathered the pages, and made a notation on one of them with the black pen he always kept in the pocket of his lab coat. Then he moved over to the aquarium where her lungs were marinating in an electrified solution.

They left me my heart, she thought. At least they left me my heart.

Dr. C. made more notations and walked along the metal table where her organs were on display like items on a steaming buffet.

And I still have my brain, she thought. But I'm sure that they tried to take that.

Her heart and her brain—but she didn't like to think about the latter, because there were a couple of times where she'd caught a glimpse of herself in the thick lenses of Dr. C's glasses, and she'd thought that her hair looked very strange—multicolored, in reds and blues and greens. Then she realized that what she was looking at wasn't her hair at all but a nest of wires, and that the wires were attached directly to various places in her brain. They had lifted the top of her head off like the lid of a cookie jar, and her brain, grayish and shrunken, seemed poor soil for the garden of wires to have sprouted from.

At first she'd thought that her brain was exposed to the air, but then she noticed that there was a big bubble of Plexiglas extending around her head from her temples. The wires were bundled at the back of her head in a thick cable that fell across her shoulder like a ponytail. Dr. C opened a panel at the front of the bubble once; she assumed it was so that he could check the wires and their connections.

If she could speak—which she couldn't, not with her lungs removed—she would ask what the wires were doing to her mind.

She had ideas—and more than once she wondered if the very

fact that she had ideas was a failing, and not a function of the wires—and none of them was pleasant.

She'd been thinking them on the day that awful boy entered her room, and they grew in scope and clarity after he did what he could to her. She knew as soon as she saw him that he was going to harm her, that he would do things. He was going to harm her, and there was nothing that she could do to prevent him, just watch and wait until it was over. Just watch as he added cleaning chemicals to the vats and jars containing her body. Just watch as he twisted dials and flipped switches on the machines that were monitoring and regulating her.

There were times when he moved out of her field of vision, and she went through a series of painful, sometimes ecstatic changes, the first of which was like a violet curtain dropping over her eyes, the next an intense taste of lemon. She imagined that he was plucking wires from her brain like they were stray hairs, or that he was alternating the amount of amperage that flowed through them. The violet and lemon went away, and she was struck with an acute memory of playing in a sandbox as a toddler, a memory that was so tactile and so rich with sensory detail that she could feel the sand, granular and cool, slipping through her tiny fingers, and she could feel her heart beating in her chest, and she was aware of her breath going in and out, and beside her in the sand a little blond boy in a red jacket sat, and he was offering her his yellow shovel and she was so, so happy. The emotion welled up inside her with a strength and purity that she hadn't known since dying.

She reached for the shovel, and then the memory was gone, its departure as abrupt as its arrival.

She then felt a desire that she'd never felt before, in either life or death: the desire to kill. She wanted very much at that moment to kill her tormentor, and that was before her next vision.

This one was as powerful as the first vision, and like the first was so real, she felt like she was living through it rather than remembering it. She could feel the weight and texture of fabric on her skin. She could feel the air moving through her lungs. But this time she wasn't a child but a young woman. She was a young woman, and she was walking from a classroom, and she was aware—pleasantly aware—that heads were turning to watch her leave. She walked out of the classroom, and the click of her heels on the polished tile was audible over the general clamor of her fellow students. She pushed open a heavy wooden door and stepped out into the sunshine of a warm spring day. She crossed a tree-lined quad of bright green grass and someone was waiting for her; she could see him standing in the shade of a cluster of birches. Although she couldn't see his face, she could feel her heart leap a little in her chest as she quickened her pace to meet him. Then the boy—not the one waiting for her, but the one with her at that moment, in her room—twisted a dial or removed a wire, and the vision went away. She wanted more than anything to cry out, but couldn't.

Unlike the vision of the sandbox, this wasn't a memory. Nor was the next experience, which was a sanity-obliterating wave of pain that racked her all over, that racked parts of her even that were no longer attached to her body.

The next experience was from something outside of her as well, a clear vision of a beautiful girl that she almost didn't recognize as being Karen from Undead Studies class—whom she didn't in fact recognize until Karen winked one blue eye that became her more familiar diamond color when the lid was raised.

The girl disappeared, and Sylvia saw her mother on her deathbed—another memory—and when the image disappeared, the feeling of desolation remained.

The torture continued. Senses, memories, emotions,

experiences—real and imagined—coursed through her at the torturer's whim until, bored perhaps by her lack of a physical response to his depredations, he moved on, giving the washing tub vat a healthy dosage of glass cleaner before walking out the door.

He had tortured her, without even being aware of the horrors he was putting her through, but he'd taught her something as well. Something that she would not forgive him—any of them—for.

Dr. C was finishing his rounds. Of all the things that she wished, she wished that the memory of what happened next would be destroyed along with whatever other damages his messing about caused. And there certainly *were* damages—Doctors C and Beck had raced into her room soon after the boy had left, panic evident on their faces, lab coats swirling about them as they moved from vat to vat, assessing and sampling. The Hunters were summoned soon afterward, which worried Sylvia. She wondered if maybe he had done damage that could not be repaired. Angela held her hand as her colleagues worked, whispering words of compassion and apology. Sylvia was looking into Angela's eyes when she heard the words that froze her soul.

"We have to take her offline," Dr. C had said. Angela was still telling her how sorry she was when Sylvia went away. That was the only way that she could describe what happened. She went away.

Where did she go when she was "offline"? There were no other words for it. She was gone. Nonexistent. This was something she'd never experienced before; when she died, there had been a time when she felt she was present in her deceased body as a being of pure consciousness, unable to animate her dead flesh but still capable of thought and emotion. And when the doctors began her augmentation, she was fully conscious through all of it, all the surgeries and removals, and although they sometimes hid what they were doing to her with a curtain or a sheet, she had still been aware.

Not when she was offline. When she was offline, she was just gone. She'd already thought that they were evil for toying with her mind, for implanting impulses and memories and feelings that she'd never had, but this was far, far worse. This was just like *erasing* her, making her nothing at all.

Dr. C gave her liver a final inspection and then went to her, smiling. Always smiling.

"I've very good news, Sylvia," he said. "You are ready for the final phase of your augmentation. Well, the final surgical part, anyhow. You are ready for reassembly."

He was beaming at her as he spoke these words, his apparent happiness for her evident. Reassembly, as though she were a broken toy being rescued from the corner of Santa's workshop.

She didn't quite share his enthusiasm, fearing, as unlife had taught her to, the worst.

And then the worst arrived.

"But we will have to take you offline. Just for a little while."

Her mouth was working, but the scream she felt building in her brain had no release.

She returned on the operating table, in time to witness most of her reassembly. The doctors acted swiftly in reattaching, transplanting, and positioning all her new or refurbished parts. Doctors C and Beck were assisted during the various procedures by a revolving cast of lab-coated assistants, and all were observed by the attentive—and somewhat sad—eyes of Angela and Alish Hunter. Alish, already ancient in appearance, looked as though he'd aged another eon since she'd seen him last. Sylvia found herself hoping that it was from watching what they'd done to her.

The thought wasn't like her at all, she observed.

She watched them return her lungs, two withered purple sacs, to her body, Dr. C placing them down into her chest as though he were lowering a baby to its cradle for a nap. She lost track of the order of the reassembly after that, closing her eyes for many of the procedures, no longer wanting to see what they were doing to her. There were mirrored light fixtures above her; she had to clench her lids tightly to keep their harsh white glare from penetrating through to her eyes. She couldn't clench her eyelids tightly before, so this represented some progress. Seeing the pieces of her scattered across the room in jars hadn't been an issue for her, but seeing them replaced in the hollow of her body cavity was. She began blinking, and it was Angela who finally realized, nearly an hour later, that she was blinking in code. Angela held her hand and whispered in her ear.

"I don't understand," she said, a statement Sylvia found extremely ironic. "I will ask you questions, and if you can, blink twice for yes and once for no. Do you understand? Can you do that?"

Sylvia blinked twice.

"Do you feel any pain?"

Blink.

"Are you uncomfortable?"

Blink.

"Would you like me to continue holding your hand?"

Blink Blink.

Through blinking alone, Sylvia was able to convey to Angela that the lights above were bothering her and that she didn't want to witness the procedures. Minutes later she was wearing sunglasses, and there was a curtain hanging above her neck. It took Sylvia much longer to request some music to listen to while undergoing the operations, and longer still to assist Angela in finding the sort of Deep House/Trance music that she had enjoyed when she was alive. She'd listen to the music in hope and anticipation of someday having the courage and the lack of inhibition to dance; now she just hoped that she could walk out of the Foundation under her own power.

Angela asked her if she was excited that the augmentation was nearly complete, and Sylvia blinked twice; but her answer didn't mean what Angela thought it did.

She tried to make Angela aware that she didn't want to hear any progress updates on the procedures, but Angela never quite grasped this, dutifully informing her of every step along the way.

"Your liver was damaged beyond repair," she said, a single worry line creasing her normally untroubled forehead. Angela had argued with Dr. C. only a moment before, telling him that it was inappropriate of him to complain in front of their patient (a term Sylvia considered to be a status upgrade—she'd heard herself referred to by many terms: "the experiment," "the project," and once, "the body," but never as "the patient" or, even more tellingly, as "Sylvia" by anyone other than Angela). Apparently, Dr. C went on a mini-tirade about how her music was "driving him crazy."

I'm driving *him* crazy? Sylvia thought. After he went tromping through the jungles of my mind, swinging his machete?

And actually, he was crazy long before I arrived at the Hunter Foundation. They all were, herself included.

"We'll have a new one for you tomorrow."

Three days later, her reassembly was all but complete. Somehow they'd replaced the front of her ribcage—Dr. Beck was going on about ceramic polymers and bonding agents, and Sylvia blinked rapidly at Angela in an attempt to get her to talk over him. She tried this technique again to silence an assistant who was talking about stitching.

An hour later, Dr. C entered the room. He was whistling a

jaunty tune, but the moment he arrived the worry line was back on Angela's brow. They whispered in the corner of the room for a few minutes. When they finally approached her, Angela would not meet her eyes, and she knew the news would not be good.

"We have to take you offline again."

Blink

She was aware that Angela was squeezing her hand in both of her own. "This will be the last time, honey. I promise."

Blink

Dr. C walked around the table and behind her, then leaned forward, his bald head like a full moon eclipsing the bright lights above.

"Your augmentation is nearly complete," he said. "Taking you offline in ten seconds. Nine."

Blink. Dr. C continued counting.

"You'll see it is for the best, Sylvia," Angela said. "When we bring you back."

Blink

Blink

Bli

When she returned from nothingness, she knew that they were playing with her brain, detaching wires, providing stimulus, because she had similar experiences to those the boy had given her when he was torturing her. She woke up drowning, her throat and her new lungs burning, unable to draw air. There was intense pressure against her eyebrows, and the pressure was building from within her. The burning sensation spread from her lungs to her extremities, and then she was no longer drowning but on fire, as though the liquid that had been clogging her lungs had been gasoline and Dr C had lit a match. After total immolation, which took approximately one thousand years, Sylvia returned to her childhood once again. She was holding her father's hand in a crowded city street, and then he let go, and she was adrift in a tide of humanity. He—neither of her parents, really—had ever been good at holding on.

The smell of wintergreen came as the vision faded. Then she was on a hill at the edge of a city—the same city where her father let go of her, maybe—and she was standing under a bruised and purpling sky, a crowd of corpses gathered at the foot of her hill. Not all of the corpses were still walking, and she heard Dr. Beck telling an assistant that most augmentations were unsuccessful. She heard the clacking of bones in the wind and then the taste of steel wool was in her mouth. The sensations were winking in and out, as though someone, Dr. C most likely, was taking her on- and offline rapidly.

The strobe-effect sensations ceased suddenly, and then she felt warmth spreading through her, a warmth that was as emotional as it was physical, and she understood herself to be in the presence of God. She could not recall what He said to her when she awoke a few minutes later, but she knew that His words had made her happy.

Angela's was the first face Sylvia saw when she returned.

"Sylvia," Angela said, all worry gone. "You're back."

Sylvia blinked twice and could feel herself blinking. She opened her mouth, and she could feel her lips parting.

"Happy … birthday," she said.

Angela had frowned then, not understanding Sylvia's little joke. She'd spoken the same words that Frosty the Snowman had said whenever the children re-incorporated him from snow and his magic top hat. Even when she'd been a small child herself, she'd always wondered where Frosty went after being melted, and how it was that he was able to retain his memories after being destroyed.

And did he want to remember? It always seemed to her that melting—going offline—in such a manner would have been a very painful experience.

Thinking of him now, she wondered why Frosty had never been angry at his destroyers—wouldn't he have wanted vengeance on those who melted him out of existence?

Or maybe, she thought, he reserved his darkest feelings for his creators, the children who brought him back time and again to relive his own destruction.

Angela brought a mirror with her on Sylvia's first day "back" from augmentation. The girl that stared back at her from the glass was prettier by far than the one that had come back from the dead nearly a year ago Her hair was glossy, not dry and withered, as it had been in death, and her skin was smooth and had tone and color. While still a shade pale, she no longer possessed the mottled, grayish pallor she'd had since returning. Her eyes no longer just reflected light, they now had a light within them; and when the girl in the mirror blinked, Sylvia gasped in surprise. She smiled—the muscles worked, by reflex—and she brought her hand up to cover the astonished "O" of her mouth.

"I'm… I'm breathing," she said. "Am I… alive?"

She was pausing because she was surprised, not because of the debilitating effects of zombie-ism.

Angela shook her head, and reached toward her. She used her fingernails to comb the hair that had fallen over Sylvia's eyes.

"No," she said. "But you aren't fully dead, either. You're something new. Something … *differently* differently biotic. We think that with more treatments…"

"Treatments?" Sylvia said, running the tips of her fingers

over her forehead, expecting to feel a ridged line of stitching; but she could feel nothing except supple skin. "Don't take me offline again."

"We shouldn't have to," Angela said.

"You don't have to… remove… the top of my head… again… do you?"

Angela laughed, but Sylvia hadn't meant it as a joke. She didn't see anything funny about the question at all.

"No, we shouldn't. You can't feel a scar, can you? We can do wonders with skin now."

Angela leaned forward to hug her, and Sylvia allowed her to. Angela had held her hand for hours at a time during the many procedures; and she'd barely left her side the entire time she had been conscious. An internal voice that seemed entirely unlike her own asked Sylvia if that had been for her benefit, or for Angela's.

First, they took your body, the voice continued. *Played with it and took it apart like you were a cheap plastic doll. Then they tampered with your mind, made you experience and feel things you've never felt.*

Then, worst of all, they erased you.

And when they brought you back, who is to say that you are still the same you?

Sylvia could feel Angela's warmth, and she could smell her perfume. After a moment, she hugged her back.

"Is there anything that you would like to do?" Angela asked, breaking their embrace. She beamed at Sylvia, and Sylvia could tell that Angela thought she was the same girl she'd always known. "Anything that you have been dreaming of?"

"Yes," Sylvia said, and she remembered to smile. "I'd like… to take… a shower."

Coming back from augmentation was far, far different from

coming back from death. Sylvia was walking and talking with few hitches and pauses almost immediately, and her abilities were very close to those she had possessed when she was alive. Prior to augmentation, she'd only been able to move her arms laterally unless she concentrated very hard, as the muscles that allowed her to twist and rotate simply did not work the way they were supposed to. But now… now she could do so much. She could run short distances; she could read an entire paragraph of a book out loud without pauses. She could shoot a basketball and once in awhile she could even put it through the hoop.

She could even type.

Angela thought that typing and light office work would be a good thing to incorporate into her overall therapy, and although Sylvia accepted the duties without complaint, Angela felt she needed to sell her on the benefits.

"Phoebe and Karen used to work in the office," Angela said. "We'd worked out a schedule, remember? The duties would rotate so that everyone would get a chance. We were hoping to do a study on whether or not certain activities helped improve a differently biotic person's functionality."

Sylvia remembered a day when some of her friends had come into her lab. Karen had looked around the room at her, fury blazing in her diamond eyes.

"Where are… my friends?" she asked.

Angela told her of the dissolution of the Undead Studies program. She didn't say so directly, but Sylvia got the sense that her friends' walking in on the augmentation mid-process had been a contributing factor.

"I hope that one day they will reconsider," Angela said. "We… I think that we were doing very important work together, work that would have a very meaningful impact on trad/db relations."

Sylvia, pretending to be studying the computer screen, did not look at her.

"Maybe when they see you," Angela said. "Maybe when they see how wonderfully the augmentation worked and they see you, they will come back."

"Oh, they will… come back," Sylvia told her. "I'm sure of it."

She was correct; her friends returned a week later for a visit. Angela paraded Sylvia before them as though she was a show horse, and Sylvia was struck by the irony of the proceedings. The comments from her friends were mostly about how well she was moving, or how pretty she looked, or how she could speak without pauses. Once again, the discussion was about her body, about the assembled pieces, and not the mind that gave those pieces life. Only Karen seemed to sense that there was something else at work behind Sylvia's eyes, but Karen didn't share whatever it was that her telepathetic powers were telling her, as was her way. They embraced, and when they were cheek to cheek, Sylvia couldn't help but think that the primary result of the augmentation was that it made her more Karen-like.

"Are you okay?" Karen whispered. "Do you want to leave with me?"

Sylvia shook her head, smiling at her friend. In her heart, which may have even beat on occasion, she did want to leave with Karen, but there were some things that she needed to do first.

Not all of her various therapies had been completed.

She'd been online—online via the computer; she herself had been "online" without cease since confusing Angela with her "happy birthday" greeting—reading about automobile construction and repair when the boy who'd tried to destroy her, Pete Martinsburg, had walked past the office where she worked. She'd never had an interest in vehicles prior to her augmentation, but now she found the subject endlessly fascinating, and she could spend up to an hour at a time looking at a single schematic. She especially liked the schematics that showed the various parts separated but ready to be joined, their connection points indicated by dotted or solid lines. She learned that these particular drawings were called "exploded drawings." "Exploded drawings"—she liked that phrase.

The idea that an engine—each operating system within an automotive, really—could be broken down into its component parts and be reassembled in a manner that actually improved the overall performance of the vehicle was both inspiring and illuminating to her.

She saw Pete Martinsburg out of the corner of her eye. She barely glanced up from the exploded drawing of a motorcycle carburetor on her flat computer screen as she palmed a pair of very small but very sharp scissors. This was a purely reflexive reaction, like reaching for a magazine or a shoe when encountering a large and leggy bug crossing the kitchen counter. It was an action devoid of conscious thought, an impulse driven by a hot wire in the brain.

Martinsburg gave her a look that was at first smug and appraising and vaguely threatening, but ultimately one that morphed into shock. He recognized her. That was good, she thought. If she'd seen even a flicker of guilt or remorse register on his handsome and evil face, she might have felt something different than what she now felt.

Angela accepted him into her office, closing the door behind him. Sylvia had never spoken to her about what Martinsburg had done to her body, and she wasn't certain that Angela was even aware of the extent of it. Perhaps Doctors C and Beck had conspired with Duke Davidson to keep the incident a quiet, shameful secret. Maybe they had been afraid for their jobs. Maybe one more botched augmentation would have been the final straw, and they would be out on the street.

Or maybe they all knew—Angela, Alish, the doctors, all of them. Maybe they all knew, and they were just too afraid to tell her.

And maybe they should be, the voice in her head whispered. That voice was sounding more like Sylvia every day.

She waited for Martinsburg to come out, the scissors hidden under her sleeve like an amateur magician's finest trick. She was breathing now, and although Dr. C said in one of his periodic examinations that it wasn't really necessary, he also said that there might be some positive benefits, so keep it up! She kept her breathing even and steady, and though she could feel the excitement bubbling out and over the edges of her mind there were no physiological effects visible whatsoever. She was looking again at the schematic of the carburetor, admiring the elegant complexity of how the individual pieces fit together.

Martinsburg emerged from the office not very long after entering, and then was taken on a detour from the exit by Duke, who steered him back into the depths of the facility. Sylvia waited until they reached the end of the long corridor before rising from her chair to follow them.

How nice it was, she thought, to feel the silvery coolness of the scissor blades pressing against her forearm. Of course, it was nice to feel *anything* at all—back when she was differently biotic instead of *differently* differently biotic, they could have driven nails into her flesh and she wouldn't have felt a thing. Now she could feel almost anything.

They turned to the left and took another long corridor to an elevator, so she took the stairs instead. The elevator only went down from this floor, so that was the direction she went.

Stairs, she thought. Old, dead Sylvia would never have been

to negotiate the stairs the way new and improved Sylvia was, with haste and a spring in her step. She knew where Duke was taking him; he was taking him to the vaults where the others were, the desperate dead. She knew of this wing of the Foundation but had never gotten farther than the door at the bottom of the stairwell for fear that the cameras would spy her entering the forbidden corridor. She'd tried once, but she had barely got it open before Duke's voice had come over the intercom to tell her that she was in a restricted area. Duke carried a Taser; she'd seen on the news what Tasers could do to the undead. Tasers took them offline. Sylvia never wanted to be offline again.

Still, she dreamed about infiltrating that corridor and revealing whatever dark mysteries contained within the rows of rooms—or cells—down at the far end; this would be fitting and partial payback for the way they had infiltrated the corridors of her mind and body.

She reached the bottom of the stairwell a moment before she heard the bland ring announcing the elevator's arrival. She waited behind the door, not daring to show her face through the slim rectangle of wire-reinforced glass until she could hear their footsteps taking them farther away.

She looked down at her hand, where the scissors were now tightly clenched, at some point having slid from beneath the cuff of her blouse as she pursued her quarry down the hall. She held the scissors not by their looping grips but farther up on the blades themselves, more like she would hold a knife. She looked up and, estimating Pete and Duke to be a good distance down the corridor, chanced a peek through the window.

They were walking side by side, and had just pulled even with the rows of doors. Sylvia counted four doors on each side, and there was another facing her at the opposite end of the hall. Light trickled from the tiny square window of this ninth door and from only two of the doors along the sides.

She knew that they were going to visit the denizen of the ninth room. She'd seen him once, his wide and staring eye blank of recognizable intelligence yet still somehow mournful even across the vast length of the corridor. She'd wondered then if he could see her, a step away from her own tiny window in case there was a camera trained there. If so, he gave no indication.

She knew the cameras would not be running. Duke wanted to prove some point to Pete, but whatever it was he would not want that point recorded.

Offline, she thought. Duke would have taken the cameras offline.

She considered flinging the door open wide and running down the hall at them, shrieking like a banshee, hoping that the surprise and shock of seeing her, the not-human, not-zombie maniac with flailing arms and flashing blades would stun them immobile, giving her a chance to harm them before Duke could get his Taser out. She realized, though, that such a plan would never work; she may have been stronger than a human girl but not as strong as either of them, and she was much, much slower. Duke had a handgun and a truncheon as well as the Taser, although that was the weapon she feared the most. She didn't know if the Taser would affect her the same way it affected a pure zombie, but she didn't intend to find out. She never wanted to be offline again.

She thought that her best strategy would be to wait inside the stairwell until the elevator bell sounded again. The elevator was only about ten feet from the stairwell door, and if she timed things right, she could slip into it right behind them as the doors whisked closed and do something very similar to what had been done to her.

Maybe she could even take one or both of them offline.

Down the hall, she caught a glimpse of the last zombie when Martinsburg recoiled at his sudden and shocking appearance at the window. Even though she had only a small square of window to view him through, and the window was far down the hall, she thought he looked like the most extreme example of the scarred, wild-haired, vacantly staring variety of living dead as she'd ever seen. He seemed to be staring past Duke and Martinsburg, right at her.

She wondered if he could recognize her for what she was, and she wondered if that recognition gave him hope, the way she used to feel hopeful in the presence of Karen or Tommy.

Martinsburg turned to the side, and Duke faced him, so Sylvia shrank back from her rectangle of glass and out of their view. A couple of minutes later she could hear their footsteps approaching. She pressed herself flat against the wall in case they decided on taking the stairs for exercise instead of returning to the elevator.

They didn't. She heard one of them—Duke probably—press the button. Pete seemed more the type to impatiently punch it a dozen times, as though each press would cause the elevator to accelerate and arrive sooner. Duke was a one-press guy, she thought.

The bell sounded, announcing the arrival of the elevator. Her grip was so tight on the scissors, she thought she could feel the closed blades biting into her skin. She heard the doors slide open, and she could hear their heavy tread on the floor of the waiting car. This, she realized, was the opportune moment.

She didn't move.

She didn't move until she heard the motor hum and the cables strain and the elevator begin to ascend.

She went back up the stairs two at a time, determined to

make it down the hall and to her seat in the office before they returned. She didn't know exactly why she'd held back at the end; it was a response as reflective as it had been to conceal the scissors in the first place. Something about a desire to do things right, to execute desired tasks completely and well. One thing that her studies of schematics and automobiles had taught her was that it was just as important to take care disassembling the parts as it was putting them back together.

Dr. C was killed in a car crash a week after Martinsburg's visit to the Hunter Foundation. His vehicle had gone skidding off the road after he'd worked a long shift at the Foundation. A shift where, a somber Angela had informed her, he'd been participating in another augmentation.

"That is so sad," Sylvia said. She hadn't been spending much time with either Dr. C or Dr. Beck since her own augmentation process had been completed.

She asked Angela if she could visit the new "augmentee," or perhaps even assist in the process, but Angela said she didn't think that would be possible.

"Not yet, anyway," she said. "Maybe when she is ready for her therapy."

The evening prior, Sylvia had risked another trip down the stairwell. She'd been reading about security systems during the hours where Angela wasn't creating busywork for her to do around the office, and she had already learned a great deal. There were so many different types of systems, and so many different ways of taking them offline.

She'd glanced at the camera. The zombie at the end of the hall was still there; he would sometimes press his pitted and scarred forehead against his window. The other lights were all extinguished. Sylvia had stared at the zombie for some minutes before returning to her room upstairs.

She wondered if the zombie possessed feelings like her own. She wondered if he had any feelings at all.

Angela sighed. "The police are saying that it could have been a mechanical failure of some sort. Brake fluid, steering fluid…"

So many fluids. "Or ice," Sylvia said. "It is very icy outside, especially… at night."

Angela started crying softly. Sylvia placed her hand on top of Angela's, and she wondered if the twitch she felt beneath her cold fingers was one of disgust, the same reflex triggered by the touch of a snake. Sylvia smiled for her. Dr. C was a broken doll now, and there would be no augmentation for him, no one to reassemble his parts.

Angela was crying, and although Sylvia's own tear ducts were working again, another happy result of the augmentation she'd endured, hers were bone dry.

MY SO-CALLED UNDEATH

MY LIFE AS A ZOMBIE

Words From a Beating Heart

Hi everyone, Phoebe here. I'm writing to let you know we'll be posting the newest road report from Tommy in just a few days. I don't want anyone to worry, but he had a very close call when crossing from New Jersey into Pennsylvania. Scary but everything is okay.

In other news, Margi told me that she talked to Colette a few days ago and that the Skeleton Crew tour got off to a rocky start. It seems that a club owner in Albany did not know that DeCayce was a zombie when he booked the band, and so he killed the band's power during their opening number. Well, turns out there is a small but very, um, energetic, crowd of pro-zombie youth in Albany and they kind of ran amok in the club. I'm afraid readers in the Albany area won't be seeing any shows there in quite awhile!

I'd tell you the name of the club but we have enough to worry about without being sued by bioist club owners.

And Margi said that she is actually going to write a piece for *mysocalledundeath,* can you believe it? She and Colette (who Margi is now calling "Yoko", ha-ha) are going to do two interviews—Margi is going to interview DeCayce, and Colette is going to be interviewing the living members of the band so each can find out a little about what "life" is like on the other side. It should be fun!

Although my big grumpy boyfriend is saying that they should call the interview "Open Hearts and Empty Heads".

Words From A Beating Heart: Round Numbers

Phoebe here, celebrating! Why, you ask? A couple reasons:

1. There are now 1500 people on the Wall! Even though so many of my friends have traveled far from Oakvale, at least we've got so many friendly faces inside the Haunted House!
2. This is the 100th post to mysocalledundeath.com! Yay!

On behalf of everyone here at mysocalledundeath.com I'd like to thank all our readers and Wall participants for your support and kind thoughts!

I won't be referring to you all as a "horde" like a certain Mr. Williams, however…

Road Report

Hi everyone—

Phoebe here, with another road report from Mr. Williams. I have to warn you—this is not a pleasant story, definitely not for the faint of heart. I'm still disturbed by it.

I can tell you that Tommy made it safely out of Scranton, but I'm not going to say just where he is, yet.

He thinks he's being followed.

Keep him in your thoughts, please, like I know you do. And again, his report is a very frightening one, so think twice about reading it.

Stay safe,

Phoebe

The Road Journal of Tommy Williams

"We're not in New Jersey anymore," Jason said.

The funny thing was that I knew it even before he said it. It was weird, because northwestern New Jersey isn't all that different from that northeast corner of Pennsylvania, but I knew we were in a different place. Something in the air, or maybe the highway signs were subtly different, or the composition of the asphalt beneath the tires of Jason's car different that the roads we'd just left behind.

Or maybe we passed a big giant 'Welcome to Pennsylvania' sign and my conscious mind did not register it because I was so busy scanning the bare trees for villagers with pitchforks and torches.

I'd been warned about PA, you see.

Jason drove a bright yellow VW bus that he'd nicknamed the Hearse because he'd used it to smuggle at least five dead people out of the state.

"Scranton, PA may be the city most hostile to the undead in the entire northeast," he told me. "And that's saying something, really."

Jason is nineteen. He's from South Carolina but he goes to school at Princeton, where he wants to major in cultural anthropology. He refers to his trips into PA as 'field work'.

"Pretty much everywhere is hostile to you guys, though. That school you have over in Connecticut is a rarity. You've got a decent db scene in New York, and I hear that there is an even bigger one in LA and in San Francisco. I think it's because all the dead get chased out of all the other states."

"Except New Jersey," I said. "Netcong was good to me."

"Yeah, 'cept Jersey."

We met at a party in Lodi (which I'm told stands for "Lots

of Dead Individuals"), where I was staying with DeCayce and his family for a few days. A dead girl from Cleveland named Tanya introduced him to me as 'the guy who saved my life."

"I was a little late," he said, looking self-conscious beneath the brim of his Nets hat. Tanya hugged him and was clearly totally in love with him. I found out later it was because he and a few of his friends have set up a sort of underground railroad for differently biotic people. He brings most of them to Lodi, but he told me that some he's brought further. In fact, a few of his passengers are now staying at the Haunted House."

"Scranton hates dead people, man," he said. "And they are organized about it, too. I think there are some people there that do what I do, except the rides they give to dead folks end in Scranton. And they are definitely one way tickets. Stacey and Rick—you'll meet them—are pretty sure there is some sort of group that meets weekly, and each week they've got a differently biotic person at the meeting. Not applying for membership, either."

On the surface, it sounded ludicrous that a group could be destroying one of my people each week as a part of some weird ceremony—they'd probably have the whole state of PA swept clean of dead kids within a year if they were—but I knew in my still heart that things like that were happening all over the country, all the time. I saw more white vans on the Garden State Parkway than I'd ever seen before in life or death, and every time we passed one I'd wonder if it was filled with assault rifles and a flamethrower. I know many of you do not quite believe in what some blog trolls refer to as "The Tommy Williams White Van Conspiracy", but maybe you should talk to Cooper Wilson at the Hunter Foundation for an eyewitness account.

My conversation with Jason would be halted every ten minutes or so for him to answer his cell phone, and every time a certain number came up he would answer the phone "Karen here." First I wondered why he was giving the name of one of my best friends. It took me a few of these phone calls to figure out the code.

"Charon, as in Charon the ferryman of the dead?" I said.

"Yeah," he said, looking at me only through the reflection in the rearview. "You aren't insulted, are you?"

"How could I be insulted by something so corny?"

(And if you are insulted in reading this I ask you to reconsider, because I won't be apologizing and I don't think Jason should either. Sometimes a sense of humor is all we have to cling to; there have been times where I have thought it is the only thing keeping us alive. I also won't be apologizing for fishing two pennies out of the cup holder where Jason throws his spare coffee change and putting them on my eyes as we went into Pennsylvania, even though doing so really seemed to freak him out).

Jason told me there was a sight he wanted me to see before he brought me over to Stacey and Rick's apartment. What he wanted me to see was the towering, wrinkled face of Reverend Nathan Mathers, his five foot tall eyes still managing to look beady and empty as he peered down at us from a massive billboard, holding a copy of his wonderful book *The Undead Scourge*. For some reason, his greedy cold eyes made me think the title was actually *The Uncle Scrooge*. Maybe I've already been on the road too long.

"That was paid for by a local church group," Jason told me as we drove by, "they raised part of the money by having bake sales and car washes that the parishioners' kids did."

We went past Mathers doing seventy, but his looming visage did not recede nearly quickly enough for me.

Rick and Stacey (who aren't really Rick and Stacey, the same way Jason and Tanya have different names and the bright yellow bug that Jason-not-Jason drives might actually be a battered old pickup; the work they do being dangerous to themselves and the cargo they transport) are twenty-year old hippies, who speak with the same fervent conviction that I have seen Mathers (the actual six foot version) utilize, although you can see a light in their eyes that is absent even in the larger than life reproduction of Mathers. They don't eat meat, they don't wear leather, and they are involved in a number of environmental issues when they are not helping the dead escape to a better 'life' further east.

"We respect the sanctity of life and death," Stacey tells me, her hand on my arm and her eyes scanning my face with an intensity I would find frightening if I were still alive and still fearful. "God created all things. Everything."

"Yeah," Rick said, his lips barely visible behind a thick brown beard that would probably let him run covert ops missions among the Amish, "the idea that you guys are some sort of demonic presence on the Earth is just crazy. I think the idea that anything other than God is responsible for creating you is even more blasphemous that what Mathers and those guys say. If God made the Earth and everything on it, and then someone says he didn't make you and you are blasphemous, isn't that blasphemy? I mean, what the heck."

Rick was practically shaking with incredulity, but luckily I had Stacey's steadying hand on my arm as she scanned my face, appreciating the sanctity of death.

"I could use some coffee," Jason said, to try and lighten the mood, I guess.

"Man, that's the most damaging drug of all," Rick said. "The uptight drug, we call it."

"You drink tea, though," Stacey reminded him.

"Yeah," Rick agreed.

I know my portrait of Rick and Stacey may seem a little unflattering, a little mocking. Don't let it distract you from the fact that these people are literally the main reason why a number of us are still walking around. But they are real people, just like any of us, and for me to portray them as anything other than who they really are would be wrong.

Jason drove. I sat in the back with Stacey who was telling me all about her theory that we, the dead, were really some type of new human/plant hybrid while Rick cycled through the radio stations without cease. I think we were going south.

"Some plants, they die… as in actual death, roots dried up and all," Stacey said. "And then they come back. With sunlight, or water. Or because someone is talking to them. Isn't that amazing, the idea that you could bring someone back to life just by talking to them?"

"Pretty amazing," I said. The car which may or may not have been a bright yellow bug was regardless cramped in the back seat. Stacey was wearing a peasant shirt and was not wearing a bra. I have a friend who has as many bracelets on her arm as Stacey had ribbons in her hair.

"Worms, if you cut them in half, each grow into a new worm. Energy can never be destroyed, only transformed. Maybe you have just found another way to transform your own energy instead of releasing it when you let go of your body. I see auras; that's how come we can find the walkaways like we do. You all have this cool blue aura, like that new color of Gatorade or certain fabric softening agents."

"Thanks," I said. "What are 'Walkaways'?"

She nodded vigorously. There were a couple feathers in the shrubbery of her hair that fluttered like tiny wings. "That's what we call the dead on the lam. Not too many of you can actually run."

"Oh," I'd said. That one, at least, made some sense to me.

"I can't tell who the bad people are versus the good ones. Jason and Ricky have such nice golden auras, really pretty. Most of the people in town have this sickly gray color. Like cigarette smoke or cancer. Ick."

"I just think we are put here on earth to constantly renew ourselves, every day. Did you know that every seven years your body replaces all of its cells, one cell at a time? Living people, anyways. I don't know if the dead actually do cell replacement. I've never studied the subatomics and molecular nature of the differently biotic before. I studied pre-law in school. Can you imagine me as a paralegal? Can you believe it?"

The funny thing was that I could, and in some ways I wished that she had become one. Jason told me as we crossed the border (after asking me would I please take the pennies off of my eyes) that Pennsylvania was one of the first states to pass legislation concerning the differently biotic (although in their laws the term used is "undead"). The law they passed made it illegal to "give occupancy" to an undead person, which meant that she and Rick had broken the law just letting me into their apartment, and it was probably a more serious crime than the one they were committing with their little horticultural experiments.

"They did it because there was a farmer in Bethlehem who was letting two dead people stay in his barn in exchange for free labor. Bethlehem, Pennsylvania, ha-ha. His neighbors complained and lo and behold there was a fire of mysterious origin in the barn. Luckily the zombies weren't in it at the time; they were inside the farmers' house tiling his bathroom or something like that. I don't even think I'm supposed to have you in my car."

It was strange hearing the story from Jason, as it was one I had heard directly from one of the zombies who'd stayed on the farm, although in his version he and his friend (who never made it out of Pennsylvania) were scaring crows out of the fields. It was weird—so much of our history is an oral history, and hearing the tale retold by a traditionally biotic person gave me an odd little thrill of validation—if not vindication.

Somehow during the conversation with Stacey, we had drifted

of Rte. 80 and onto some twisting and hilly back roads, roads more likely to be lined with brush and cattle fences than street lights.

"You are going to wish you'd taken the long way," Rick said to me over his shoulder/ "This isn't pretty."

Jason took a sharp left onto a "road" that was really just a set of tire ruts in a hard packed grassy field. He drove about a third of a mile in and stopped within about fifty feet of a metal pole set in a hillock of dirt as if hurled there by an angry deity. The dirt of the hillock, as well as the grass immediately around the hillock, was packed down hard, as though trodden frequently by many feet.

There was a blackish lump, about the size of a small suitcase, at the base of the pole. When I opened the door the smell of gasoline on the air was strong enough to hit even my less than sensitive nose, not the scent one would expect in the middle of an open field.

I looked back at my three living companions.

"I'm stayin' here, man," Rick said. Stacey, who was crying silently, squeezed his shoulder and followed me out of the car.

Jason reached the pole first. The suitcase was the charred remains of one of my people, just a lump of charred ash and bone. The pole, which in more human settings would have had a basketball net attached, was streaked with greasy soot.

"They chain them here," Jason was saying, looking down at the poor thing that used to be a person, the pile listing to the side. "They chain them and douse them and light them up. End of story."

"Every week?"

He looked at Stacey for the answer, but Stacey had knelt in close to the remains and I realized that she was saying a prayer. "Poor thing," she said, "poor little girl."

She stood, and beckoned me to the other side of the hillock. I wasn't prepared for what I saw on the other side. I wasn't really prepared for seeing the charred body, even though Jason told me that's what we were going to do, but the trench on the other side of the hillock… I could not even guess as to how many bodies burned into ash it had taken to fill that trench, a trench that was long and wide and filled with a crumbling black substance that looked like charcoal until you realized that the dots of white, some as big as my palm, were bone fragments. I didn't even know there were that many dead people living.

I thought I felt the wind then, looking down into that trench. At that mass grave.

Some people, the people who might be scared of us but not scared enough to want to burn us like monsters, say that we are ghosts wearing human flesh. Looking at the trench I could feel the ghosts of my people; they were tugging at my sleeves and whispering in my ear and urging me to do what I had taken this trip to do.

I don't know how long I stood there. Eventually Jason said that we shouldn't hang around.

I stopped at the burning post again on the way to the car, and when I got down on one knee I blinked; I thought I was hallucinating because I thought I saw a flash of light in the center of the burned remains. I looked again and saw that what had flashed was a tiny lump of metal glinting in the sunlight. I pried the lump, a flat melted disc of gold no bigger than my thumbnail, with fingertips that came away black with soot. The disc came free of its charred prison with a brittle snap.

A locket, I thought. This was once a locket, given to her by someone, a relative or a boyfriend perhaps, someone still living who had no idea that the little girl who they'd given it to would spend her last moments on this earth chained and aflame, ringed by a throng of blank-faced men.

I put the disc in my pocket and wiped my fingers on the

sides of my jeans. Jason started the car and Rick, without turning around, said that they needed to get me out of Scranton.

Margi Interviews DeCayce

Hello—I'm turning MSCU over to Margi this week for her interview with DeCayce! Hope you enjoy it!

—Phoebe

Hi this is Margi Vachon and I am sitting with DeCayce, the lead singer of Skeleton Crew. If you aren't familiar with Skeleton Crew—and why would you be, because it isn't like you can buy their CD in a store or anything—they are a punk band from New Jersey that is unique because they have a zombie lead singer. DeCayce the zombie and this is my interview with him.

Margie: Hi, DeCayce

DeCayce: Hi, Margi

(**Note**: DeCayce has a lot of pauses in his speech but I'm not going to try and type those out or anything. It is hard enough trying to type along with this stupid recorder. Sometimes I think the pauses are because he's a zombie and sometimes I think it is just because he thinks a lot before he says anything)

Margi: So is DeCayce your real name?

DeCayce: Sort of my. My real name is Casey Dimello. So, Casey D. D. Casey.

Margi: Well plus that's like a cool name because it is like a pun about zombies. You know, like 'decay'.

DeCayce: Oh, you caught that?

Margi: So anyway, you've been in Skeleton Crew for how long?

DeCayce: Since about a month after I died.

Margi: Seriously?

DeCayce: Yes. Before I died the band we were in was called The Polynesian Gods of Southern New Jersey.

Margi: What?

DeCayce: We were a surf band.

Margi: You were in a different band with the same guys? Before you died?

DeCayce: Yes.

Margi: That's so cool! How did you die?

DeCayce: I leaped to my death from a hotel balcony tower while shouting "I am a golden god."

Margi: No way. Really?

DeCayce: No.

Margi: Come on, how did you die?

DeCayce: I prefer not to say.

Margi: Fine, be that way. Well, were you always the singer for the band?

DeCayce: Yes. When I was alive I also played guitar, but it is very difficult for me to move my fingers fast enough on the frets now. But I am relearning.

Margi: Wow. That's kind of sad.

DeCayce: Yes. It is.

Margi: I heard that you write a lot of the songs.

DeCayce: Yes. I write most of the lyrics. We all help write the music.

Margi: What about *I'm Only Dead on the Outside*? Did you write that one?

DeCayce: Yes

Margi: What about *Differently Biotic, Differently Neurotic*?

DeCayce: Yes. The lyrics.

Margi: *Living is Like Dying*? *Lost the Plot*?

DeCayce: Yes. And yes.

Margi: *Across the Universe* ?

DeCayce: No.

Margi: Hah! Just kidding. That was Fiona Apple.

DeCayce: Actually, it was—

Margi: I know who it is dummy I'm just kidding you. So, do you have any wild stories about being on the road?

DeCayce: You mean like when bioist jerks throw bottles at me?

Margi: I was thinking like whether or not you have groupies. Other than Colette.

DeCayce: Colette isn't a groupie. She's my soul mate.

Margi: Ew, whatever.

DeCayce: I wouldn't call them groupies, but we have some fans, I guess.

Margi: Do you have more dead ones, you think, or living ones?

DeCayce: Hard to say, because sometimes it is hard for differently biotic people to get to the shows. I'm glad we have so many traditionally biotic people cheering us on.

Margi: Lots of girls think you are really hot. Which I think is pretty weird.

DeCayce: Yeah. Thanks for that.

Margi: Even beating hearts. You guys are pretty good, though.

DeCayce: Thank you.

Margi: Not as good as the Misfits were, though. Or The Damned.

DeCayce: Well, those are great bands. Legends.

Margi: Or the Others. Or Blitzkid, or Son of Sam.

DeCayce: Those are some great bands, too.

Margi: Or. Michale Graves. Or the Morgue Staff Rejects. My

Chemical Romance. Paramore. The Rosedales.

DeCayce: Ok, I get it.

Margi: Green Day. You aren't bad, though. For a local band. Buckcherry.

DeCayce: Yeah, thanks.

Margi: So what's next for Skeleton Crew?

DeCayce: More practice, apparently.

Margi: Come on! Don't be so sensitive!

DeCayce: Well, we're thinking about recording a CD once we have enough money to get the studio time. I'm not sure if we'll do it as a digital download or what.

Margi: Any new songs? Or the same old stuff I've heard you play at your last three shows?

DeCayce: We've got a new song that Dominic wrote. It is called "Karen".

Margi: No way.

DeCayce: Way. We're not sure what we're going to call the album, though. We're thinking either "Love Never Dies" or "Generation Dead".

Margi: Go with the first one. The second will never fly.

DeCayce: Yeah, thanks for your always trenchant commentary.

Margi: No problem. Just make sure you thank me in the liner notes.

That's all for today, everyone! This is Margi Vachon, intrepid girl reporter, signing off! Skeleton is on tour right now playing all ages shows anywhere that will have them! Check local club listings!

Road Report: Cleveland

Hi, Tommy here with the latest from the road. Thanks(?) to Margi for filling in.

I wasn't sure what to expect for my trip to Cleveland. My fiends in Pennsylvania arranged for me to stay with the Thomases (names changed to protect the innocent), who have two zombie sons who I'll call Greg and Dave. Like me, Greg and Dave both died in a car accident. Unlike me, their injuries are both visible and horrific. Greg can still walk, albeit with a pronounced dragging limp, while Dave is confined to a wheelchair. Greg's face was so disfigured in the crash that he wears a mask like my friend Melissa, although his is a Spiderman mask and not a white theater mask.

Greg doesn't speak at all; Dave is talkative but isn't what you would call a fast talker. Both of them are deadly poker players, however. I gathered that Greg and Dave had been popular students at the school prior to their demise; a photograph on the Thomas's mantel showed them both in the school's baseball uniforms, smiling for the camera on a sunny day. There was also a prom photo of Greg and a pretty smiling girl nearly a foot shorter than he was. No prom for photo for Dennis; he must have died too soon.

Of course he died too soon.

I thought I would just be talked to them and whatever network of zombie friends and maybe parents that they had, so I was a little surprised when Mr. Thomas told me that I was invited to go speak at the high school where his boys still were allowed to attend classes. I said sure, I'd be glad to.

When I followed the Thomas family down the hall, with Spiderman Greg pushing his brother down the hall, using the chair to balance himself, I was pleasantly surprised by the number of their classmates that said hi or called to the boys by name. Dave always waved with his one good arm, although by the time he was able to raise his hand the person he'd meant to greet was already long gone down the hall.

I was thinking it would be something like Undead Studies class, with maybe fifteen students and a teacher or two.

I was wrong. There were over a thousand people in the school's auditorium, students and many of their parents.

I don't get sweaty palms or shortness of breath, and when my speech hitches people assume it is because I'm dead and not because I'm nervous, so overall the talk went pretty well. I spoke about what people were doing to zombies across the country, and I encouraged living people everywhere to try and be more understanding of the difficulties that undead Americans deal with on a daily basis. When I was done speaking, everyone clapped. The clapping wasn't like I was at a U2 concert or anything, but I'd like to think the applause was more than polite.

The principal took the stage, and he shook my hand.

"Does anyone have any questions for Mr. Williams?" he said.

Lots of people did. The parents, especially. Questions about how they could get involved, questions about politicians I had never heard of that might be sympathetic to our cause, questions about how they might get laws to change.

Many of the people that spoke to me didn't have questions as much as they did ideas, or statements about things that could help. A young girl spoke up and said that a city bus driver threw some "hoods" (her word, which I just loved) off his bus because they were making fun of a zombie and his mother. I told her that was the one thing that beating hearts could for us: speak out.

One elderly woman spoke up and said that she'd invited a couple of runaway zombies to stay with her at her house.

"I love those kids!" she said. "They're quiet, respectful, and they take my trash out for me. And I don't even have to feed them!"

That got a big laugh, but she wasn't done yet.

"They're so much better company than cats!"

After the applause died down, she looked around at all of her neighbors, her grip on her purse tightening.

"No one should be lonely," she said, and she sat down, rather hastily.

I wasn't sure if she was talking about "those kids" or herself, and clearly, it didn't matter either way.

Like I said, I wasn't sure what I was expecting out of my trip to Cleveland, but this sure wasn't it.

Zombie Meme Redux

Hello—

Last year Tommy posted a meme that I wrote. We now have over *three times* as many members on the Wall than we did then, so I thought it would be a good time to invite all you new zombie kids to post your meme into the comments.

Here it is, the Zombie Meme:

1. **How did you die?**
2. **How long have you been gone?**
3. **Death age/true age?**
4. **What do you miss most about being alive?**
5. **What, if anything, is cool about being a zombie?**
6. **How did your family react to you coming back?**
7. **Most humiliating moment as a zombie?**
8. **Visible signs of zombiism?**
9. **Goals/ambition?**
10. **"If I were alive today, I would..."**

Tommy says he has some "big news" about his trip to Omaha, and Colette has finished typing up her interview with the traditionally biotic members of Skeleton Crew, so we should have more news to post soon. Until then, post your memes!

Road Report: Omaha

I'm sorry it has taken me so long to post; but thank you to all the zombies who have been posting your memes. I asked Phoebe if she would post this for me when I was on the road, but she said that it was one I really ought to do myself.

I met a girl in Omaha. Her name is Christie Smith and she's a zombie.

I met her at a small gathering of zombies and we really connected. I'd really like to write more about her and how we met—I tried to get her to do Phoebe's zombie meme—but she's really, really shy.

But Christie and a few of the other zombies I met are going to be joining me on the rest of my travels. Right now there are six of us. I'm no longer hoofing it or catching Greyhound, either—the mom of one of the dead kids is driving us around in—get this—a white van.

Although, the van is so old it is really more of an off-white van. But I thought you'd think it was funny, anyhow.

Death To Zombies

So we get to Denver. And as cities go, this one is actually fairly hospitable to the differently biotic. We're able to line up a few places where we are welcome to speak about what it is like to be undead in America without much hassle or heckling, and a number of zombie teens want to join up with us on our travels, so we've now got a caravan of three vehicles, and we've got three traditionally biotic supporters who are driving, including the mother and the older brother of one of the new recruits. All and all, a pretty good trip. Except during one of our stops—in the community room of a senior center, no less—we come out of the building and someone has painted "DEATH TO ZOMBIES" in still-dripping black paint on the side of our white van. We're outside staring at this lovely piece of artwork, a whole host of thoughts and emotions going through our head, when Justin, one of the newlydead kids, say "I can fix this." We all looked at him—it was sort of like when Jeff Spicoli trashed the car in *Fast Times at Ridgemont High* and says his father has 'awesome tools' or whatever. But we play along and drive Justin to the local hardware store. He comes out with a couple brushes and cans of paint.

"Watch this," he says, and he opens a small can of black paint and makes a few marks. We wait until he's done, and then we see that the van now says:

"DEATH,TO ZOMBIES..."

He opens a can of red paint, and in tiny letters writes:

"another chance to get it right."

"You try," he says, handing brushes out to some of the other kids. In a few minutes there are a number of messages in various spots on the van, messages like

"a sobering experience."

"the great equalizer."

"a laff riot."

"a pain in the brain."

"heaven deferred." (That one was Christie's)

So now whenever we stop we ask local zombies to add their thoughts to our travelling billboard. Thank you, nameless vandal!

What will you write on the van when we stop by your town??

(thx to Dee for the inspiration)

Dead in Hollywood

I could write an entire book on the adventures that we had in California. In some respects, California seems like its own country within our country, there is so much diversity within the state in terms of lifestyle. I'll keep today's entry quick though, confining my comments to the time that we spent in Hollywood.

I've got to admit, that the trip to Hollywood was really more about satisfying my own curiosity. What would America be without Hollywood? I really didn't expect to find a very big undead population there, and I was right. I mean, the Sunset Strip was loaded with zombies, but only at night, and most of them were doing their best to blend in with the rest of humanity. If, that is, you consider them to be a part of humanity.

We didn't stay long. Not because we pelted with rocks or driven to the edge of town by angry villagers or anything like that, but I'm not sure that any of us felt less comfortable in a place than we did during our trip to Hollywood. I was talking about it with Christie in the van when we driving away, heading east. It wasn't that the beautiful people there were hostile, or even curious. It was more like they were completely indifferent to us—like we didn't even show up on their radar. Like they were so inside themselves and their own concerns that they didn't even notice we were dead.

I've got to tell you, in some ways I found that even more terrifying than the guy who pulled a gun on us outside a gas station in Utah.

We didn't stay very long. The police kept us moving along and didn't really give us a chance to talk to anyone. They weren't violent—actually they were probably the most polite of any of the cops we've dealt with thus far, but they kept us moving, like we were trash they would like to see swept out of town.

The only thing that even came close to a normal human

interaction was when a bearded guy stopped Christie and I and told us really liked our "look". We were too stunned to speak, at first. He went on to tell us that he was a filmmaker and that he'd really be interested in having us do a screen test. I don't even think he was aware that we were dead, not at first. He was sort of a heavy-set guy, which set him apart slightly from most of the people we saw in that town, and when he looked at us he seemed to be staring right through us; I felt like he was staring at something that wasn't even there.

I told him no, thanks. After I spoke he looked at me like he could see me, the real me, for the first time.

"Why not? Really? You really wouldn't want to get some screen time? I'm shocked. I'm really shocked that you would say that."

I started to reply, but he kept going. For such a large guy he moved around a lot, shifting from side to side and punctuating his words with his waving arms. Christie would tell me later that his sneakers cost upwards of $500 dollars.

"Look, you people need to get some screen time. Images. Image management. All that newsreel stuff, it doesn't do you any good. I'm talking positive images, film, documentary. Images people can relate to. Beauty. You're beautiful. That will translate."

I remember turning towards Christie in the exact moment that she turned towards me. Whatever it was that would translate, it wasn't anything the bearded man was saying.

"Look," he said. "I know. You're busy. I understand this. You have things to accomplish. But I think we've got something hear. Death as attractive. In the right light, makeup, some slice of life, I think we could really make a statement. Do you have a card?"

"A card?" I said.

"Here's mine," he said, and fished one out of his jeans, which Christie said were the least expensive thing the man was wearing.

I took his card, which was creased and torn at one corner. It had his name and a phone number, nothing else.

"Kid, call me," he said. "When you are ready, call me. You can't get anything done in this country without Hollywood."

His Bluetooth lit up and he pressed a stubby finger to his ear.

"Yeah?" he said, and, turning, started walking away without another word to us, this hands fluttering and making forms in the air that would remain unseen to whoever he was speaking with.

Christie and I had a long talk about this encounter. Had he understood? Was he offering us something real? Some of the things he said made it sound as though he knew who we were, and what we needed. But most of what he said left of feeling like he had no clue at all.

I kept his card, though.

Actually, we had one other interesting encounter just before we left, again at a gas station. A girl and a boy about our age, beating hearts, walked over to Christie and I as we stood outside the van. They were so tanned and healthy looking; it was hard not to think of them as the our living reflections, the image of what we'd be if we were truly alive. The girl asked if she could add a slogan to the van, and Christie found her a can of blue paint.

"Death, to zombies…" the girl wrote, and a thin drip of blue paint slid down her bare leg, "… is an endless sunset."

She drew a big blue smiley face, and then she stood up and gave Christie a big hug. Weirdly—or I thought it was weird anyhow—the boy hugged me as well.

"Good luck," he said, and then he took the girl's hand and off they went.

I left as confused as ever. Maybe someday I'll come back to Hollywood, someday when I have the time to figure things out.

Membership Drive

Hey everyone, Phoebe here. I'm writing to ask you if you have any friends, zombie or otherwise (werewolves, pixies, and creatures from the black lagoon are welcome, also), who you think might be sympathetic towards the issue of rights for the undead, that you would consider encouraging them to add their names to The Wall at right. We're hoping to get as many people as possible to sign up in anticipation of Tommy and team arriving in Washington.

We're hoping to get the total number of names on The Wall to two thousand in the next two weeks. Can you help us?

Here's a silly "joke" from Adam:

Who won't get any older this year?

Answer: Zombie kids, and Phoebe. (I was born on February 29th—no birthday for me this year!) Conan O'Brien, he isn't.

He'd better not think he's getting out of giving me a present…

Membership Drive: Success!

Wow! In just a little over a week, you helped us get over the 2000-strong mark! We're hovering at 2001 at the moment—thank you!

And there's always room for more…

On a Dark Desert Highway

Driving through the desert for seemingly endless miles, working our way back east. We stop every couple hours or so, so that the living among us can stretch their legs and breathe. There further we go the windier it gets, so that at our last stop you could actually see thin curtains of sand rising and falling away. The living people don't like to stand out in it for very long, but I wish that I could feel the grainy air abrading my skin. We wear sunglasses, even at night, when we are outside. Not to look cool but to keep the sand out of our eyes.

I could look out at the desert sky all night and get bored. Sometimes I think that, rather than go on to Washington, that I should just gather up as many zombies as I could and more them all here to the desert, where there isn't anyone to bother us. We could move into the Grand Canyon. Or maybe Death Valley would be more appropriate. We don't need to worry about water, and while the wind, sand and sun would most likely take a toll on our skin, it wasn't like we could feel sunburned. We're immune to rattlesnake bites, too. We could find the ghost towns of the old west and move right in and create our own town.

The thoughts make me smile, because the idea of being able to get away from everyone that hates us certainly is appealing sometimes. But I know it isn't the answer, not really. It might be nice to have a secluded corner of the world, but the world will always turn its eyes on you, eventually.

It would be great if zombies established some communities outside of "Normal" society—in the desert, at the poles, under the ocean. For all I know we could colonize the moon—we could go Anywhere we could be safe and free. But only if it was by choice, not because we were forced there or in hiding. Maybe if things go well in Washington we'll have some of those options.

Those were some of the thoughts I had as we moved sleeplessly through the desert.

Companions

I know it has been awhile since I've written last. Texas… things happened in Texas. I can't even put them into words yet that's how terrible they were. The images are there in my head, like they were etched there by a ragged fingernail, but my body and my hands resist pressing the keys that would turn those images into words.

Our first few stops in Texas were pleasant… but nothing had prepared us for what was going to happen. Nothing. The look in their eyes…

That was weeks ago. We—those few that remained—stopped in New Orleans afterwards and although that city opened its heart to us we really couldn't enjoy the hospitality. The news never reported what happened; the story was squelched. When we tried to explain no one could really understand what it was like. Not unless you were there. I called Phoebe, and told her as best I could what had happened. If I don't find the strength to write about it soon—or if something should happen to me—I've asked her to help me get the story out. But without Karen to help her, and with everything that is happening in Oakvale, and don't know that anyone would listen.

All I'll say now is that the little caravan that we had has now been reduced to one vehicle, our hand painted van. There's only a few of us still traveling; some went back to where they were from, others we had to leave in Texas. We had to leave them in Texas and they won't be returning.

"I'd almost forgotten what it was like to not exist," Darius, one of the guys who'd joined us in Denver said when we were miles away from the attack. It was the first thing that any of us had said in a few hours.

We're on our way to Memphis now, a stop I swore we'd make to help three of our brothers and sisters who need our help. We're doing almost all of our traveling now at night, and during the day we have to be careful where we park so that our living drivers can get some sleep in the van. The miles roll past and I'll think about people I thought I knew and then I'll wonder if they were ever really there at all.

I feel like my whole life right now is staring out a car window, looking for something that that I'll never find.

Memphis

We rolled into Memphis the day after a week of heavy rains. The river swelled against its banks, and again I had to fight the urge to leave the van, to leave my friends and just start walking towards the river, and keep walking until the muddy water covers my head.

"What's with you?" Ty said, just after slapping me in the back of the head. "You look like a zombie."

I turned towards him just as he lets loose with a manic giggle. Truth be told, Ty is the one that looks like a zombie. He's been driving for the last six hours, a during which time I watched him consume two cans of red bull and eat two large Snickers bars. There's only three living kids still traveling with us, and all three of them seem to regard ferrying the rest of us around the country as some sort of holy mission. There's an odd sort of symmetry among the three—Ty, Chris and Kyle all wear hats or bandannas, all three have tattoos on their mountain-bike hardened calf muscles, muscles which are always visible because all three wear cargo shorts constantly. All three are addicted to the new Stone Sour CD (Ty, when the others are asleep, will sometimes put Hendrix's "Valleys of Neptune" on the dashboard. They are the sort of athletic, easy going sort of guys that you can totally picture running two dozen miles over rough terrain to get medicine to an injured party lost in the woods. They are the guys you'd want with you in a fight.

"Sorry," I said to Ty. "I'll try and look more alive."

Ty laughed his jangly laugh and tapped me on the back of the head again.

Affectionately, I think. Ty was a basketball player; that's what basketball players did on their way to the bench, tap each other on the head. Before my one-play football career with the Oakvale Badgers, I'd been a baseball player. I think the basketball guys had the better idea.

"We going to try and find Elvis?" Ty said. "I hear he's dead like you."

"Funny," I said. "I think his followers believe he never died, which is a little different."

Ty shrugged. Kyle and Chris were helping our dead friends out of the van—for some reason they thought stretching was as beneficial for us as it was for them.

We made a few stops. Most everywhere we went people were supportive and kind. A girl gave Chris her phone number. An elderly couple brought three dead kids to us and asked that we take them with us, which we were glad to do. The girl who gave Chris her phone number painted a hot pink heart on the side of the van and I started thinking that the world had possibilities again.

We went to the Lorraine Hotel before we left town for D.C. The hotel is a museum now, and if you don't know what it is and what happened there you need to look it up on Wikipedia. Hard to believe that happened within my mother's lifetime.

On to Washington. Wish us luck.

What Happened To Karen?

Posted by Tommy Williams

Open Letter to Phoebe

Phoebe, I lost my cell phone in Texas, which is why I haven't called.

But I've been doing a lot of thinking. I've been thinking about Evan and Texas and what happened to Karen and more and more I'm coming to the conclusion that life is short. Even differently biotic life is short, it seems. Some of us—zombies, I mean, but I guess trads too—act like we're immortal. Nothing could be further from the truth. We disappear a bit more every day. I've been thinking a lot, Phoebe.

I've been thinking of you.

I know you're with Adam now. Adam is my best friend in Oakvale; he's the first trad guy to stand up for me and I'd never do anything to hurt either of you. He gave his life for you, and I will always owe him for that.

But Phoebe… things weren't over between us. You know it and I know it. I may have stepped aside, but I was lying to myself. I was lying to you. I thought that time and distant would change the way I felt but if anything my feelings have only grown stronger.

I think you know what I'm talking about. I think there's a part of you—and maybe, right now, it is only a tiny, fragile part—that feels the same way.

When I'm done here in Washington I'm going back to Oakvale. I'm going back to Oakvale because there's a lot that I have to say to you.

Please listen.

T.

MY DEAD HEART

I WASN'T EXPECTING A parade. I arrived home from my months on the road to an empty, or nearly empty trailer. The screen door whisked shut behind me, drawing the attention of my cat Gamera, whose tail stopped in mid-switch as he regarded me with active disgust.

"Hi, kitty," I said, and stooped to pet him. He hissed, bearing teeth as his paw lashed out and laid open three perfectly symmetrical scratches on the back of my wrist before he bounded off into the kitchenette, probably to seek a higher perch from where he could launch a new and more devastating attack on me. And all I wanted was to make friends.

I lifted my slashed hand and waited for the blood to well up in the cuts, but of course the blood never arrived. That spring dried up months ago.

"Quite a welcome," I said. But it was no less than I expected, no less than I deserved. A smarter person than I am would never returned, except for holidays and birthdays. A smarter person than I am would have kept walking. But a smarter person—a dead one, anyway—wouldn't fall in love.

I dropped my backpack on the floor and sat in the kitchen chair facing the door, slouching as though fatigued from my long trip. The truth is that the dead don't get tired, although some have told me that their "lives" are like a constant state of being tired. I don't feel that way. I may not move quickly, but once I'm moving I can go forever, like some relentless machine composed of dry veins and dead flesh. I can't evade the claws of the cat, but I don't feel any pain from the scratches I receive even though they will never heal. We are all the sum of our scars, a wise man I met on the road told me, and he was still among the living.

I've been on the road these past months talking to people about rights for the undead. My travels have taken me to many parts of the country, some strange, some so normal they seemed strange. I went to the nation's capital and found sympathetic ears and now there are a few legal rights and protections for "my" people that there weren't before. Time will tell if any of those rights are upheld or any of those protections enforced. Already I have heard of retaliatory strikes against the dead around the country, many in places that I had visited just days before. But my part, on that larger stage, is over for the moment. I returned home because of unfinished business. I returned home for the truth. The truth, or so I am told, has the power to set you free.

I don't know how long I sat before my mother came home; my relation to time hasn't been the same since the car crash that killed me. Faith is a nurse at the hospital, working all sorts of strange shifts. Recently she's become a sort of midwife to the dead; she wrote me an e-mail while I was on the road telling me that the hospital has her counsel the recently returned and their grief-stricken families. It is a job she is ideally suited for.

Her eyes found me the moment she walks through the door, as though every day or night that she comes home from work she has expected to find me here. She looks as though she is seeing a ghost, but a ghost that she's been waiting for years to arrive.

"Tommy," she said, already crying.

Turns out I can move at nearly human speed when I put my mind to it. I tell myself that I may not be able to feel the scratches and the scars but that I can feel her hug.

The next morning I went to the Haunted House, and almost everyone else was at school. Everyone I knew, anyway. You would think I would beeline toward Phoebe, of course, but I never get proper credit or recognition of my shyness. My unfeigned shyness, by the way. People who see me speaking on television, in front of cameras, cannot understand the difference between personal and public shyness. But there is a difference.

Takayuki is the only person that I recognized at the Haunted House. Two or three other zombies appeared during the course of our conversation, but I don't recognize them. One nodded, one flashed heavy metal horns in what I guess is an affirmation or tribute, and so I assumed they recognized me. The dead like to acknowledge but not necessarily meet me, I've noticed.

Tak was on the porch, watching the way a vulture watches dying prey. It is though I've never left, in a way. He looked up and his hideous smile was veiled and then it wasn't. I said his name and he nodded in my direction. His arms were crossed on his chest, but not as though he was trying to restrain the furnace of anger I've known to burn within his chest; if anything he seemed at peace, almost Buddha-like in his serenity. I climbed the creaking stairs and stood before him.

"Congratulations," he said, and in his greeting lay the essential conflict between him and me; where others say thank you, he congratulates me, every syllable laden with sarcasm. Others assume that my deeds are about them; Tak assumes they are about me.

"Thank you," I replied, because there is nothing to be gained in arguing the point. I knew from the moment I met him that Takayuki Niharu and Thomas Williams were opposite sides of the same coin, and for me to debate minor semantic points is to debase us both. He knows the value of what I accomplished; I know where my accomplishments have fallen short.

"Thank you," I repeated, in case he had doubts about my sincerity, "and thank you for what you did for Karen."

The dead don't flinch, and Tak is the deadest of us all. But I saw that the mere mention of her name hurts him, causes him actual pain, and I am embarrassed for the both of us. His feelings for her are something I've often suspected but never witnessed; the shadow that crosses his gray face is all I need to know. Phoebe had sent me a message detailing what had happened to Karen in my absence, and the risks Tak took to help her.

"You...... weren't...... here," he told me, which is as close to admission of weakness I've ever heard from Tak, but at the same time there is pride; pride and defiance. I can only nod. I owe him a debt, one that I am unlikely to be able to repay. I too would die another dozen times for Karen.

"Mal?" I asked him. He focuses his attention on me, eager to banish the too-bright specter of Karen from his mind.

"Mal is still... beneath... the Oxoboxo," he said, and I have the sense that he is being purposeful with his speech pauses, as though he needs to remind me of just how dead we are. "Many... think... he awaits... you."

I nodded, not wishing to address the implied insult. "Colette?"

"On... tour," he said, showing me his teeth. "She... fell in... love... in your... absence," he said.

Many did, I thought. I was nothing but happy for her.

"Kevin?" I ask. "Tayshawn?"

"In... school," he replies. He almost looked confused when he says this, and for a moment I imagine that his hatred for me is tempered by a warped form of gratitude. I've never hated Takayuki, but after learning what he tried to do for Karen I can't even dislike him. "Popeye, too."

"Popeye is in school? At Oakvale?"

I couldn't help but laugh, and although the result is somewhat grotesque I think the attempt brings an authentic smile to Takayuki's ruined face as well.

"Well, then," I said. I could ask him if he is planning on attending school, but I already know the answer. I turn; no need for good-byes. I will go back to school and see if they will have me back.

"Wait," he said. "There is something… I think you… should see."I followed him through the woods. We walked for miles and I knew I wouldn't be getting home until near dark, because as yet the dead have not learned the art of teleportation. We exchanged maybe two dozen words during the hours that we were traveling; when I grew tired of staring at the back of his head and at his long hair brushing along the silver-studded shoulder pads of his leather jacket I looked around us into the woods. Spring was coming; green had begun to mix in with the grays and browns. New growth was budding at the tips of the thin branches of birches that stretch toward us as we made our way; skunk cabbage, ferns, and other ground-level greenery brushed my sneakers and his boots as we walked. I imagined the air that I no longer have to breathe as having a rich, loamy smell. Squirrels danced away from us, weaving in and out of the holes in a crumbling rock wall half-hidden behind a veil of brambles. Their play became headlong flight, and I wondered if they were spooked by my dead companion and me or the echoes of gunfire that I could hear in the near distance.

My father had never been a hunter and I had no idea if it was a legal hunting season or not; but I'm also guessing that the gun-bearing citizenry of Oakvale wouldn't let minor quibbles like legality keep them from blasting creatures that offended them from the face of the earth. The dead have moved to Oakvale in droves since the high school reopened its doors to them; my efforts in

Washington may have helped create conditions making it illegal to reterminate us, but very few states other than Connecticut took the next obvious step by allowing basic freedoms or rights, like the ability to attend school, to the dead.

See what happens when I'm given a few moments to think? Do I linger long over the beauty of new life emerging from the ground, do I stop and smell the roses (roses, at least, are typically pungent enough for even my dulled senses to recognize), as it were, or do my thoughts immediately return to how easily that new life is denied or destroyed?

There must be something deeply wrong with me, I decided.

I actually laughed out loud, just two short but loud barking sounds. Tak looked back at me over his shoulder and at first glance I thought he was sharing my sudden change of humor, but then I realized he wasn't smiling at all; the missing half of his cheek just made it look that way. He turned back without saying a word.

In life I had terrible pollen and mold allergies. I was briefly thankful that I no longer had to deal with them, but given too much time to think, I realized that I missed sneezing, even, and I wished that we would arrive at our mysterious destination.

But we walked at least another two miles before that wish was granted. The sound of gunfire was very close, and I couldn't help but recall how a single bullet ended the life of my friend Adam, ending along with it any possible chance of happiness for me. There was a smaller popping sound even closer than that of the gunfire and I realized that I'd balled my hands into fists and the sound I'd heard was that of my knuckles dryly protesting the tension I'd put upon them.

Tak was looking at me. When he felt he had my full attention he lifted a finger to his lips, motioning for me to be quiet, and then he started crawling through the underbrush. We crept and crawled, two dead things, toward a heavily wooded outcropping that looked over a small camp a short distance below. I could see two small weathered buildings, white paint flaking off boards that had been warped and bowed, their gray-shingled roofs covered with pine needles and bird droppings. Between the buildings, three boys no older than Tak or I were shooting with handguns at a trio of paper targets posted maybe thirty feet away from their firing line. They worked under the watchful eyes of a man I first mistook for Duke Davidson; his bearing was the same, as was his tight expression of mild dissatisfaction, but then I saw that he had dark black hair trimmed just above the white collar of his shirt. He wore a blue baseball cap, dark sunglasses, and ear protection; and like Duke he gave off an aura of being ex-military or ex-police. He watched the boys shoot without comment; each of the three also wore ear and eye protection; I couldn't see their results from my vantage point beneath the bushes but it looked as though the boy in the center had the steadiest and surest stance.

"They are… members… of Oakvale's newest church," Tak said, the slurred, almost lisping quality created by the tear in his cheek made more evident by his whispering. "They arrived… a few… weeks ago."

"Newest church?" I said, watching as the shooters placed their weapons and their gear on a small folding table behind them before stepping out onto the range to retrieve their targets. The one in the center paused to rub his gun, as though the barrel or the handgrips had been soiled and that such a thing was intolerable to him.

"Reverend Mathers himself has come to town," Tak said, without pause.

If my heart beat, it would have stopped. If I had breath, it would have caught. Butterflies would have been released to flutter in desperation against my rib cage, a cold chill would have danced along my spine, my legs would have grown rubbery and weak. The dead have no greater enemy than Reverend Mathers, who has been preaching hatred against us from pulpit and publication from the day Dallas Jones picked himself up from the puddle of his own blood spreading across a filthy convenience store floor.

"Mathers?" I said. "Really?"

"His first… service… was last Sunday. It was… well attended."

The central shooter paused again, and he lifted his head toward the tree line where Tak and I lay. He was a slight, skinny kid one that looked vaguely familiar now that his earphones and safety glasses were off. His gaze lingered in our general direction for a few moments before turning away.

"I thought… you should know," Tak said to me. The shooters were inspecting their targets; their coach was walking toward them, saying something I couldn't hear. "Your work… isn't over."

"My work?" I said. "My work?" Tak didn't answer.

"The boy in the middle looks very familiar to me," I said. He was wearing black jeans that looked too big for him and a black T-shirt with some band logo. The shirt was so baggy it seemed to be floating above his wiry frame. He didn't look insane; if anything he looked too normal and that was more disturbing to me. The three boys turned towards their coach, he was the only one not smiling.

"I think I recognize him. I think…"

My voice trailed off, because I realized that Tak was no longer beside me. I looked over my shoulder and saw him moving like a shadow through the trees.

I watched the people below awhile longer. When I finally did withdraw and begin the long walk home I can't say that I was any lonelier than when we walked out.

I went back to school the following day. Mom dropped me off, kissing me on the cheek before I stepped out of the car.

"I started making you a sandwich for lunch this morning," she said. "Isn't that funny?"

I smiled at her. "Pretty funny."

I leaned over and kissed her again, and then I went into the school.

Walking into the school was a bit strange—it is always strange for the new kid, even the old new kid. Most of the people I saw in the foyer and down the hall recognized me; some nodded in greeting, some looked away, some whispered behind their hands to skulking companions. I'd almost made my way to the office before I was attacked.

I heard her shriek before she slammed into me from behind, pinning my arms against my sides as she screeched my name.

"Tommeeeee!" she said, and I recognized her voice even before I was able to wriggle around enough in her iron grip to see her face. Actually, not her face but her hair. Her pink, pink hair that rose up in spiny tufts that would have tickled my nose and chin if I could feel them. She was squeezing me tight enough to crush the life out of me, so I'd have been unlikely to notice the tickle in any case.

"I missed you so much, we missed you so much. All of us! You look great, Tommy! You smell great, too! Is that Z? Are you still wearing Z? That bottle Phoebe bought you, are you wearing that you are aren't you? Tommy, we're all so proud of you, and you..."

"I..." I managed to say. Ever articulate. Margi released me from and took a step back, looking me over a moment before again wrapping her arms around me and pressing herself close in yet another fleshy embrace. Somehow she managed to do this without slowing her mouth down even a beat.

"... and you are back here with us now, I'm so happy, so, so, happy! Wait until Phoebe sees you, she's going to flip! And Adam, and..."

"Margi, I..." I managed. I wished that I could feel more. I imagined that Margi was very warm, a small furnace, a dynamo. It wouldn't have killed me to hug her back but my body was a slab of ice.

"Margi Vachon," a stern voice behind us said. "Are you aware that PDAs are punishable by detention at Oakvale High School?"

Margi released me, her cheeks already turning the color of her hair. I turned around and saw Principal Kim standing and glowering behind us, her hands on her hips. I'd often wondered how such a strong, authoritative voice could come from such a slight woman.

The principal's dark look cleared as she broke into a smile; a rare moment of good humor from her. "But I think we'll make an exception in this case. Welcome back, Mr. Williams," she said. Her hug was not as aggressive as Margi's was, but it was every bit as surprising.

Thirty minutes later I was walking to class my first class. Principal Kim made it very clear how happy she was that I'd returned, and she made it very clear how happy she was at the increase in what she termed "undead enrollment" had grown so much—forty-three new students—since I'd left, but she was also very clear about letting me know her concerns about me being back.

"You aren't just a student," she said. "You are a media personality. A sort of celebrity. And like any figure that has caught the eye and imagination of the public, you have to expect a certain degree of... undue attention."

I'd remained silent as she spoke; there was no point in denying what she was saying. I'm not entirely naive and any disavowal of my "status" in the community would only be false modesty.

"You are also a symbol now," she had said, and looked away as though embarrassed by what she was saying. "An important one. I hope you'll agree that we should take certain... precautions with you being here at Oakvale High. Don't you agree?"

"I agree," I said, and asked her what she was thinking in terms of precautions.

She mentioned security guards, metal detectors, bag and locker searches, zero tolerance for any bullying or harassment of the differently biotic. Oakvale was a rural community, one that prior to my baby steps towards becoming "a symbol" had been relatively free from violence and crime, but what she was suggesting were measures more likely to be found in tough inner city schools—or prisons.

"I might be a..." —and here my pause had more to do with me carefully choosing my words—"... media figure... but I'm also a person. I think that what you are proposing will cause even more people to... hate me."

She nodded. "And possibly the other forty-three as well," she said. "But I have to think that it will be safer for them if we go that route. Safer for everyone. The Hunter Foundation has graciously offered a sizable grant to properly equip the school, so I won't even have to try to squeeze money from the already tight school budget."

Sitting there, I thought about how odd that the principal was discussing what amounted to policy decisions with me. But I knew the subtext of what she was telling me as well: be careful.

She shifted in her chair. "Unless you have other ideas?"

I didn't. For the moment, I didn't.

And now there were a thousand different ideas, thoughts, and words rolling like a swift tide through my mind, the same thoughts I've had on every moment of every endless night since I left Oakvale a few months ago.

In just a few short steps I would arrive at the classroom, and I would see her.

Phoebe.

I've very rarely been thankful that I was dead before, that all but a small range of my physiological functions have been shut down, but I was thankful then. I could only imagine how my body would have reacted during those moments, what havoc the swirling pools of my mind would have caused a living body to experience. Sweaty palms, upset stomach, shortness of breath, dry mouth, extreme nausea, convulsions, heart attack, instant death. I shuffled forward; I opened the door.

The class was silent, in the middle of a quiz or a test, but most turned to look at me as I crossed the threshold. My eyes found her immediately, in her usual seat near the window where the sunbeams streaming through the blinds made her long dark hair shine and catch the light like a raven's ring. She turned as well and even across the room I could hear her breath catch, a slight, barely perceptible gasp that I could feel move through me and reverberate against the walls of my heart. Her green eyes flashed and lowered and I imagined a spot of color rising on her smooth, white cheeks.

"Tommy," Mrs. Rodriguez said, a slight tone of surprise and delight inherent in her voice, the way she might thank a student for leaving a chocolate bar on her desk. "Welcome back. Please take an open seat in the back row."

I nodded at Mrs. Rodriguez, but then my eyes drifted back to the beautiful girl sitting beside the window. Some moments later I noticed Adam Layman sitting at the desk behind her; he lifted his chin toward me with the slightest of acknowledgements. I might have detected a trace of wry humor glinting in his unblinking eyes, but it may have just been a trick of the same light that bathed his girlfriend so beautifully. I nodded back and started to take my seat.

And that was when I noticed the boy from the shooting range, staring forward at Adam's broad back as though his eyes could bore holes through his flesh. I was certain now that I recognized him; not only from the previous day, but from an incident of some months ago when his photograph appeared in a free zombie newspaper that friends of mine put out called *The Underground*. I sometimes linked articles from their site to my blog, mysocalledundeath.com. If I was remembered correctly, the boy was responsible for the retermination of two zombies, people like Adam and me. Of at least two zombies—if there were some, there were likely to be more.

The boy didn't glance at me. He just sat with his arms at rest on his desk. He wore blue jeans, black sneakers, and a zip-up gray hoodie over a white T-shirt. His pencil and his quiz lay before him on the desk, and I could see rows of neat, uniform writing toward the bottom half of the page. I was almost certain it was him.

Dorman, his name was. Davis or Denny Dorman, something like that. I wasn't certain of the story exactly, but I know it had something to do with reterminating zombies in either Louisiana or Texas, in a state where he wouldn't be reviled for his action but praised as a hero.

None of the zombies in the class—five of them, including Adam—rose when the early "undead bell" sounded to give them an additional five minutes to let them get to their next class. They all stayed so they could stop by my desk to say hello or to thank me. Even some of the living welcomed me back, chucking or slapping my shoulder as they passed with what I assumed was an expression of solidarity. The gestures from the traditionally biotic were unexpected and especially appreciated.

The boy in gray—Dorman—wasn't among my well-wishers, however. I watched from the corner of my eye as he lifted his books and headed for the exit. He seemed to take special care not to look at me as he walked out. He moved very deliberately but managed not to look hurried.

I was certain that he wanted to destroy me. He didn't do anything to telegraph this desire; he didn't leer or wink like Pete Martinsburg might have done, but I could sense this desire burning within him as fiercely as my desire for Phoebe burned within me. He said "excuse me" to a larger boy blocking his path, and I could hear a slight lisp in his voice. Then he was gone, slipping into the flow of student traffic in the hall beyond.

Adam and Phoebe waited until most of the class had left before approaching me. Adam seized my hand in his with a grip that I'm certain would have painful if I could have felt it.

"I'm glad you're… back, Tommy," he said. I think he meant it, too. I was sort of touched by his sincerity. Phoebe, though—her smile looked painted on her pretty face, and I thought she was blinking an awful lot when she finally spoke to me, like maybe I was something causing her vision to blur. Her voice—the voice I'd heard in my head every free moment ever since I'd left—was soft and tentative. I'd only heard those qualities in her voice once before, when we first met, really met, that night long ago at the edge of the Oxoboxo woods.

"Yes," she said, and I'm sure I would have shivered if I'd still been alive. "We're all glad you're back."

"I'm glad to be back," I said. I stared at her too long, too openly. I didn't possess the willpower to take my eyes off her. She noticed; Adam noticed.

But he didn't haul off and hit me as he might have. Adam may be the best person I know in terms of heart; certainly the best male. I was glad to see that he was moving and speaking far better than he had been when I left; but then, if Phoebe's affection—her love—couldn't bring him back from the edge of death, nothing could.

"You and… Phoebe," he said. "Have some… catching up… to do."

I couldn't tell if Phoebe was thankful to him or wanted to crush his instep with the heel of the calf-high boot she was wearing. Probably both.

"We do, I suppose," she said, flipping a stray strand of hair over her shoulder with her fingertips. "Do you have sixth period free?"

"I do," I told her. I really had no idea; I hadn't memorized my schedule yet.

"Great," she said, and for the first time I thought that her smile slipped into something real. "Want to walk? They started letting us outside just last week."

"Sure," I said, wondering if the elimination of that newfound freedom was going to be one of the first "precautions" that Principal Kim undertook to keep her school and it's student body—and bodies—safe.

"Great," she repeated, and I saw the nervousness return to her smile, and I heard it in her voice. She looked up at Adam and clutched his arm, as though for support. "Meet me by the bleachers?"

I told her I would. The bleachers was where we had a fight, where I decided that I should leave Oakvale. It seemed fitting.

"Later," Adam said, and the hand that had just gripped mine enclosed Phoebe's as he led her out of the room. I willed her to look back over her shoulder at me, but she didn't.

"Go ahead and follow them, Tommy," I heard a voice behind me say. Mrs. Rodriguez; we were the only people left in the room. "You don't want to be late on your first day back."

She was right; I didn't want to be late. But I was already too late. Far, far too late.

I stopped by my locker after my next class was over and spun the dial to enter the three-digit code of my combination. The locker sprung open on my first attempt, and I saw that someone had left me a gift. There was a white card taped to the shelf, just below eye level, with a single word written in blue, the letters even and delicately formed but formed, also with confidence.

Boom

I plucked the card from where it hung, the tape tearing away from the metal with a soft rasping sound, the sound of a bandage being ripped free from an unhealed wound. Whoever had hung the card there had managed to unlock my locker; either by breaking the code with the expertise of a safecracker or by having gotten the combination from someone who knew it. I'd been careful not to let anyone see me work the combination earlier—and even if they had been watching they would have been unable to decipher it, because it typically took me three or four tries—and so to find the card taped there, perfectly centered rather than merely slid through the vents, was a bit of a shock. A shock, but not the biggest one.

I flipped over the card and found it wasn't a card at all but a photograph. The pale blond girl in the photograph was smiling at someone, posing almost, but it wasn't at whoever had taken the picture that I held in my hands. This photographer was behind and to the left of whomever the girl was smiling at so that her pretty face was almost in profile.

Karen.

And on the other side, that one word: *Boom*. I didn't recognize Karen's surroundings; she was sitting on a shaded bench or a table on the edge of what looked like a small parking lot, her long legs drawn up beneath her. I could see cars behind her. I thought that maybe she was at a fast-food restaurant or someplace like that. She was wearing cutoff jean shorts and a white blouse and her feet were bare. I didn't think the photograph had been taken in Connecticut, and at first I thought that it was an older photo, one taken before she'd died, because she looked so lively and healthy in this shot, but there was something about the photo that made think it had been taken recently. I hadn't heard from Karen in a while, but then I had been pretty hard to get hold of for some weeks.

I realized that I was stroking her image with my fingertips, as though I could reach into the photograph and touch her and assure myself that she was all right. It bothered me that she hadn't been aware of this shot being taken. It bothered me that someone was able to open my locker undetected and tape it there. It bothered me that I didn't know the nature of what was obviously a warning—no, not a warning, a threat. Was it myself or Karen that I was supposed to worry about?

I looked around. I was almost certain that it was Dorman who put the picture in my locker, but I had no proof. If it had been Pete Martinsburg, he would have been waiting at the intersection of the hallways with a few of his cronies, grinning like jack-o'-lanterns as they waited for my reaction. But whoever had put the photo in my locker, it wasn't Pete. The amnesty granted to the undead at Oakvale had not been granted to him; he was still not allowed to attend school. This was someone who was far more calculating, someone paradoxically far less emotional about the way he hated me.

This was the way "life" would be for us now, I thought. Now that we'd made some progress and were granted some protections and rights, we no longer had to huddle in the shadows and were free to shamble out in the light. But that didn't mean that we'd overcome our enemies. All we really did is switch places with them, because they were still out there and we would be forever looking in every darkened doorway and every place where shadows gathered for the next bioist threat.

Boom.

Time slowed to a speed agonizing even to one with the patience of the dead as I waited for sixth period to roll around. I thought of her, I thought of Karen, I thought of Tak. I thought of Margi and of Adam and I had a sudden flash of insight. I knew why Adam didn't hate me, even though my inaction had led to his death and zombification. He didn't hate me because my inaction also allowed him a slim window to pass through and capture Phoebe's heart. One's life for her love? It seemed a fair trade.

My train of thought was interrupted when I realized that the differently biotic boy who sat down next me in my fourth period biology class just as the final bell rang was someone I recognized.

"You again," he said, which may have been the warmest greeting he's ever given me.

"Popeye?" I said. "Is that you? I didn't recognize you without the pins and studs." He still wore his sunglasses, though, which was a good thing for all of our traditionally biotic classmates.

"Once again your sense of… humor… underwhelms," he said. "I will not… be your… lab partner."

The next time he spoke was to ask the teacher if he could dissect his own arm rather than the fetal pig she was going to assign. I laughed along with the other DBs—and a few of the braver traditionally biotics—and I thought about the irony that the only laughs I'd had since my return were provided by humorless guys like Popeye and Tak. He was on his best behavior for the rest of the class, and I tried to pretend it was normal for the living and the dead to discuss cutting up another dead thing. Alas, poor piggies, what secrets do you hold? I would have to look forward to those secrets on another day, because apparently it took a whole day to discuss the dissection before the dissection could actually begin. Popeye, for his part, looked very eager.

Outside of class I was stopped in the hall by Kevin Zumbrowski, and unlike Popeye, at first I didn't recognize him at all. The pronounced hitch in his walk that I remembered from our time together in Undead Studies class was nearly gone. He was carrying books in his left arm, and from what I remembered he could barely move his arm a few months ago. He and Sylvia had been the most severely limited zombies in our class in terms of their mobility, and here he was, getting around nearly as well as Adam or I could. I took my seat wondering if Kevin had met someone like Phoebe that was bringing him back to life.

I learned that it was not the affection of a girl that was giving him new spark and verve. I said hello to him after he called me by name and gripped me by the upper arm. I didn't have the sensitivity to gauge such things any more, but my sense was that his grip was strong, surprisingly strong for a boy who hadn't been able to grasp a pencil just a few months before.

I saw that his expression hadn't changed from when I'd seen him last; the placid, slightly surprised grin he always wore on his face was still fixed in place. But that would come, I thought; control over the facial muscles was much harder to regain than control over the larger muscles.

"Tommy," he said to me. "It is not… too late… for you… to repent."

"I'm sorry?" I replied. He was speaking more normally than before, the pauses in his speech shorter, but I could not have been more stunned to hear him talk about repentance than if he'd been talking about purple elephants gathering for a touch football game on the field outside.

"You can still… ask… for forgiveness," he said. "It isn't… too… late."

"I'm not sure what you mean, Kevin. I…"

He held his free arm out toward me, and there was a piece of paper half crumpled in his clutching hand. Hands, like the muscles of the face, were difficult; his fingers didn't bend as I slid the paper from his hands.

"Please… read it, Tommy," Kevin said, expression never changing. "Please."

I smoothed the paper out. It was a pamphlet, and at the top were the words One Life Ministries, which was the church organization founded and run by Reverend Nathan Mathers.

"Kevin, what..."

"Please, Tommy," he said, releasing me and lifting his clawed hand between us. "Just... read... it."

I watched him walk away. Kevin always had a very pronounced limp to his walk, as though the entire right side of his body had been switched off, but his movements almost seemed jaunty as he walked down the hall. He disappeared into the slipstream of the living, many of whom had less bounce in their step than he did.

I took a closer look at the pamphlet he'd pressed into my hand. There was a crudely stylized painting beneath the name of the church depicting a glowing, vaguely human form standing or riding a platform of white clouds. The form stared down from his misty perch, rays shining down from his featureless face onto a throng of ragged figures gathered below. Many of the figures were on their knees; most were raising their arms in supplication, or in fear, their pale and mottled flesh visible through the holes and tears in their shabby garments. Their eyes were wide and staring and ringed with black; their shaggy hair ideal for the nesting of vermin. These were meant to be my people, but in caricature, the hideously stereotypical depiction of my people. In the sky next to the glowing figure was a question, written in a flowing cursive script, the final word bold and twice the height of the others. "*Are you among the* **Damned**?"

Below the writhing and wretched figures was another line of text: "*And the truth shall set you free...*"

I opened the pamphlet, but I wasn't expecting truth or freedom inside.

"*You have died and been spat from the mouth of Hell to return and walk the earth as one of the* **Damned**. *But is your punishment to be* **Eternal**????"

Kevin, I thought, distracted by another crude drawing of a

zombie, a rotting skull face taken right out of an old comic book. What are you doing? What have you done?

"*It may not be* **Too Late** *to* **Repent**!" the pamphlet informed me. I read on through the next few paragraphs, which held out a slim hope for me and my kind to again regain our Creator's favor. By following a strict regimen of atonement, one that included sequestering myself from others of my kind (the **Evil Dead**), praying a minimum of twelve hours a day, and devoting the remaining twelve hours to furthering the anti-Evil Dead teachings of Reverend Mathers and One Life Ministries, I could possibly open the filthy vessel of my worm-infested body to the Creator's touch and allow it to be rejoined with my missing soul. The pamphlet implied that this reunion of accursed body and immortal soul was an outside chance, however, but the promise of **Everlasting Hellfire**, which was to be my fate if I was reterminated while in my fallen state, made every attempt, no matter how desperate, a worthwhile endeavor.

My head spun; I felt as though **Everlasting Hellfire** was blazing a charred furrow in my mind. I crumpled the pamphlet and took aim at a trash can outside the gym, but then I thought better of it and brought it to my locker, smoothing it out and sealing it in a pocket of my backpack. I closed my eyes and I was back in the woods with Tak, but now when we looked down at the line of shooters there were four of them, the one on the end a little more unkempt, a little more gray of complexion and sallow-cheeked, but no less steady as he squeezed the trigger of his gun. My first emotion wasn't anger but guilt; how could we have let this happen to Kevin? What level of loneliness on his part or neglect on ours had allowed One Life's vision of an undead-free America (and afterlife) seem more appealing than what we—what I—was working for? What good was it to march and make speeches if in doing so we overlooked the people just across the hall from us?

The bell rang, shattering my concentration. I began walking, aimlessly, and then I realized that sixth period had finally arrived.

I met Phoebe at the bleachers. She was already waiting for me, high up and all the way down at the end. She was bent over book on her lap, one finger marking her place, but her chin was propped on her hand and her eyes were following the path of a Frisbee arcing between two kids on the field before her. One of the kids made a diving leap as the wind threatened to pull the spiraling disk out of reach, and his companion cheered on his athleticism and the flair he'd employed to make the catch. Phoebe's reaction, if any, was hidden to me. She caught sight of me, and lifted her book in a little wave which I returned as I climbed the metal bleachers.

She said my name, and for just a moment I forgot that I was dead.

She was wearing black again; she'd gone through a period after Adam's death where she avoided wearing her usual goth-garb so as not to look like she was in mourning; but whereas once the darkness of her clothes served as an ironic counterpoint to the joie de vivre she projected with her smile and her carriage, they now seemed all too appropriate. The world has weighed upon her these past few months; there seemed to be an air of tragedy hovering around her like a gray halo. She was still the most beautiful girl I had ever seen, but it was hard to look at her and not to hate myself for my role in the darkening of her light.

"Congratulations," she said. "Everyone is so proud of you, Tommy."

I glanced at her; she was still tracking the spinning disk. "Thank you."

"Not everyone, maybe, but you know what I mean. They missed you."

"I missed them, too," I said. Speech was suddenly a difficulty again, like when I'd first returned. "I missed you."

Her green eyes flickered in the sunlight. "I liked reading about all the people you met on your travels," she said, her words coming quick as though to compensate for the slowness of my own speech. "How's Christie?"

"She's… fine," I said.

One of the figures below us rose up for a high-flung disk that sailed just over his outstretched fingers.

"I'd love to meet her."

"Soon, maybe," I said. Staring into the sun would be less painful than looking at her. I tried to watch the Frisbee instead.

"Now that you are back, what are your plans?" she said, waving her book, an old paperback with a garish reptilian creature on the sun-faded cover. "I mean, are you still going to speak out, you think?"

I didn't answer right away. The truth was I didn't have any real plans for a change and I couldn't think of one with her sitting so close to me.

"You are going to rejoin Undead Studies, right? We didn't have it for a few weeks—there wasn't much point when zombies were outlawed from the school. Adam took a page from your book…"

Here she stumbled, just a fraction, but I caught it and so did she. "… and kept going to school even though it was illegal. His big protest move."

She laughed. Music. "I don't think it was quite the same with him, though. Everybody knew him, knew him before, so…"

"Phoebe," I said, cutting her off. I touched her arm and she startled, her book slipping from her hand, bouncing off the bleacher below us and flapping end over end to the ground below.

She'd gasped when I touched her, with surprise or revulsion or both. She peered between the gleaming silvered bleachers and then she turned toward me, smiling.

"Sorry," we said, in unison.

We walked down the steps and went under the bleachers to rescue her book.

"You were going to say something?"

She was walking in front of me, which made it harder for her to see me lie.

"I was going to tell you how much Adam better seems since before I left."

She murmured in affirmation, but went on to another subject.

"I've been reading a lot lately," she said as we went down. "Old stuff, new stuff, anything that looks interesting."

"Have you been writing anything?" I asked. We walked under the bleachers, striped by the light that slipped between the metal benches. I found her book in the grass beside a soda cup and cleaned the cover off with my sleeve. We were talking now, having a conversation, whereas before it had seemed we'd just entered into some strange mannered ritual of communication, a verbal dance where the things we said were just there to obscure the things were weren't saying.

"Poetry, you mean? Some, I guess. I don't really show it to anyone, though."

I held the book out to her. There was a shout of joy from the field beyond, and then there was another sound, that of the lid being removed from a can of tennis balls, and then a whistle and an impact, a wet impact, and a spray of red flew from my arm and the smile disappeared from her face.

"Get down!" I yelled, and in turning I half felt another whapping impact on my side and then on my thigh. I willed myself to be twice as tall, twice as wide. I willed myself to be a magnet for bullets, for slings, for arrows, for all manner of harm. There was no pain, there is never any physical pain anymore. The shots were coming from the tree line beyond the bleachers. I saw the slightest movement, a branch displaced, and I was running. I was running, a target as large as a school bus, a target with a gravity strong enough to pull down the sun and the moon. They would not hurt her. I would not let them hurt her anymore.

I was hit again, a solid thump in the chest like an echo of a heartbeat, and the next one struck me directly in the center of my forehead. Head shot—the only way to permanently kill the dead was with a head shot like the one I'd just received. An explosion of red filled my eyes and cascaded down my face and I knew it was over. I sank down to my knees, half the distance between her and the Oxoboxo woods.

And I was happy, happy like I hadn't been since she had followed me out into the woods on a cold moonlit night. Happy like I hadn't been since I'd held her in my arms in the humid glow of lights at a school dance. Happy like I hadn't been since I thought that there was something other than the cold, dead existence my "life" has become.

No one knows why we, the dead, have returned. Theories both logical and ludicrous abound, though no one has solved that mystery to the satisfaction of anyone concerned. But in that moment as I was kneeling, head-shot, in the grass, the sun shining down upon me, I thought at last I knew.

I'm not certain how long I remained on my knees, but eventually it occurred to me that zombies, when they bleed, do not bleed red. I wiped some of the stickiness away from my eyes. The "gore" covering me was a viscous and pinkish, almost Day-Glo color. I'd been shot, yes, but not with bullets. Paintballs.

They—or he—had shot me with paintballs. The goal this time had been to terrorize, not to reterminate. **Everlasting Hellfire** would have to wait.

I heard Phoebe running toward me as I struggled to my feet.

"I didn't hesitate this time," I said over my shoulder. My vision was blurry; my left eye sticky with the paint.

"Are you all right, Tommy?" she said.

I was more than all right; I was elated. I hadn't hesitated and I was about to repeat that fact when I noticed the splash of pink-red on the black sleeve of her left arm and knew then that acting quickly wasn't always enough. I faced her, a ridiculous clown spattered in paint, a mockery of my supposed heroism.

"There was no Christie, Phoebe," I told her. "At least no one that mattered. There was only you. There was always only you."

I couldn't see her reaction, but I knew that my words had stopped her as surely as the shot to the head had stopped me. The Frisbee players had trotted over to the bleachers by this time, one of them proclaiming how I got "pasted," the other asking me if I was okay. I turned and walked into the woods. I knew that whoever attacked us was long gone, his gear stowed, the evidence removed, and that he would be whistling softly to himself as he returned to class. I walked into the woods without any plan or purpose. Maybe I would return to school tomorrow, maybe I wouldn't. Maybe I would "live" every moment wondering if someone close to me was going to be harmed because of me; maybe I would find some way to overcome that fear.

Maybe I could forget Phoebe like I should. But I knew I wouldn't.

I walked into the woods, and this time it was she who hesitated, or worse, made a conscious and deliberate decision not to say my name, not to stop me.

Of course I went back to school; I was there the very next day. I hugged Margi, I told Kevin that he would always be my friend, I forced eye contact with the boy I now knew to be David Lee

Dorman from Pitkin, Louisiana, and I wished him a good morning. If I was a "symbol," as Principal Kim had termed me, then I was going to be the best and most visible symbol that I could be. And if they reterminated me, so be it. Few symbols had greater impact and influence than a martyr for the cause.

I found Adam and Phoebe, and I told them that I loved them. Adam looked at me like I was crazy but as I turned I imagined that I could hear Phoebe whisper, "Thank you." I couldn't entrust her protection to anyone else, not even Adam. I won't be leaving Oakvale again anytime soon.

My mind seemed clearer now, as though that shot to the forehead opened a path to insight in my mind, a chakra, a portal to enlightenment and truth. The truth shall set you free, as Kevin's pamphlet reminded me. I have finally told the truth about my feelings, both to Phoebe and to myself, and my fleeting hope, one born of surviving what I thought was to be my second death, was that by telling her my truth I would find the freedom that the many months and the many people I'd met along the way couldn't grant me.

But my truth has not set me free. If the telling of that truth was supposed to produce a key, the purpose of that key was not to open, but to close and lock away forever.

I am careful now not to be seen with her unless it can't be helped, and when it can't be helped I make certain we are not alone. It is crucial that I give the impression she is no more or less important to me than anyone else we are with. The closest that we come is a classroom away, a quiet boy who patiently longs for my destruction just one of the many obstacles between us. Even then, I try very hard to not even glance in her direction, and some days I am almost successful. When I am fortunate enough to look at her, it is usually from a distance. The distance is safer for her and less painful for me.

Miles and miles, and the truth I carried within me seemed to beat at the bars with each step I took away from her. But my truth wasn't the jailed—it was the jail itself. My truth imprisons me; my dead heart sits shackled and still within a cage of dry and brittle bones, never to beat again.

MY SO-CALLED UNDEATH

MY LIFE AS A ZOMBIE

All You Zombies

Hi everyone—Margi here. This blog is more cob-webby than the Haunted House, isn't it? It will say "posted by PhoebeKendall" at the bottom of this post but that is just another example of how the Internet is a total liar. And why is Internet always capitalized, anyhow?

I asked Phoebe if I could post something here and she said sure go ahead here's my password. PSA: Kids and kid-like people, never ever ever give anyone any of your Internet account passwords. Or your wallet, your favorite stuftie, your ATM card, your mojo, or your car keys if you are old enough to drive. You wouldn't want some creeper getting a hold of that stuff would you? Luckily for Phoebe, I am not a creeper, I am her best friend. And besides, she says that she is never going to post here again, anyhow. She doesn't want me to get into it, but she was a bit embarrassed by Tommy's last post. You'd think that maybe she'd be over it and all now that Tommy is back home from his trip and back in school, but I guess it is more complicated than that.

But um yeah I'm not supposed to talk about that. Next topic, please?

So yes Tommy is back in school. And Colette! And we're having a blast every day except when she's being all mopey about missing DeCayce and everything (he's back in New Jersey with his band but they get together like every other week so I don't know what she's complaining about; at least she has a boyfriend), and Adam, and Melissa, and Cooper, and Tayshawn and Jacinta and Popeye (yes! even Popeye!). Pretty much every zombie kid I know in town is back at school, except for Tak.

Tommy, you see, was pretty successful. Politically, at least. Although Prop 77 didn't go through exactly as it was written, a number of limited rights were granted to the differently biotic, including the right to get an education. So the zombies are all back, shambling through the hallways, moving just a little faster than Phoebe before her morning coffee. Which is great! Yay, zombies!

Except, now our school is really, really crowded. *Really* crowded. And there's um, conflict. Not bullying exactly, at least not the same sort of obvious bullying that was happening back when Tommy was first starting to speak up. More like… intimidation. I don't know how to write about it yet so I won't. Soon, maybe.

Anyhow, I'm going to try and get Phoebe and Tommy to post eventually. But not until *I* get to have some fun first! I'll be answering questions, too, so post lots.

Bye!
—Margi Vee

OMZ!

That's my new catch phrase—OMZ, as in "Oh my zombie!" I always thought it was kind of blasphemous dropping the "G" word for every little silly thing that happens online or in life.

Omz, that's such a pretty dress!

Omz, Adam, you are so funny!

or

I can't come over tonight, Phoebe. Omz, I have so much homework to do.

I looked up Omz on Wikipedia and it turns out it is also the initials of a large Russian-based international heavy industry and manufacturing conglomerate. Oh well. Sorry, large Russian-based international heavy industry and manufacturing conglomerate! Omz is now the official catchphrase of Margi Vachon!

Don't know if you have following the news, but ever since Tommy's successes in the nation's capital, there have been more and more reports of international zombie-ness. There's bunches of 'em in Canada and Mexico. There's dozens in the U.K. and France and Spain. Yay, Euro-zombies. And, omz, there's supposedly some in Tokyo, too! How cool is that?

Of course, not all these reports are credible, and supposedly some governments are suppressing zombies just like in the United States, and etc., etc., etc.

So if you know any international differently biotic folks, tell them we support them. Tell them to stop by, even! I'd love to hear zombie spoken with a French accent! Omz, that would be great!

Living with the Dead

So now I have my very own login and password, courtesy of Mr. Tommy Williams. I asked him if he wanted to post anything and he said that he didn't really feel like it.

"Really?" I said. "But what about being the voice of the Dead Generation? What about all the people that supported you in your trip to Washington? Don't you want to update them on your, ah, life?"

He just stared at me. Whatever you do, don't try and win a staring contest with a zombie. Ain't gonna happen.

Some of you have asked about Phoebe posting as well; I wish I could give you an update but she's kind of not speaking to me because of my last post. I'm sure she already regrets giving me her password (remember kids: don't give out yer passwords), just as I'm sure Tommy will regret it in a couple days, too. Oh, well. She'll get over it. If I can't be me, I can't be me.

Colette is still talking to me, of course. She dyed half of her hair metallic blue and it looks super cool. I'll stick with pink, though.

Oakvale High Update: Classes are way way over-crowded now that the db kids have come back. There's got to be over thirty of us packed in a class now. And I get to sit next to that charmer, Popeye, in one of those classes. His real name is Chad, can you believe it? Chad Doyle. He absolutely flipped out when Mrs. Rodriguez called him Chad, though. He took off his sunglasses and everything. And his shirt, which was not a pretty sight, believe me, because he's done some really disgusting things—bodifications, he calls them—to himself. Like removed layers of skin right down to the muscle and stuff like that. Too nauseating to write about, really.

"Please put your glasses on, Popeye," Mrs. Rodriguez told him.

"Why?"

"You know why. And your shirt."

"I don't get it. Pinky Tuscadero over there gets to do whatever she wants to her hair, and gets to wear like three thousand bracelets, but I can't…"

"The school has a shirts and shoes policy, Popeye," Mrs. Rodriguez said, interrupting him. "And pants, before you get any ideas. It's all in the handbook."

"Oh, well, if it is in the handbook," he said. "That's like being in the Constitution itself. Or the Bible. The handbook. What about the sunglasses, Mrs. Rodriguez? I bet 'the handbook' has a policy on those as well, doesn't it? And the policy is that they need to come off."

He's such a jerk sometimes. He didn't even seem to notice that Tori Simmons was crying, she was so scared of him.

Mrs. Rodriguez sighed. "We're willing to make an exception for you," she said.

"Maybe I don't want to be the exception. Maybe I want to be the rule."

She told him that if he didn't sit down, put his glasses and shirt back on, and spend the rest of the class with his mouth closed and his hands neatly folded in front of him, she would make certain that he was suspended from school.

He complied, taking his time about it. I don't think he really cares about being suspended, but I think he wouldn't want to miss a few days of getting in people's faces and offending them.

He's in trouble all the time and the weird thing is I know he's trying to get into trouble. I think I'm pretty close to telling him off.

PURPOSE STATEMENT

THE DEAD BOY drummed his fingers on the desktop, the steady rhythmic ticking of his nails sounding like the approach of a slow metal insect. Popeye had replaced his original fingernails with pieces of thin curved copper; he'd first used shortened razor blades until Principal Kim made him remove them, telling him that he'd be expelled if she saw them again. Popeye wasn't really interested in school at this stage of his unlife, but he was interested in finding out what the far edges of his boundaries were, and so he removed the razors.

"Chadwick," his teacher said. "Please stop the tapping."

He considered continuing—he hated being called by his meatlife name; it triggered memory cells in his brain that he would prefer remain dead. Chadwick Sebastian Appleton; if anyone needed proof of his parents' deep hatred of him, there it was. Not that many called him "Chadwick" when he was alive; usually it was "Chad" or "Sebby" or "Seb," all of which he found even worse.

But he didn't continue. He stopped tapping. The goal, after all, was not to push the limits of normal human jerk behavior—there were plenty of breather goons like TC in his class who could provide the normal, everyday irritations. What he wanted to do was to continue to shock the living with the fact of his being dead. Any beating-heart idiot could drum on the desktop; only a zombie like Popeye could empty a room just by taking off his sunglasses.

"Thank you," Mrs. Rodriguez said. He waved a little mock salute.

There were seven dead kids in his current class. Since Saint Tommy Williams made his zombie march on Washington last year, many individual states began protecting the rights—scratch that, began *allowing* rights—to their undead populations. Despite Pete Martinsburg's best efforts, Connecticut was one of the first states to pass some laws. So Oakvale High, which had been emptied of undead students—Adam Layman being the last holdout—now had more teenage corpses within its cement walls than the local cemetery.

The undead bell rang—zombie kids were given an additional three minutes to proceed to their next class. Popeye watched the dead rising—ha-ha—from their desks. Cooper Wilson; that red-haired chick; Kevin Zumbrowski, who curled his lip at him as he walked by. Zumbo could beat him easily in a footrace—in fact, the kid seemed like he was getting more spry by the day—but unlike Popeye, he always took advantage of the undead dismissal bell.

Unlike most kids, living or otherwise, Popeye never wanted class to end. He'd stay there all night if he could. Not for any lust for learning, but because being in class was the single best way he knew to offend the status quo.

That has to be a wig, he thought, watching the willowy red-haired girl walk by. Her hair was too shiny and lustrous to be real zombie hair. He didn't like it.

A few minutes later the bell for the normals rang, and Popeye got to his feet. He heard the tendons of his neck stretching as his neck swiveled from the left to the right. He realized that he was being stared at by two kids—that lumbering imbecile TC, and some quiet mousy kid that sat behind him, forever eclipsed by the larger boy's hulking shadow. The boy looked quickly away, as though he could feel the weight of Popeye's return stare even through the dark lenses of the sunglasses stupid Principal Kim made him wear.

Popeye waited for TC to walk by, gesturing expansively with his copper tipped fingers toward the door, as though he were the maître d' at a fine restaurant and TC a frequent—and frequently ridiculed—customer. TC glowered at him as he walked past.

The slight boy hadn't moved from his spot. When at last he looked up at Popeye, Popeye could see the fear in his eyes.

"Can I help you?" Popeye said, and the words came out smooth, barely a hitch between them. Practice, practice, practice.

"They," the boy said, and there was a long enough pause between this word and his next that Popeye wondered if he were secretly dead and just hadn't notified anyone yet.

But then when he spoke, Popeye got the idea that the fear he saw on the boy's pale face was not of him.

"They are going to attack you," he said, his voice a quiet whisper, like he didn't want their teacher to hear. "Today. After school."

Not fear *of* him, Popeye thought, itself unusual. But fear *for* him.

They stood there a moment, the boy clutching his math text and a sketchbook to his chest; he realized the kid was in his art class as well, the one class of the day that Popeye actually put some effort into. He realized that he even sat at the same table as the kid.

Popeye opened his mouth, and the boy's eyes flicked downward, perhaps taking in the filing job that Popeye had done to his teeth.

"Is there a reason why you boys aren't headed to your next class?" Mrs. Rodriguez asked. "Chadwick? Derek?"

Derek, Popeye thought, the question on his lips answered. He'd never bothered to remember any of the beating hearts' names.

Unlike Mrs. Rodriguez, who apparently just loved the word "Chadwick."

"No… problem," he said, turned on the heel of his boot, and stalked out of the class.

At first he didn't realize that Derek was hurrying behind him. He looked over his shoulder at him and Derek was so startled he nearly dropped his sketchbook.

"We have study hall now," the boy said.

Popeye didn't answer. He didn't want anyone in the hallway to think he was having a conversation with a beating heart.

"I… I wanted to tell you that I really liked your last piece in Miss Quin's class," Derek said. "The painting with all of the figures? With the reds and the oranges?"

Popeye continued walking, but maybe he slowed, just a step.

"What did you call it?"

Popeye glanced to the right, and then to the left. People were trying hard not to pay attention to him.

"*Vision of Hell Number Fifty-Three,*" he said.

"Yeah, that's it," Derek said, having pulled even with him. "Are there really fifty-two others? Can I see them?"

"No," Popeye said. The little breather looked hurt, which normally would have made Popeye happy, but the kid was flattering him. Beyond that, he'd tried to warn Popeye that trouble was coming his way. "No, there… aren't… fifty-two… others."

"Oh," Derek said. "Oh, okay. I just really love that painting, you know? It… it makes me feel… I don't know. Strong, or something. Powerful." He was looking at his feet, as though embarrassed by his sudden confidence.

"You can… have it," Popeye said.

"Oh, really? No, I couldn't. I…"

"It is yours," Popeye said. "Just… shut up… about it."

"Oh. Yeah, okay. Thank you. I've... I've got to run to my locker before class, okay?"

Popeye waved him away, like he was shooing a puppy out the door. The kid could have the painting; Popeye was done with it. But maybe it would make more sense to rip it into strips before giving it to him; the kid could learn a number of valuable lessons from that.

Study hall. Popeye was the only zombie in this one, and took his usual seat in the center—the dead center, ha-ha—of the classroom. Best possible position to freak out as many beating hearts as possible. He'd made a girl cry just by ruffling the gills he'd cut into his neck. She didn't attend the study hall anymore—Popeye was rather proud of the fact that the school had instituted a whole new class because of him, an offshoot of the whole stupid Undead Studies class. This class was for living kids that couldn't deal with the presence of the dead in their daily lives, spoiled pampered breather kids who would begin to twitch and shake and have some sort of seizure just being in the presence of the dead. He thought—

"Hi there, Mr. Friendly," an overly perky, yet sarcastic voice said, landing on the seat beside him with a solid thump. He didn't have to turn to know that it was her, the chubby pink one, who was there to ruin what was already a less than optimal day.

"Begone, NF," he said.

"Oh, don't be that way," she said. "You know how I hate being called that."

"I do," he said. "Enn... Eff." *NF* stood for Necro-Friendly, a derogatory name he liked to credit himself for inventing. He hoped it would catch on, but so far there weren't many takers.

She wore a mocking pout on her face as she leaned over his desk, her absurdly large flesh bags coming far too close for comfort. Although he couldn't really feel it, Popeye abhorred the touch of the living, which he knew was an unfortunate weakness because he could terrify far more of his living enemies if he could just bear to reach out and graze them with the dry pads of his fingertips. But he couldn't.

"So…" she said, and again he wondered why the living wanted to emulate the dead with their pauses and false starts. "What's new at the Haunted House? How's ol' Takky doing?"

"He is… on a murder… spree," Popeye said, cursing himself for all the pauses.

"Hey!" she said, peering closely and ignoring him at the same time. "Your horns are gone. What did you do with your horns? Did Miz Kim make you remove them?"

His left hand moved to his forehead, to the raised perforation where he'd hammered in one of the two horns he'd carved by hand from a block of wood.

"Yes," he said. "Yet another… example… of discrimination against the undead… by the living."

"Oh, totally," she said, her ample flesh bouncing as she tucked her chair in beneath her desk. If he could still have thrown up, he would have. "Those horns were awesome. I really liked the ring of nails, too, but I guess I can see why they made you get rid of that. Kind of pointy, after all. Weaponlike."

He stared ruefully at the black holes that ringed his wrist. He'd pounded nine-inch nails pointy-side out through his wrists the day before school, and was made to remove them by the principal before he'd even made it through homeroom.

"Now that I think of it, the horns probably could be considered weapons, too. They were pretty long. And pointy. Pointy is kind of a theme with you, isn't it? Pointy, pointy, pointy."

"Do you have… to sit here?"

"Not really," she said, squirming in her seat, bracelets jangling one way, insipid pink hair flopping that way. She was constant motion. "I want to. I mean, with everything that happened, it gets lonely sometimes. All my friends..."

"Why don't you... sit with them?"

"Well, most of them aren't around here anymore, are they? Ever since Phoebe..."

Popeye nearly cringed—would have, if his body still took reflexive cues from his mind—just upon hearing the name of her, the ultimate NF.

"Sit with... your own... kind... then," he said.

"Oh, you're my kind, Pops," she said. "Believe it."

Realizing that there was nothing that he could do to make her go away—even some of his more nauseating stunts, like lifting his T-shirt to reveal the patch on his side where he'd carved away layers of skin to reveal pink-gray muscles, like half-cooked pork, only amused her. He steeled his heart on ignoring her. She'd spent too much time with the dead, had too many friends among them, to be fazed by any of his pranks.

Derek came into the classroom a few minutes later, followed by TC Stavis. TC thumped Derek as the much smaller boy was taking his seat, knocking him forward. TC either pretended not to notice, or he actually didn't notice—does an avalanche notice a sapling before crushing it? Derek, face red, didn't dare call any attention to himself. Popeye had no love for the little breather, but TC's action angered him.

TC walked by Popeye's desk, giving him the stink eye the whole time. Popeye smiled at him as he went past.

As if, Popeye thought. Giving *me* the stink eye. I *perfected* the stink eye.

At the front of the classroom their study hall proctor, Miss Quin, was talking to Mrs. Rodriguez, who often stopped by on her way to the teacher's lounge. Miss Quin was also Popeye's art teacher, a young woman fresh out of college who was the school's first art teacher in five years. From what he understood, the school had laid off the last one. He'd heard mention of how horrible it was that Oakvale High could sink money into an Undead Studies program but couldn't afford liberal education staples like art and music.

He actually worked in Miss Quin's class, although he never bothered to do any of the class work she assigned. She didn't seem to mind, though, accepting whatever he handed in and commenting on it with enthusiasm, which only irritated him more, as many of his works—*Vision of Hell #53* included—were intended to offend the living.

At least he was able to steal plenty of art supplies, he thought.

She and Mrs. Rodriguez looked deep in conversation. Popeye turned around, and saw Stavis in the back row with his math book out and a frown of concentration on his face.

"Hey, Stavis," Popeye said, trying to keep his voice low. TC's dull and angry eyes rose from his paper. "I hear you are going to kick my ass after school."

He heard Margi trying to shush him, but he kept his eyes locked on TC's

"That's right, wormfood," TC said. "Twice dead."

Popeye opened his mouth, ready to deliver another goading reply, but Mrs. Rodriguez' voice filled the gap.

"Stavis. Appleton. Detention. After school today."

"What? What?" TC said. Popeye turned from him in contempt.

"Why do I get a detention?" he asked. "For enquiring if he is planning on kicking my ass after school?"

"Oh, no," Margi whispered, trying to hide behind a textbook. Light, nervous laughter rippled around the room.

Mrs. Rodriguez was old school, and not easily rattled. "For instigating. Keep it up and you'll have a week of detention."

"*Instigating*? Seriously? He..."

"Chadwick, I'm serious."

She was immune to his glaring. Mrs. Rodriguez could maintain eye contact with him even when his glasses were off; she was a solid teacher and authoritarian, completely unflappable and unassailable. Miss Quin beside her looked a little nervous, and if it had been her he might have kept going, but he'd gain nothing in continuing the argument with Rodriguez, and so he returned to his drawing.

"Watch those two," Mrs. Rodriguez was saying to Ms. Quin. Popeye shook his head and began sketching Mrs. Rodriguez, putting her trapped on the third floor of a burning building.

"That's one way to avoid a beating," Margi said after she'd left, leaving Miss Quin, who looked queasy behind her desk, in charge.

"What?"

"I'm saying that was a pretty clever way of getting out of the fight."

Popeye didn't realize he was pressing down so hard on his drawing until his pencil snapped in half.

"That's what you… think?"

"Well, sure. He can't smack you around if he's sitting in detention with you, can he?"

Popeye tore the ruined page out of his sketchbook and crumpled it. "You are… an idiot," he said.

When their class was over, TC left without further incident. Popeye watched his wide shoulders as he lumbered towards the door. Popeye got up with the intention of following him into the hall and provoking him, but Miss Quin must have heeded her colleague's advice because she stopped him at the doorway.

"Chad," she said.

"Popeye."

"Popeye, what are you planning?"

He grinned, showing her his pointy teeth. "Why, Miss Quin, whatever do you mean?"

"Why are you provoking him?"

That was the first question that anyone had asked him that day that he felt compelled to answer honestly, the first one that was worthy of real thought. He didn't get the chance, though, because she wasn't done speaking.

"You getting into a fight with TC isn't going to improve things for anyone in the school, differently biotic or otherwise. Whatever the outcome of the fight, it can't make things any better for you, either."

"Now that's… a point… on which we must… disagree … Miss Quin."

"You have such talent, Popeye," she said. "Such gifts. Your artwork is really, really special. Those portraits you did… they are among the best I've seen in any high school class."

That's because you've been teaching about eight months, he thought, but didn't say. Flattery was like chocolate to him, and he didn't care who was feeding it to him. He knew their words were empty and off-track but he liked them too much to stop.

"I'm afraid that if you continue down the path that you are on those gifts will be squandered. Wasted."

"Thank you… for your… concern."

She wavered, but didn't look away. He didn't hate her as much as he hated the other bloodbags that ran the school, although he did think she was ridiculous and clichéd in her sandals and her hippie dresses. She didn't wear makeup and she usually tied her short hair back with a ribbon. She looked, to him, like she put a lot of effort and thought into looking arty and casual.

"I *am* concerned. I really do hope you will think about what you are doing with your life. My door will always be open if you want to talk."

"Thanks," he said. Normally he'd close with a sarcastic retort about her "your life" comment, but she was trying to be helpful in her own way. Even if her brand of "help" showed a complete lack of understanding of him and what he was trying to do.

First Derek and now Miss Quin, he thought. Maybe you are growing soft, Popeye.

She had no idea of the bottomless depths of anger swelling inside him, vast oceans of fury that he could feel surging though him even though his blood did not circulate and his heart did not beat. He often wondered why he could have these feelings—what bizarre brain chemistry could create this barely controllable rage, these violent passions for destruction—in a body that was essentially cold, lifeless, and unfeeling?

He used the edge of a copper fingernail to dig at a phantom itch on his wrist as he walked to his final class. On his way he caught a glimpse of TC at the center of a ring of fellow bioists, their eyes shining with hatred.

He blew them a kiss.

There were three kids besides him and TC in detention, none of them zombies. He sat in the very back of the room, TC in the front. They were supposed to use their time in detention for silent study and homework, but Popeye didn't feel much like studying so instead he brought out his sketchbook and began drawing TC's wide back and squat, lumpy head. The proctor of the detention was Mr. Allen, who Popeye thought to be one of the most bioist teachers in the school, miles away politically from beating hearts like Quin and Rodriguez on the necro-friendly continuum, and so he had decided to "behave." It wasn't that Popeye feared reprisals or punishments, it was more that he didn't see much of a point in agitating when he only had an audience of four, and with the others probably being as dull and atavistic as TC was. No sense in wasting good material on clods, he thought.

He reconsidered when he realized that every five minutes or

so his enemy would twist in his seat to cast his most horrific stink eye back at him, his cold demeanor and twitching jawline meant to convey how much he was looking forward to delivering a beat-down to Popeye. Instead of replying, Popeye instead drew a series of TCs on his paper; TC hunched over his desk, TC with a Clint Eastwood-esque glare and thin cigarillo, TC with a thick finger up his wide and flaring nostril.

Mr. Allen, heedless of the reasons why the students were in detention, released the detainees all at once when the hour was up. Popeye hurried to catch up to TC on his way out the door, and TC slowed to let him.

"You're dead," TC told him.

"You're very… observant," Popeye replied. TC looked confused for a moment, and in that moment Popeye saw that Miss Quin was waiting in the foyer, two huge canvas bags lumpy with books and papers at her feet.

TC had recovered his composure. "When we get outside, you better start running. You…"

He stopped when he saw Miss Quin walking toward them.

"Popeye," she called. "Could you help me bring some things to my car?"

TC sneered at him. "You coward," he said. "You are only delaying the indelible."

"*Inevitable*, you utter… moron," Popeye said. "Tomorrow after… school. Behind… the… concession stand. Bring… friends."

The look on TC's face was one of utter shock. Popeye couldn't have taken him more off guard if he'd turned around and socked him in the solar plexus.

"Popeye," Miss Quin called.

"I'm gonna mess you up," TC was saying. "I'm gonna kick…"

"Yeah, yeah," Popeye said. "Sure." And then, speaking loud

enough for his voice to carry into the foyer and down the many halls that ran off it, he called, "Okay, TC! I… accept… your apology!"

He walked over to Miss Quin, leaving TC fuming like a dormant volcano trying to erupt.

"Why didn't… you ask… the meathead?" he said to her. "He's… so much… stronger than… me."

Miss Quin smiled, although he could tell she was trying not to. "The 'meathead' doesn't need a ride home. You do."

He was going to protest and tell her than he'd rather walk—it was his policy not to accept kindness from the beating hearts—but to do so would be to waste hours getting home, so he decided to keep his mouth shut.

"Great," he said, lifting her bags. "Lead… the way."

Miss Quin drove a small beige compact car, the bumpers adorned with stickers proclaiming a love of peace, a fondness for certain dog breeds, and a predilection for failed political movements. There was a paper cup from Starbucks in the holder in the front seat and a couple of CDs from earnest coffeehouse-quality singer/songwriters who'd somehow made it big. When she turned the ignition key the radio came to life; Popeye was unsurprised to find it tuned to NPR.

"Do you live at the farmhouse at the edge of town?" she asked. "The one on Fire Street?"

"Yes," he said. "We call it… the Haunted House."

"Mrs. Rodriguez told me that it really was haunted," she said. "She'd had a couple of the children that lived there in class when she first started teaching. There was a tragedy of some sort, and for years it was empty. The locals said it was haunted with…"

Her voice trailed off. Popeye smiled.

"With?"

"With the spirits of the dead," she said. "Ghosts, I mean."

"Ah," he replied.

"What about your family, Popeye?"

"My only family… are the… dead," he said. "If you mean… my livemeat… family… my parents… we parted ways… before I died."

"You ran away?"

"I did. I went… to the city… seeking fame… and finding… death."

"How… how did you die?"

Popeye was surprised at her directness. Most beating hearts did not like to broach the subject of death, feeling that it was a topic too sensitive and taboo to bring up.

"Overdose," he said, keeping his voice flat.

"I'm sorry."

"Why? Be sorry that… the drugs… don't work… for dead people. That's something… to be… sorry about."

He hoped this embellishment would curtail further questioning; he thought this story was far more romantic and fitting than the reality, which was that he, weak from not having eaten in days, died from hypothermia on a park bench after trying to beg for bus fare home. The dollar eighty-seven in his jacket pocket was stolen between the time he died and the time he returned as a zombie.

"Do they know… ?"

"That their son is a disgusting… zombie? No. But it wouldn't… surprise them."

"Have you thought about contacting them?"

"Every… day," he said. "That's why… I don't."

They drove in silence for a few moments, moments Popeye spent watching the trees fly by his window. The perspective was completely different from the one he saw from his seat on the bus every day.

"Popeye," she said. "Have you thought about submitting work to the Congressional Art Competition I mentioned in class last week? That winter landscape you did, or any of the portraits, really… I think…"

He cut her off. "I have… no intention… of submitting… my work anywhere."

"Are you sure? There could be scholarship money involved. You are one of the best artists in the school, and…"

"No," he said, again interrupting her. "I am… *the*… best artist… in the school."

"So prove it! Get your work into the competition, and…"

"Look," he said. "I don't know… why… you are so… concerned… about me. But… understand… this doesn't… have an after-school… special… ending. You will not… *reach* me. This is not… one of those… stories… where the… tired but… passionate… teacher… breaks through… to the troubled… student… through art and… creativity. Those things… will not… happen. Waste… your time… elsewhere."

She cycled through a half-dozen expressions in a second or two, finally settling on one that, though weary, was more bemused than defeated.

"You've really figured out everything," she said. "It must be nice. How old are you, really?"

"I'd be nineteen," he said, lowering his age by two. "I was… seventeen… when I died." He'd died when he was nineteen, making him one of the oldest zombies in Oakvale, and he "walked the Earth" for about two years after that. He'd be legal now, if zombies had legal status. If he wasn't dead, he'd be able to drink, vote, and drive a car—but legally he was prohibited from any of those basic rights.

She nodded, as though that confirmed certain suspicions. "If you change your mind, my offer to talk still stands."

"Don't be… angry," he told her. "I'm just… trying… to be respectful… of your… time."

"Oh, I appreciate that, I really do. I'm not angry."

"Okay."

"Just disappointed. The hardest thing for a teacher to endure is witnessing potential being wasted."

They were getting close to the Haunted House, and he asked her to drop him off at the edge of the long winding driveway. She complied without asking for an explanation. One could just barely catch a glimpse of the Haunted House through the trees.

She pulled to a stop.

"Oh, and Popeye?"

"Yes?"

"If you need art supplies, just ask me. I'll get you what you want. Please don't steal them."

Popeye didn't know how he should respond to that, so he kept his silence. He opened the door of her car and stepped out.

"See you in class tomorrow," she said.

"See… you," he repeated.

He walked down the driveway. There were two zombies sitting under the large oak tree in the front yard. Popeye ignored them and waved to Tak, who was standing on the slouching porch.

Tak was one of two Haunted House zombies who had elected to not return to Oakvale High once its doors were reopened for their kind—the other being Mal, who had yet to return from the refuge he had found at the bottom of Lake Oxoboxo.

"Learn… much?" Tak asked him.

"Always," Popeye replied.

That night, Popeye worked on a painting with his stolen materials. He had a single lamp that he ran from a very long extension cord powered by the generator downstairs. He liked working in the upstairs room that contained the Wall of the Dead—which had grown to encompass nearly two walls at this point—and he sometimes incorporated faces and images that he saw there into his own work. He found inspiration everywhere but the Wall was so powerful—it was one of the few works of art he knew of that could make him feel jealous that he had not created it himself.

Unlike his time spent at school, which passed at a slow crawl, his time spent working sped by. School time was like dead time, and time spent creating moved at the speed of life.

"You were a… topic… on the bus home… today," Tayshawn said. Tayshawn seemed to enjoy hanging out with him while he worked. Since they'd returned to school, he and Tayshawn were spending more time together, and more time alone. Tak was more of a loner than ever since that business with Karen.

"Do tell," he said.

"Said that… you… purposely got… a detention… so you wouldn't get … beaten up."

Popeye added more burnt sienna to his palette.

"Idiots," he said.

"Yeah," Tayshawn said. "I didn't think… that sounded… much like you."

"No… it… doesn't. How did you… manage… getting on… the bus?" Tayshawn had been hit by a skidding ambulance; the impact shattered his leg and he'd been limping and unable to put weight on it ever since.

"Thorny… helped me."

"That's the… little one? The… beating heart?"

"He's a… good kid. If he was dead, you'd be… good pals."

"Sure. I'm… sorry… I wasn't… there… to help you."

"No… worries. Feels better… every… day. I think… my leg… is healing."

"Really?" Popeye said, turning toward him.

Tayshawn's skin almost looked healthy in the amber light of their single bulb. He nodded.

"I really… think so."

Popeye turned back to his painting. Karen had healed; why not Tayshawn? All he knew was that his many wounds—the holes in his wrists, his gills, the patches where he'd removed his own skin—none of those were getting any better.

But this, he thought, adding more color to the foreground of his work, this does the trick. This does the trick just fine.

At school, everyone seemed to know about the battle royale that was scheduled to happen soon after the final bell; everyone, that is, but the teachers. Excitement hovered over the hallways like a warm mist, and all throughout his day, people were whispering and pointing at him like he was the most interesting creature in the zoo. Not all of them were smiling at him as they did so, either. Popeye knew that he hadn't made many—*any*—friends at school, but even he was surprised at the amount of hatred and ill-will that seemed be directed at him.

But that was okay, he thought, because my purpose here was never about making friends.

Unfortunately, that attitude did nothing to prevent the interference of people he tried very hard not to be friends with. People like Phoebe Kendall, Saint Tommy Williams himself, and Adam Layman, the three of whom were all waiting for him at his locker after his first class of the day. The super-hypocrites, all pretending that they cared what happened to him. At least Layman had the decency to look as though his girlfriend was forcing him to be there.

"The beautiful people," he said. "Have you come to… inform me… that I'm… Undead Prom King?"

Saint Williams spoke first, because that, in Popeye's experience, was what Saint Williams did.

"We just want you… to know… we… support you. We're…

here for you." Popeye wasn't certain, but he thought that Williams' speech was more studded with pauses since he'd returned to Oakvale.

He was still talking.

"We… will have… twenty… zombies waiting… at the field."

"What? No. No, no, no… no."

"You don't have to face him alone," Phoebe said. "Or at all. We could tell…"

"No, wait. Just… stop. First, there is no… we. There is… *me.* And second… do not… tell… anyone… anything."

"You don't have… to fight him," Williams said. He might be speaking with more pauses since his return, but Popeye thought he also seemed to walk down the hallways bathed in a corona of white light. Or maybe that was just the fluorescent lighting playing tricks on him again—sometimes wearing his sunglasses for most of the day caused Popeye to experience strange optical effects.

"He's a bully, Popeye, but…"

Popeye turned his anger on Phoebe.

"Who asked you, you blood… bag?" he said, noting Adam's big hands immediately bunch into fists. "Don't pretend… to know… anything about it!"

Tommy stepped between him and Adam—protectiveness really was a reflex for him, just like Adam's angry reaction. Their movements delighted Popeye immensely; it was like having a real life puppet show where he could pull all the strings. With just a little more pressure in the right places, he could really get them all dancing.

"Just because you… hang around… dead guys… all the time," he said, keeping his focus on Phoebe, "it doesn't… mean… you know… us. I…"

Adam was actually baring his teeth, he was so angry. Just a little more encouragement and the lunkhead would be tossing Williams aside to get at him. And then maybe Saint Williams will charge ahead, hoping to restrain him, and…

"Popeye," Tommy said. "We're only… trying… to help."

Popeye realized that Phoebe had placed her hand on Adam's disturbingly large bicep. Watching the effect of her touch was like watching an elephant get hit with a tranquilizer dart; Adam visibly relaxed, and his lips closed back down over that winning smile. Fun time was over; Popeye realized he'd have to talk his way out of this one.

"If you really… want to help you'll… stay away," Popeye said. "It doesn't… matter… how many you… bring. There will… always… be more… humans."

Tommy had the nicest blue eyes, Popeye thought. They always appeared as though they were looking right into your soul.

"The bullying… will end today. I… promise you that," he said. "I need… to do this."

He leaned forward, hoping that Tommy could see right through the dark lenses and into his soul—if he had one—like he'd imagined.

"I would think… if anyone… you… would understand."

Check and mate. "Your way, then," Tommy said. "Good… luck."

They left, and he thought that their type of nuisance would be over. But of course, he was wrong again.

"Just so you know, I'm going today," Margi told him, having once again dropped beside him in study hall. "You can't stop me."

"Go… away, pink-haired… flea. Take your… jangling chains… with you."

"I heard what you said to Phoebe and the boys," she said. "Not nice. Not at all nice. Shame, shame."

"Will you please… stop… chattering?" he said.

"But I know why you did it. You are really just trying to protect the other zombies. I think that's really noble of you, Popeye."

He slapped his desk so hard one of his copper fingernails broke off and went skipping across the room like a discarded pull tab.

"Your ability… to completely misread… *all* of my motivations… is truly… astounding you… idiot!"

"Is there a problem, Popeye?" Miss Quin asked from the front of the class.

"Yes!" he said, aware that the entire class, TC included, was staring at him. "Yes! May I… change my seat… please?"

Miss Quin nodded her assent, and Popeye took an open desk next to the quiet kid who had warned him about the beating the day before. Derek. His groupie, his greatest and only fan. As he approached, he saw that the boy was working on a sketch of his own, one that he was covering with his soft-looking hands.

"Let me… see," Popeye said.

With obvious reluctance, Derek removed his hands. Popeye was looking down at a small drawing—a portrait, not a caricature or a cartoon—of himself, done with careful marks of black ink on lined white paper. Derek had sketched his horns back in.

"Not… bad," Popeye said.

He looked at the kid for a moment, as Derek stared up at him with scared but curious eyes. How many classes did they have together? Three, at least—art, math, and this study hall. Derek opened his mouth, but Popeye shook his head.

"Don't speak. I… know. I know what… you are… going to say. You are going… to ask… why… did I… provoke him. Or why… am I… going through with it or… why don't I… tell a teacher. I'm going to tell you… and only you… the answer. Although you won't… realize… it is the answer… unless you… really think."

Derek looked at him in a way he'd never been looked at by a

living being before; he looked at him like he really thought that Popeye might have the answers to hidden questions.

"The answer is… that art… changes lives. That's… all. Art is not… about empowering… anyone… or making someone feel better… or beauty… or revealing… great truths. It may do… all of those things or… it may do their… exact… opposite. But at its… hot core… its only aim… is… to change lives."

Derek stared up at him and Popeye couldn't tell if the confusion clouding his eyes was breaking or gathering, but he knew it didn't really matter.

"Remember that," he said.

There were about thirty people at the field already when Popeye made his way toward the concession stands; they were clustered in little groups of twos and threes and there was an ebullient, carnival atmosphere surrounding them. Many people seemed surprised to see him, others were curious, but the emotion he could most readily identify on most of their faces was hatred.

TC was there, the center of the largest group of people, the ringleaders of the school's main bioist faction. Holly Pelletier, Steve Winter, this newer kid they all called Dorman. TC, already jacketless, his large muscles bulging under a thin Oakvale Badgers T-shirt, saw him and cracked his knuckles. The sound they made was like thick twigs breaking.

"I can't believe you actually came, wormburger," he said. "I am *so* going to enjoy this." He rolled his shoulders and turned his neck from side to side, loosening up as he hopped from leg to leg.

"Yes… you will," Popeye said. He walked within ten feet of Stavis, and the gathered throng, driven by some primal instinct, formed a wide ring around him.

"He's going to kill you." This from Holly Pelletier, the look on her sometimes pretty face hungry and feral.

"Dead meat," one of their companions added.

"Twice dead," Stavis said, shadowboxing a few rapid jabs, any one of which looked to have the force to launch Popeye's head from his body.

"Sure," Popeye agreed, taking off his leather jacket. He couldn't honestly say that he was nervous, because even if TC ground his bones for his breakfast he wouldn't feel anything. He was beyond any physical pain. He supposed that the afternoon could end with Stavis opening his head like an Easter egg and scattering its contents on the field—that would be the true and final end for him—but even the prospect of final death didn't frighten him. All he felt now was the vague sense of excitement and unease, the sensation that anything could happen. This was the very same sense of excitement he had looking at a new canvas, a blank piece of paper, or an unmarked patch of skin.

"Get ready for a crushing defeat," Stavis said.

"I'm ready," he replied.

"Yeah, he's ready," he heard a voice from the crowd, a shrill, warped echo of his own voice. He turned and saw Margi, her pink hair the lone daub of color in the otherwise Brueghelian landscape. She stood behind him, alone, her bunched hands on her hips, glaring at TC and his friends. Popeye didn't know whether to laugh or to chase her back down the hill.

"Who is this, Freak?" Stavis said. "Your girlfriend?" This earned him a round of laughter—chortling, really, the sort of haw-haw-haw type of empty-headed laughter emitted only by the dullest of the dull at the most base attempts of humor. As much as Popeye wanted to chase her away, he had to admire her courage. She may have been there for different reasons than he was, but he supposed that they were no less valid.

There were no other friendly faces in the crowd. He didn't know whether to be pleased or disappointed that Saint Williams and his followers had honored his request. Part of him, he was surprised to realize, was actually glad that Margi had come, after all. He was glad that there would be a witness—one to whom the beating hearts and his undead brothers and sisters would actually listen—to what he was about to do.

"Yes, she's my… girlfriend," he said, walking over to her.

"Am not!" she whispered when he was near.

"I know," he replied, not bothering to remind her that he'd never had a girlfriend, and never would, because he wasn't in the least bit interested in girls. "Would you… hold this… please?"

She regarded the garment like it was a tissue he'd just sneezed in.

"Only because you said please," she said.

"And these." He took of his glasses and set them on the jacket as it lay in her outstretched arms. "Also this," he said, removing his shirt.

"Oh, ick," Margi said as he lay the shirt atop his jacket and coat. A collective "eww!" rippled through the crowd as they beheld his various "bodifications"—the gills, the lidless eyes, the three places on his abdomen where he'd pared back his skin to reveal the muscles beneath. "You'll pay for this."

"Oh, definitely," he told her, and stepped back to the center of the ring, raising his arms shoulder-height and turned so that the crowd could get a good look at him. He was thin to the point of emaciation, having not eaten for many days leading up to his death. He drank in the sounds and expressions of their revulsion, lifting his head as though their hatred felt like cool water on his skin.

He now saw that Margi wasn't his only supporter among the massed groundlings. Derek was sitting in the bleachers above the field, watching from a safe distance. Popeye hoped that he had his sketchbook with him, or that he had the sort of memory that would allow him to remember and record what he was about to see.

"You are one hideous freak, Freak," TC said. Popeye looked at him then; he looked both nauseated and outraged, like Popeye was an unknown insect that had just walked out of the sandwich he was about to bite.

"I'm going to mess you up even more than you already are," TC said.

Popeye, his arms still upraised, showed his pointy teeth.

"Bring it," he said.

TC brought it. He came in faster than Popeye had expected he could move; he was such a lumbering ox he hadn't considered him capable of such a quick burst of speed. His first punch, a left, caught Popeye right under the temple, and TC followed with a right that struck him square in his grinning mouth. The delighted crowd hooted and crowed. Popeye felt a splash of liquid roll down his chin, and when he touched it his fingers came away red. *Blood.*—TC's blood, not his, because his wouldn't have been red anymore even if he had enough to make a splash. His attacker had cut his hand on Popeye's filed teeth, one of which was still embedded in the flesh between TC's knuckles.

"Ouch," TC said, plucking the tooth out and tossing it on the ground. He shook his hand and when he made a fist a bright red bubble rose up between his knuckles. Mad before, he was furious now as he stepped toward Popeye. His fists thumped solidly into Popeye's abdomen with a swift, flat rhythm. Popeye couldn't feel them, and he thought of the scene in *Rocky* where the Rock was tenderizing the hanging beef carcasses as part of his training. The tempo of TC's blows slowed, but only so he could get more force into the individual punches. Popeye thought he heard one of his lower ribs crack.

"Cover up!" someone yelled. "Cover up!" He didn't know if the advice was directed at him, or at TC, whose all-out assault left him wide open for retaliation.

Popeye leaned forward, as though doubled up by the shots to

his stomach, and TC drove his bloody fist up into Popeye's nose, mashing it flat with an audible pop that made the crowd gasp. His nose was undoubtedly broken. Popeye didn't mind; he'd been considering removing it anyway in a show of solidarity with George.

He straightened up. The punishment he'd already absorbed was brutal, and the once-cheering crowd was mostly silenced except for the encouragement of a few of the hard-core zombie haters. A lone voice, not Margi's, from somewhere on the field urged him to hit back. He stood and grinned at TC with his ruined mouth.

"Protect yourself!" he heard, this time from Margi. One day, he thought, one day she'll get it right.

TC was breathing heavily, and his shirt was damp with sweat. He bellowed and then charged like a mad beast. Popeye could almost feel the anticipation of the crowd on his dead skin; he knew they were waiting for the moment when he would lash out at TC, maybe at the height of his exhaustion and fatigue, and catch him by surprise by planting a bony fist in his eye.

That moment never came, never would come. TC rocked Popeye's head back with two shots to the cheek, punches that he got his shoulders into, and he followed them with a devastating punch to the stomach that probably pulped half of his internal organs.

Popeye had to admire his technique. He took another jab across his jaw, one that spun him half around. The accompanying crowd noise was more of a series of anguished cries rather than cheers, he noticed. Even they had their limits. He tried to smile, but didn't think that he could any longer—the beating he was taking was certainly causing him damage, even if he couldn't feel it.

TC picked him up and squeezed him like he was trying to crack his rib cage, and then he hurled him to the ground. Dirt and grass that he couldn't blink away came into contact with his eyes, interfering with his vision. TC kicked him. He stomped on his hand—his right hand, the one that he drew and painted with—and broke bones. He continued to kick him, and TC grunted with each strike, as though it were he and not Popeye that was feeling the force of each blow. Popeye thought that more of his ribs were cracking or breaking under the relentless assault. Then TC wound back and launched a field-goal worthy kick that completely unhinged Popeye's jaw, flipping him on his back like a turtle.

"Stop it, stop it, stop it!" a shrill voice cut through the sudden silence. Popeye thought it was Margi, but as he tried to clear his eyes with the hand that still worked he could see that Holly Pelletier was standing in front of TC, her hands against his heaving chest. She, this little tart of a bioist, was begging him to stop the slaughter. Tears were streaming down her cheeks.

"Stop it, please stop it!" she said, actually *wailing*. "Stop hurting him!"

Popeye tried to sit up, and couldn't. Parts of him were broken, muscles moved out of place. But even from his low vantage point on the ground he could see that Holly's wasn't the only face wet with tears—many in the crowd were crying, or wore the humbled, contrite expressions of bystanders at the scene of a traffic accident. Even TC looked bewildered and on the verge, as though he'd been a survivor pulled from a burning and twisted wreck.

Cry, Popeye thought, turning his gaze toward the crowd. No amount of tears will ever wash away what you saw today, what you participated in today. My image will be fixed in your brains forever.

Margi was kneeling beside him, using his T-shirt to wipe TC's blood off his chin and cheeks. He was aware also that the crowd was beginning to disperse, the ring of people surrounding him loosening like the knot of a pulled sneaker lace. From where he lay he couldn't see if Derek was still watching, but he hoped he was, and he hoped that he was sketching away. TC opened his mouth like he was going to say something, but no sound came out save that of his ragged breathing, and finally he just walked away.

"Popeye," Margi said, placing his sunglasses back over his eyes. "Are you all right?"

She still didn't get it, and probably never would. He hoped that Derek remembered what he had told him, because if he remembered, he might understand.

"Pop… Popeye?" she said.

She didn't understand, but he felt compelled to answer her, his audience. He owed her that much. He lifted his arm, intending to answer her with a thumbs-up, but he realized that the twisted bent claw that had been his hand probably wasn't going to convey what he wanted it to. His jaw was dislocated, if not worse, and he seemed incapable of speech. Communication would be even more difficult for him than ever before

Margi backed away from him a little, but he couldn't blame her. She had no way of knowing that the sounds he was making, filtered and altered as they were through the loose bones rattling in his chest like wind chimes only to exit past his broken nose and shattered jaw, were laughter—real, mirthful laughter—and not the forlorn howl of one of God's lowest creatures, crying out in mortal agony.

MY SO-CALLED UNDEATH

MY LIFE AS A ZOMBIE

Wow! Look at the Wall!

Since I've been away, we've had our three thousandth member join the Wall! OMZ! Trads, zombies, and I think one werewolf!

In other news, by using a very complex mathematical formula, I have determined that incidents of bullying the undead are down 17.63% percent at Oakvale High (if you would like a copy of my highly scientificalogical study you can post a request here). Since that terrible incident with Popeye, I mean. Differently biotic kids are becoming much more active—no wait that doesn't sound right—they are becoming much more animated—no wait that's not right, either—they are becoming much more *involved* in school activities. There are a few zombies in the upcoming school play, *The Crucible*, there is a zombie on the wrestling team, and my pal Melissa (also a zombie) has joined the yearbook committee. Zombies everywhere! And still more coming to the school all the time.

Karen is back at school, did I mention? We already had an adventure! With Phoebe!

Are zombies attending your school? How is that going? What sorts of activities are they doing there?

STILL SMALL VOICES

KAREN HAD ONLY been back a few hours, but already her unnerving and exciting aura had swept through the gloomy halls of the Haunted House, suffusing the rooms and walls with a new vitality. Friends she hadn't seen in months—and more recent loss souls, all marchers in a steady slow parade that had begun since the early days of *mysocalledundeath.com*—reached out to touch her pale bare arms, or just to stand near her, as though warming themselves by a campfire. She accepted their attention with poise, grace and good humor. She was by far the most vivacious dead girl that Phoebe knew.

And there was something different about her, Phoebe thought. She'd come back from whatever journey she'd taken changed. Or was that just Phoebe's own projection, an outgrowth of her anticipation and worry for Karen, bottled up for these past few months?

"She looks great, doesn't she?" Margi "whispered", loud enough for everyone including Karen to hear. "I mean, considering."

Collette, to her left, gave a slow shake of her head. They were on the far side of the foyer, watching Karen greeting all of the newlydeads she'd never met before, smiling at them and shining with celebrity glow. The Weird Sisters had been the first to greet Karen, but politely stepped aside to share her with the others.

"Come on, Mother Theresa," Margi said, again too loud. "We've got stuff to talk about."

"Hush," Phoebe said, but she agreed, they did have "stuff" to talk about. Phoebe wanted time alone with Karen also so that she could discuss the weight on her heart over Tommy's—and her own—unresolved feelings, and of all her friends she thought Karen might understand. Phoebe knew she would have to wait patiently until everyone else had a chance to talk to their returned celebrity.

After a final discussion with an earnest young zombie, Karen turned and found her three best friends waiting for her. Her pale diamond eyes found Phoebe's, and she smiled before embracing her.

"Missed… you," she said, her mouth against Phoebe's ear.

Hugs all around, and then Karen asked if they could go upstairs to be alone, just the four of them.

"You bet," Margi said, the first steps creaking in response to her compact weight. "We can't wait to hear all the dirt re: your adventures."

"We'll… be… alone," Colette added. "The others… visit… The Wall… but don't stay… there."

"So why'd you take off, DeSonne?" Margi said, having reaching the top floor before Colette could get all the words out. Phoebe worried about Colette sometimes; she didn't show any of the "coming back" signs that many of their dead friends like Tommy and Karen did. Even Adam, who'd only been dead a year, was moving and speaking at a faster pace.

"It's complicated," Karen said.

"It always is," Margi agreed, stepping aside to let Colette pass. "I'm interested in those complications. Was it because Smiley got a case of the grabby hands?"

"Margi!" Phoebe said, after an odd snoring sound from Colette that might have been an attempt at laughter. Phoebe looked over her shoulder at Karen, three steps down, but Karen was smiling, too.

"What?" Margi said. "I can't be the only one who has noticed Tak was crushing on her in a major way."

"Have you seen Tak recently?" Karen asked. It was a question for the whole group but Phoebe answered.

"Not often," she said. "He stops by, but spends most of his time in the woods around Oxoboxo with his friends."

"I'm sure he'll crawl out of the ground once he hears you are back," Margi said.

"Well," Karen replied, "I hope so."

Margi and Phoebe used light provided by their phones to enter the room where the Wall of the Dead was, where dozens of zombies had placed photographs of themselves.

"Wow," Karen said. "There are so many… more. People I've never seen."

"Yeah, it's a regular zombie apocalypse," Margi said, flopping down against the near wall closest to the door. her long skirt kicking up a billow of dust.

Karen looked back at her before more gracefully seating herself on the floor, leaning against the Wall where snapshots and printed photos of the dead surrounded her. Phoebe moved to the wall facing her, and Colette to the far wall, just below the covered window where cracks between the boards let the moonlight in. She and her friends were the points of a compass, with Karen at true north.

Phoebe cut her phone, and the moonlight stretched for the dead girls, giving them bluish coronas with its caress.

"So," Margi said, giving the ruffled hem of her skirt a few shakes, as though shaking spiders free. "Give."

"I'll give," Karen said. "And give and give. Heartbreak and hope in nearly equal measure. I want you to tell me… Oakvale news as well. But first…" —and here Phoebe thought her pause was for dramatic effect and not symptomatic of her differently biotic state— "… a story."

"Oh, goody," Margie said, mock-clapping her hands. Phoebe couldn't speak for the other girls, but she felt a brief thrill. She loved stories.

"Imagine you are in a haunted house…" Karen began, after a second dramatic, not differently biotic pause.

Margi wasn't reached by the moonlight and Phoebe couldn't see her, but she imagined she could hear Margi's eyes roll wetly heavenward in their sockets.

"I'm *so* there," Margi drawled, apparently having taken Karen's intro as a pun on their current location. This house, abandoned since they could remember, had always been known as the Haunted House, even before the dead kids had started moving in.

"Margi," Colette said. "If you don't… quiet… down…"

"Yeah, yeah," Margi interrupted. "You'll kill me and make me one of you. Got it."

"Oh, do be quiet," Phoebe heard herself say. The light seemed to shift; now only Karen was illuminated, her eyes flashing as she glanced southward at Phoebe.

"Not a safe house," Karen said, and Phoebe thought she could feel the old telepathetic bond returning, a tickle at the back of the skull. "Not a house of comfort like the one within whose walls we currently take… shelter. Not a home, but a house of… gloom and invisible drafts and of… doorways best left securely closed."

Phoebe couldn't make Colette out anymore; her last image was of her with her knees up and her arms folded across her chest, as though she were cold.

Karen continued after a brief pause, perhaps waiting to make certain that Margi had no more distractions to offer.

"Imagine you are drifting through the halls of this haunted house, and your bare feet are making no sound on the uneven floors. No sound at all, not a shuffle or a creak, almost as though you were a ghost yourself. Imagine there is no sound at all, not even the sound of your own… breathing."

Phoebe flinched when she heard Margi lean over toward her.

"Is this supposed to be autobiographical?" she stage whispered. Phoebe shook her head with disapproval though she knew Margi couldn't see her; the moonlight hadn't found her. Despite Margi's disruptions, she could feel something in the air between them and the dead girls; a sort of presence conjured up by their proximity and, possibly, the complex feelings they had for one another. Their positions in the room gave their gathering a ritualistic feel, and the words Karen spoke the feel of an incantation meant to further bind them.

"You are searching for something as you walk these halls and enter these rooms. Always… searching. What you are searching for may be there, hidden in the house. You aren't sure. You aren't certain what you are searching for, and you aren't certain what you are searching for even exists."

The fingers of light were receding through the slats, the moon swallowed by darkness or passing clouds. The doorway beside Margi was already a pitch black portal that seemed to pulse; Phoebe's eyes had already begun to play tricks on her in the gloom. When she closed them, she thought she could make out the outline of the bodies of her friends, which was stranger still.

"You are the one that is searching," Karen continued. "But sometimes, you are the one that is found. It wasn't there a moment ago, but now you know that something is in the haunted house with you. Something unknown, something with mysterious intentions."

Phoebe felt the skin on her arms stipple. She brushed at her hair, having the sensation that the legs of a spider, perhaps shaken from Margi's skirt, had become entangled there. She turned to her right and then to her left, her eyes still securely shut, like the doors in Karen's story. Margi, outwardly the most brazen, the most brash, inwardly the most fearful and insecure, had retreated inside of herself, her comments silenced. Colette, Phoebe knew, was still hugging herself, afraid that no one outside of this room ever would, her self-embrace making her colder even than death. When Phoebe again heard Karen's voice she shuddered, a dozen spiders now dancing on the back of her neck.

"And then, just at the point when you are so… deep… inside the house, the point where you could not return, you hear a voice. A soft, whispering voice, as though the act and effort of forming the words caused the unseen speaker great… pain."

Phoebe realized that both she and Margi had stopped breathing, like the character in Karen's story. She realized also that her hands had left her lap and were at her sides, palms up, knuckles touching the dusty floorboards, like she wanted to link them with those of her friends—but they were too far away.

"What frightens you more?" Karen said, her voice faint, fading. "The spectral voice that says… 'Get out?'"

Phoebe wanted to scream, but there was no air in her lungs.

"Or the one that says… 'Stay… with me?'"

MELON HEADS

DAVID LEE DORMAN was adjusting to life in Oakvale better than he'd initially imagined he would. Back home in Pitkin, Louisiana, he'd always imagined Connecticut and the rest of New England to be a cold, barren tundra, its natives as frosty as the air they breathed. He'd been surprised at how much farmland and wilderness there was, and how different the farms and woodlands were from those he'd roamed in Louisiana. There was an orderliness to them that he appreciated; the farms were laid out in sober, mostly flat patches of land, with the crops in rows, and the trees and foliage of Oakvale forest were spaced out in a way that looked and felt designed, like God had taken his time with the plantings here but got bored and threw handfuls of seeds all around Pitkin. Even better, there were low stone walls everywhere, crisscrossing the woodlands and bordering the farms.

David Lee—or ZK—as he liked to call himself, although he was Dorman to everyone else except for the Reverend, was snug in the corner of where two such walls intersected, just inside the far border of the Oxoboxo wood. He was peering through the scope of his rifle, which was braced in the crook of his shoulder and against a nice flat gray rock.

Just like a Minuteman in the Revolutionary War, he thought, or maybe a Yankee in the war between the states, although official fighting had never spread this far north. He'd read up on the history of Connecticut, paying special attention to the strange tales and legends that were an abundant crop in every state.

He could see three people, a tall, rail thin farmer with by-God an actual straw hat atop his head, one of the farmer's kids, and a large woman whose produce he was bagging up. Summer squash, maybe—it was still pretty early in the season.

Smiling, he put the farmer's straw hat in the center of his crosshairs. The farmer had four kids, his eldest, a girl, was a damned dead thing. ZK hadn't gone so far as to kill a living person—yet. The Reverend told him that killing a living person was not the same as reterminating a zombie, but ZK wasn't fully convinced. He personally thought that removing a few sympathizers might go a long way to removing critical pillars of support propping up the zombie community.

Thupport, he thought, feeling the familiar wave of shame and rage ripple through him. A chronic lisper, ZK sometimes heard his inner voice, normally confident and slur-free, lapse into his real voice, especially when his ideas were too brash and/or high-falutin'. "Removing critical pillars of support"? They just had to die, that's all. Die and hasten to final judgment, where they would be found severely wanting for consorting with demons and devils. Off to the fiery furnace with them.

ZK breathed deeply, steadily, visualizing the tide of emotion coursing out of his body. His ability to master his emotions is what made him such a good shot, conversely Martinsburg's inability to do the same rendered him hopeless despite ZK's best efforts to teach him. ZK reckoned that if that boy Martinsburg put down hadn't been standing right in front of him, ten feet away, he would have found a way to miss.

"Damn it," Martinsburg had said, after failing to hit a single one of the soda cans he and ZK had set up on a similar stone wall forty feet away. "I'd do better with a pocketful of rocks."

"Boy I knew in Louisiana used a machete," ZK had told him, only slightly slurring *used.* More often than not his lisp disappeared when he held a gun in his hands.

"Was he a lousy shot, too?" Martinsburg said. ZK had noted that his chest was heaving, as though they'd been running laps and not been taking turns shooting cans with the rifles Reverend Mathers had bought them.

"Naw," ZK told him. "He just had a preference for close work."

He brought his rifle up, and fired five times, hearing a satisfying *pank* after each report that kicked the cans flying off the wall. What echoed in his head though was *just* and *preference* and *close*, which he'd manage to enunciate without even a trace of his speech impediment.

You shore do enunciate purty, he thought, the smile returning to his face. He liked to leave others with the impression he was a hillbilly, in the rare moments he said anything at all. He liked to be alone. He knew the Reverend wanted him and Martinsburg to be fast friends, and if he was friends with anyone it should be Martinsburg, what with all the similar interests and passions they shared, but ZK preferred to be alone.

At the end of his next deep breath, he squeezed off three quick shots. Three watermelons sitting atop a wooden stand just to the left of the farmer exploded in rapid succession, casting a rain of red pulp and rind four feet into the air and all over the large woman. The farmer dove to the ground, but she stood there with her mouth hanging open, fruit-gore sliding down the front of her yellow shirt.

Even better than paintballs, ZK thought, looking through the scope. He saw the farmer's kid—a boy, maybe twelve years old, peeking out from the one the cash register stand, the only one with the presence of mind—or lack thereof—to try and spot where the shooter was. ZK didn't think it mattered much; he was pretty far away and mostly hidden behind the wall.

But he turned the scope on the kid anyway. If he'd been the dead one, ZK would have fired a fourth time. But he wasn't, so he brought the rifle back.

This time.

"So what's it like?"

ZK looked over the edge of his book, *Uncanny True Tales of Connecticut,* moving only his eyes. He was back at the dormitory at One Life Ministries, calm and content after a morning spent assassinating melons. He was comfortable reclining on his bunk, his sneakers off and his legs crossed at the ankles. The question was phrased in an innocent tone but ZK paid very close attention to words and the way that people said them and he could sense the hooks trailing beneath the surface.

The question wasn't directed at him, but at the boy who had the bunk opposite his. Martinsburg. He was widely acknowledged to be the Rev's favorite, even after recent events, and that didn't sit well with most of the rest of the youth group—all boys, all orphans or abandoned boys between twelve and eighteen. He was staring out the window beside his bunk; he didn't even glance up at his interrogator or his two companions flanking him like bank guards. The smaller of the two—who was still bigger and thicker than ZK—looked over at him as though to warn him to stay out of what was going to happen, but he thought better of it midway through, his expression faltering as he turned away.

No one would have called David Lee Dorman one of the Reverend's favorites, but that didn't mean that the Rev didn't consider him special.

"I said, what's it like?" the center tough repeated. There were at least a dozen boys of various ages in the dorm; his question had captured their attention and they were all watching now.

"What's what like?" Martinsburg said, his voice that flat monotone of the dead, just without the hitches in speech. ZK could see his reflection in the window, and it was utterly without expression. If he'd been looking at him through his scope, and at a distance of greater than ten feet, ZK would have thought he was staring at a zombie.

He waited with the others for the response. He'd been enjoying *Uncanny True Tales of Connecticut*; he'd just read a "true tale" that seemed to add a new dimension to his activities of the morning, and had just begun another story about Dudleytown. But he could feel that the exchange between Martinsburg and the other boy was about to get interesting.

The big mouth felt it, too, and sneered as he answered.

"Putting your mouth on a dead thing. Kissing a…"

He didn't have the chance to complete his statement. Martinsburg spun and was off the bed in a heartbeat, his first mashing the other boy's nose before he could finish his taunt. The smack of flesh on flesh hung on the air like a gunshot, and ZK had to suppress a smile.

The boy reeled backwards, stumbling against the next bunk, knocking it askew as he went down. Martinsburg was on him, straddling him; one of the two cronies moved in as though to tackle him off but instead took a wild, knob-knuckled punch to the abdomen just above the belt and he sat down hard on the bunk.

The boy who'd tried to look all tough and threatening, made the mistake of looking at ZK before getting involved. ZK barely moved his head, but the boy understood the message implied and remained frozen in place with slumping shoulders.

ZK wanted to laugh. He was no good with his hands, he weighed a hundred and ten soaking wet. The boy would have beaten him in a fair fight as handily as Martinsburg was tearing up his friend. But what he was good at was reputation management; there wasn't a boy in the dormitory—Martinsburg included—who'd have come at him with his fists.

"It felt like this," Martinsburg was saying, his fist drawing back and then swiftly down with practiced brutality, his voice still oddly dispassionate, as if he were trying to teach an important lesson to a child rather than win a fight. "It felt like this."

He punched twice in this manner. From his bed ZK couldn't see the blows hitting their target, Martinsburg's broad back and mop of black hair obscured the boy from view. He could only hear them connecting. Martinsburg drew his fist back again and as he did a crimson drop landed on the open page of ZK's book.

"It felt like this," Again. The other boy, the one who had been beaten only by the force of ZK's will, made a sick, tortured noise and looked away.

A flurry of activity, bodies entering the frame, people—a few of the Reverend's deacons as well as some of the others in the youth ministry—pulling an unresisting Martinsburg off of his victim and then snapping fingers in the prone boy's face.

Deacon Roberts, who had tattoos on the backs off both hands that were not designed in an artists' studio, announced that "the show was over", although ZK wasn't aware of a crowd watching. he watched another one of the burly deacon's drag the boy up to a sitting position while another tapped him lightly on blood-smeared cheeks. The eye that wasn't swelled up and purpling fluttered open and glanced up in a confused, lost manner. The Deacon held up his hand in front of the boy's face, raising his middle finger from his clenched first.

"How many fingers am I holding up?" he asked. The boy looked up at him, or in his general direction, not comprehending. His nose was clearly broken, pushed off to the left with bleeding freely from both nostrils. Laughing, the other deacon dragged him to his feet, where he wobbled unsteadily, barely able to move his feet as he was walked/dragged toward the door.

Deacon Roberts looked down at Martinsburg, who was staring up at the ceiling like he could see through the sheetrock.

"You better go see the Reverend," Roberts said, and then he told the other two boys, once still clutching at his stomach, to do something very irreligious and undeaconlike. His squat bald head swiveled on his thick neck and shoulders. "You, too, Dorman," he said. "Come see the Reverend."

ZK didn't know why he was involved all of a sudden, when he didn't do anything other than watch—he could argue that he actually cut down on the violence by warning the other boy out of it. But he shut *Uncanny True Tales of Connecticut*, without complaining and without wiping away the crimson globule that had been flicked there from Martinsburg's knuckle.

Reverend Mathers's office in their new Connecticut home was a far cry from the one he'd kept out West, which had been austere and gloomy, with heavy dark furniture and somber artwork. The office had but one window, and the Reverend had used it to blind rather than illuminate, drawing the curtain only when he wanted to be sheathed in a bright glare that made him hard to look at directly. ZK remembered the large portrait behind his desk, the painted figure of the Reverend was unsmiling and had eyes that tracked you when you crossed the room to take your seat. There was an antique looking painting of an angel stabbing a snake; ZK had liked that one.

The new office had high windows, and the Reverend often had the curtains open and the blinds up but the light filled the room rather than concentrate solely on the Reverend. Instead of the massive portrait he had a much smaller framed photograph of him beaming warmly as he shook the hand of an aggressively coifed presidential hopeful whose usual pout had been replaced with an equally wide grin. ZK noticed that as he and Martinsburg entered the Reverend tried on a smile that landed somewhere in between that of the old portrait and the new photograph.

"Boys," he said, gesturing for them to take the two chairs in front of his desk. Once they were seated, he spoke again. "You were in a fight, Peter. Again."

There was no reprimand in his voice, ZK noted, resisting the urge to look over at his companion slouched in the plush chair beside him. Instead he looked calmly straight ahead, at the Reverend.

"Yes, sir," Martinsburg said, in that same dead voice. "Because of my association with the zombie."

The zombie, ZK thought. When he'd first heard about Martinsburg's "association" with zombie—they'd *kissed*, for God's sake—he'd thought that Martinsburg must be insane or moronic to have been tricked by a cold corpse. And Martinsburg didn't help disprove either of those theories, shuffling around half catatonic and staring into the middle distance, pausing in his speech like he was a zombie himself. But after a few weeks of surveilling the corpse girl, ZK had come to change his mind. Sure, she'd looked like a total freak with her beyond-pale skin, ultra-blonde hair and creepy diamond-chip eyes, but even up close ZK couldn't see any of the normal "tells" that made the abominations easy to spot. She spoke well and without pauses, her face was expressive (and pretty, he supposed, except for the demon eyes), and she moved swiftly, fluidly, and with more grace than most of her living classmates.

Martinsburg claimed that she could change the color of her eyes like a chameleon, but ZK hadn't seen her do that particular trick.

The Reverend nodded, as though his suspicions had been confirmed.

"I see," he said. "That is unfortunate. Your sins have long been forgiven, and yet it seems that you are still suffering for them."

"Righteously," Martinsburg said, automatically.

"Perhaps. But perhaps also I have erred in keeping you close for so long. There are different forms of ministry, as you know, and I believe it is time for you to start yours."

The Reverend glanced briefly at ZK, who'd felt a brief spark flare in his chest when he'd said the word *ministry.*

"You need an outlet for all of the emotions inside you, a different outlet than administering beatings to the less spiritually advanced boys in your youth group. I believe it is time for you and David Lee hear to begin more of an… outreach program."

"Outreach, sir?'

The Reverend smiled. "You had a list once. You showed it to me, do you remember?"

Martinsburg said that he did.

"I have a list as well," the Reverend said, opening a drawer in his desk and taking out a yellow file folder. He withdrew two sheets of paper from the file and turned them around so that there was one in front of each of the boys. ZK realized that was another difference between the old office and new; Reverend Mathers last desk was a massive expanse of oak, so wide that you would have to lean over to be able to shake his hand if he were seated. This new one was so narrow that he half expected that the Reverend was going to kiss the top of his head when he leaned forward to read the paper.

"My list has some of the same names as yours did, as you can see. But you will note that mine only has abominations on it; you are not to practice your ministry on any living person."

They scanned the identical lists. Each name had a number in front of it.

1. *Karen DeSonne*
2. *Tommy Williams*

3. *"Tak"*
4. *Adam Layman*
5. *"Popeye"*
6. *Sylvia Stelman*

"These are the abominations most in need of the help that One Life Ministries can provide," the Reverend said. "Of course, if you are able to minister to other abominations, so much the better."

ZK nodded. He knew by sight all of the names on the list. He also knew what the Reverend meant by *ministering.* He could feel the excitement welling up in his chest because he was sick of shooting paintballs at abominations and sicker of shooting real bullets at melons. He'd been waiting for the Reverend to turn him loose, and it seemed he was finally getting his chance.

He didn't care why these particular names were on the list, nor did he pay any particular heed to the order that they were in. They were all monsters, and he would be glad to *minister* to each of them. He figured Martinsburg would have felt the same way and was surprised when he asked a question.

"Why Layman?" he asked. "I get why most of the others are on here… except maybe the last one, I don't even know who that is."

The Reverend asked his question with a few of his own.

"Does seeing his name here upset you? Or Miss DeSonne's, perhaps? Would you prefer not…"

Martinsburg was shaking his head, coming the closest to displaying an actual emotion that ZK had seen all day. Even when he was pounding on the other kid he didn't look as angry as he did just then.

"I killed Layman once, I can do it again," he said. "That bitch, too. I just don't know why he's there."

The Reverend actually looked pleased, even though he'd been interrupted—which just wasn't done.

"Symbolic value," he said. "The first three are leaders. Different sorts of leaders, but their being shown the One Life path will have vast positive repercussions among their fellow abominations, not only in this wretched town but across the country. The second two—Adam Layman and that freak, the one who desecrates daily the former temple of his body—they could have significant symbolic value for their demonic friends and their deluded sympathizers. And Miss Stellman… she's a hunch. She has gone through what the fools at the Hunter Foundation call "augmentation". I don't know what necromantic ritual of pseudoscience that process entailed, but it can't be good. She needs to be shown the path."

He let his words sink in a moment before turning to ZK.

"David Lee, do you have any questions?"

"No, sir," he said. "I am very clear on the subject."

"Good," he said. "There are a few names on your list that are not on mine. One in particular is to be spared full ministration, if only for a little while."

He leaned back, pressing a button on his desk phone.

"Deacon, please escort Kevin to my office."

A few moments later Deacon Roberts returned with an abomination, a young looking-male who looked like he could barely drag his carcass down the hall. He was slow, but his round face was stretched in a wide pumpkin-like grin that had probably taken him weeks to fix. ZK did not think this was one of the expressive ones.

"You may remember Kevin Zumbrowski," the Reverend said, to Pete. "He has taken the first step on the path of One Life by accepting the spiritual message of our ministry."

The zombie began to lift his arm, perhaps in a greeting. "Kevin knows he is lost, lost to the fiery furnace, the eternal torment of the damned," the Reverend said, but his gaze was pitiless. "He knows that the only chance—the *only* chance—to avoid the everlasting hellfire is to accept in his heart the full nature of his sin, to reject his debased nature, and to walk—if not run! On the path, to fully embrace One Life."

The thing finally got his hand in the air, but his eyes were dead, soulless, a stark and horrific contrast to the mirthless grin he wore. ZK wished he'd had one of his guns.

The Reverend smiled. "Kevin understands also that he has a rare opportunity to help others of his kind accept One Life, and in doing so possibly increase his own chances of avoiding the flames. He hopes to minister to his fellow abominations—and if he cannot minister himself—he will help us in our cause."

Great, ZK thought. Can he shoot?

"Kevin," the Reverend said. "Tell them what you know."

An hour later, Martinsburg and ZK were in one of the many cars owned by One Life ministries, a black sedan. Martinsburg was driving, because ZK had never learned how. The headlights cut through gloom ahead, revealing the twists and turns of winding Oakvale backroad. Pete was doubling the speed limit but somehow it didn't feel like they were travelling at an unsafe speed.

"I thought that would never end," he said. It was the first words either had spoken since Roberts had brought them back to his office and tossed Pete the keys to the car. "And I don't think he told me a single thing that I didn't already know."

"I didn't know that Julie… I mean DeSonne was staying at that derelict house they have,"

Martinsburg said.

ZK thought that he sounded engaged and interested, the monotone dropped since being given his mission. He was a good driver, too, at least by ZK's own standards. He'd wished the Reverend had let him put Zumbrowski on the path; if not for being an abomination than just for being so boring.

He debated egging Martinsburg on, maybe with a comment

about how he'd have thought he'd keep better tabs on his former girlfriend, but he knew the Reverend thought it was important that the two of them became good buddies. Plus, he remembered what that kid's nose looked like after Martinsburg tuned him up for making a similar comment.

"She's number one on the list," he said instead.

Pete nodded, and ZK almost laughed when he swerved to avoid killing a squirrel who'd ran out into the road.

"And it sounds like at least a few of the others might hang around the same place," Pete said. The monotone was definitely gone. Funny what a little purpose did for someone. ZK normally liked working alone, but maybe he would give the team up thing a fair shot.

"They call it the Haunted House," he said. Pete looked at him.

ZK shrugged. "I just listen. People will say anything if they don't think they should pay attention to you."

"I killed Adam there," Pete said. If he'd been speaking slow before he now sounded like he was speaking too fast. "Right outside that house."

ZK had almost forgotten that Pete had done something with a gun that he had never done—killed a living person. He had an idea.

"That's right, you did," he said. "Your aim was true."

Pete looked over at him, the first time that night that he'd taken his eyes off the road. ZK wondered if maybe he'd tapped into the well of Martinsburg's anger that had gotten a kid better than ZK was beaten up.

"I wasn't aiming for him," he said. "Williams."

"Ah, yeah, Williams," ZK said. "I suppose you want him for yours, right. To *minister* to?"

Pete nodded.

"Prolly the girl that tricked you, yeah?" ZK continued. The Louisiana was coming out in his speech, but he wasn't stuttering.

"I want the Japanese kid, too," Pete said. "Tak." ZK noticed his big hands were tensing on the steering wheel.

"Well, son, that's the top three! You going to leave any for ol' ZK?"

He laughed as he said it, because really he didn't care which ones he got as long as he got a lot of them. He was gratified to see that Pete was grinning.

"You can have Layman," he said. "Been there, done that."

ZK let out a hoot, and gave Pete a soft punch. Martinsburg's upper arm was like a rock, and ZK was beginning to realize what a true partnership with Martinsburg could be like.

"You think ZK wants your sloppy seconds, now?" he said, keeping his bantering tone. "You think I'm the sort that will settle for that?"

"You're a better shot than I am," Pete told him. "You'll probably get all of 'em."

"Uh-uh. You want the top three, they're yours. Or One Life Ministries', I 'spose. This here is the commuter lot. Go ahead and park."

Pete turned into the lot as instructed. "I can't shoot, ZK," he said.

"About that," he replied. "We're going to fix that tonight."

Pete parked the car, cut the engine.

"How?"

ZK had a theory, one he wasn't going to share. He thought that Martinsburg's inability to hit the broadside of a barn, much less a can on a fencepost, had a lot to do with how the events went down outside this "Haunted House". Shooting at a zombie and killing one of your former friends was certain to leave a mark on the brain, he thought. Martinsburg's problems in using a firearm weren't physical; they had everything to do with how his head had been rewired that night.

The solution was simple, he thought. He just needed to do some rewiring.

"You ever hear about the Melon Heads?" he said, then he got out of the car. "Pop the trunk, now."

"Huh?" Pete said complying.

ZK took one of the rifles out of the trunk, waiting until Martinsburg joined him before answering.

"The Melon Heads. It is one of your foremost paranormal legends."

Pete took the outstretched gun, slamming the lid once ZK had his.

"I have no idea what you are talking about."

ZK smiled, because he knew then he had him hooked. Maybe ol' Reverend Mathers wasn't the only one who had some skill rewiring brains, he thought. He knew that he had to get in Pete's head just a little bit and disconnect that part of his brain that thought the zombies, or demons, or abominations, whatever you called them, really were human beings deep down. Martinsburg, somewhere, was carrying guilt over killing Layman and turning him into the very thing he thought he hated and feared. That guilt and confusion probably helped him to mistake that Karen DeSonne thing for a living, breathing girl.

"The *Melon Heads,* son. One of Connecticut's greatest paranormal—or cryptozoological, depending on your definition—legends. Right up there with the Jewett City vampires, the black dog of Devil's Hopyard, the left-handed green ghost of Stamford?"

Martinsburg's middle-distant stare returned.

"Come on," ZK said. "Don't you know anything about the state you live in? You haven't heard of any of these creatures? Not even the ghost?"

Martinsburg shrugged.

"The dog, maybe. I've been to Devil's Hopyard. Was this in that book you were reading."

ZK nodded, and alternately shook his head in mock exasperation. They started walking down the road.

"Unreal. But then, reading these strange legends is a hobby of mine, I guess. We got plenty in Louisiana—thought I caught a glimpse of our skunk ape once. And don't even get me stated about all the weird stuff in New Orleans."

"You read a lot," Pete said.

"I do," ZK said. They were about five miles from the One Life Ministries campus, right on the edge of town. ZK could see the green "Welcome to Oakvale" road sign, pocked with bullet holes, just a little way down the road. None of the bullet holes had been made by him. "Anyway, these Melon Heads—they look supposedly like human beings, sort of, but they have twisted, deformed bodies and big ol' hairless heads. Hideous creatures, to be sure. I invite you to look them up on your phone when we've stopped to see if I am telling the truth as I know it."

"Like zombies," Pete said. ZK stopped and looked at Pete like he'd just said something remarkably profound.

"Like zombies," he repeated. "*Exactly* like zombies. You sure you haven't heard about them before?"

"I'm sure."

"Huh," ZK said, and stepped off the road and into the woods. He didn't like having the car so close by; he normally liked to make the five-mile trip on foot, through Oxoboxo forest, and by himself. "We'll set up over there, on the other side of that stone wall. Mind the poison ivy. So you mentioned zombies, and if the legends are right these Melon Heads were sort of like zombies in that they were human-shaped, but very hideous as I said. No one really knows who the Melon Heads were, or how they got to be so foul looking—and again there are similarities to the Reverend's abominations. Some say they were a lost tribe, forgotten by everyone, who survived only by constant inbreeding some people say aliens. Some say they were the survivors of a terrible fire at an insane asylum. There is one point, however, on which all the legends agree."

They'd each taken a seat on one of the large flat rocks that had fallen from the wall. ZK recognized the spot; he'd done some of his best and most recent work there.

"And what's that?" Pete had fished out his phone and was tapping with his thumbs. ZK wanted the light to go away, but he wanted him to look, too."

"That they were cannibals, Pete," he said. "That they would lie in wait, and attack and then devour any man, woman or child that had the misfortune to pass their way."

"Shit, ZK, you're right!" Pete said, then held the phone out for him to see. "Check it out! Melon Heads!"

"I wouldn't lie to you, Pete," he said, solemnly. "We're partners, and partners don't tell each other lies. Know that. Now put that phone away before someone drives by here and wonders what we're up to; you can read all about their cannibal tendencies later. We should keep our voices low, too."

"I guess they shouldn't be considered cannibals if they aren't likc us," Pete said.

ZK wondered what Martinsburg had been like prior to accidently killing Adam Layman. He'd been a football star, he knew, and apparently had no shortage of girlfriends—and now he sounded like he was half melon-headed himself. There must have been some serious brain rewiring going on, long before they'd met.

"That's a good point, Pete, because that's part of what I'm building up to. I'm building up to telling you my own life's philosophy, and in its own way I think it is as important a concept as the Reverend's ideas of One Life and us being missionaries. Do you want to hear it?"

Pete nodded, and ZK continued.

"I don't care if we call them zombies, Melon Heads, or left-handed green ghosts, Pete. It doesn't matter. What matters is they are something other than what we are, and anything that is other than what we are wants to devour us. It wants to eat us up. Maybe not by chewing and swallowing, but by absorbing or replacing or minimizing. I don't want to let them do that."

"Zombies," Pete said. "They pretend to be like us."

"They do. And they ain't, not at all. They want us gone. And I don't want to go."

ZK thought he could see Pete nodding, but it was dark and gloomy and whatever moonlight there may have been was caught in the canopy of leaves above. There was a single streetlight half a block up the road they'd just walked down, but its illumination did not reach where they sat.

"That's what I think about every time I take aim, Pete. I think, 'I don't want to go'. And whatever creature is there in the center of my scope, it's something that wants me to go. But I won't let it."

He lay the barrel of the rifle atop the wall and gestured toward the distant streetlamp, hoping that Pete caught the movement through the darkness.

"You know why I come out to this place, Pete?" he said. Pete replied that he didn't know.

"That commuter lot you parked in is right of the highway exit ramp," he said. "We just drove through five miles of backroads, and then right there around that turn is the on and off ramp for the only highway that runs close to Oakvale. And what comes to Oakvale, Pete? What comes to Oakvale like they come to few other towns this size in the whole country?"

"Zombies."

"Sure, zombies. A damn lot of them come to Oakvale, and you know what? I figure a lot of them follow that highway to get here.

I figure a lot of them travel at night, because *they* figure it's safer for them to do so. And so I figure that a lot of them will cross the bright, white beam of that very streetlight over yonder. And I more than figure it, Pete. Because I've seen it happen."

Pete was no more than an outline in the dark, but he had the sense he was hanging on his every word.

"What I'm seeing is that I've actually *seen* it happen. Six times, point of fact."

"Six," Pete said. "Wow."

ZK realized that he probably hadn't talked this much in a single night since his mother had been alive. He almost did feel like a minister, a preacher, and with a thrill of pride he realized he'd barely lisped the entire time he'd been talking.

"I think number seven—or your number one—is going to walk through that light tonight. You can think of it as a zombie, an abomination, or a Melon Head—heck, you can even think of it as a human if you want—but whatever you do, don't think of it as anything other than *other*. Because anything else will get you devoured."

They were silent for a few moments, and ZK thought he heard Martinsburg turn to get a better view of the shaft of light.

"My number two," Martinsburg said, eventually.

"What's that?"

"I said, 'my number two'. I put one on the path months ago."

ZK couldn't see, but he swore he could hear Martinsburg's mouth stretch into a wide grin.

"Close work," he said.

"Shiiiiiit," ZK said. "You want to keep score, then?"

"Makes it more of a game. More competitive."

ZK snorted. "Well, let's start at zero-zero. That'll give you a chance."

They laughed, and then were silent, their eyes on the light.

Sunrise was only a few hours away when one of them dragged itself into the light. ZK couldn't tell if it was male or female at this distance; it wore ragged dark clothing and moved with an awkward, uneven gate, it's arms drawn close to its body.

"You first," ZK whispered. He heard Pete settle and he heard him breathe in and then softly exhale before the sharp retort of the shot.

This time, he didn't miss.

He let Pete drag the thing off the road and into the brush along the roadside. There were fresh liquid blotches on the pavement beneath the streetlamp; ZK used to try and do something about those but after the fourth or maybe the fifth he stopped bothering. Animals went under the wheels every day.

When Pete trotted back he was breathing heavily, either from his exertions or his excitement, or both. He looked at ZK with eyes that were so bright they seemed to project their own light.

"I know where we should go," he said.

THE PAIN OF BEING ALIVE

"NOW… IT REALLY is… a haunted house," Popeye said. "No one… will dare visit… with all that… noise."

Takayuki looked back over his shoulder at the Haunted House. He and Popeye stood at the far edge of the yard where it bordered the Oxoboxo forest. Someone in the house had told him Tayshawn had crawled out of the house and into the woods a few hours ago.

"Sounds like he's dying… all over again." Popeye said. Since his beating, his speech was even slower, more slurred, and there was a sharp clicking noise as he finished certain words, like his lower jaw didn't quite line up correctly. He sounded like he'd been gargling with crushed glass. He was harder to look at, too—some of the fishhooks he used as earrings had been mashed into his neck and he'd chosen not to remove them. His nose was pushed flattened and hooked to the left.

A dead face appeared at one of the unboarded windows on the first floor, stark white and looking startled in the moonlight.

"Jacinta said… he's been… screaming… all day," Tak said.

Tayshawn howled again, his low moan rising into a higher pitched cry, almost a shriek. He didn't sound very far away.

"He's in… pain," Popeye said, and for some reason Takayuki

thought of the crumpled and broken animals George used to pull off the roadside. "How can he be… in pain?"

Tak felt guilty for leaving Tayshawn as the pains began, but he and Popeye were working on figuring out how to get George out of the Hunter Foundation's clutches. They'd heard from Colette that a zombie named Sylvia might be able to help them; their meeting went well but still George—literally—rots.

Tak realized why he thought of George and the animals; wounded animals also crawled into the underbrush to die. But Tayshawn was already dead…

More faces appeared at the windows. The Haunted House family wanted to know what the Sons would do for their stricken brother.

Death is strange, Tak thought. Some of the faces at the empty windows were wide-eyed, their expressions frozen in place and making them look perpetually surprised. Others were complete blanks, as though nothing would ever surprise them again.

And then there was Popeye, who'd among the many "bodifications"—his term—he'd made had clipped off his own eyelids. Most days he hid his round staring eyes behind thick lensed sunglasses but since being beaten he hid them less and less. His assailant had broken his favorite pair, he'd said.

On the other end of the dead living spectrum was Karen, who was more expressive, more beautiful, and more *alive* than many of the traditionally biotic people Tak knew. Since returning from Idaho or Indiana or wherever it was she was from, an emotional distance that hadn't been there prior existed between them, a barrier that mystified him as greatly as the one that separated life and death. She'd been spending most of her time with Phoebe and the other girls.

"Tak?" Popeye said, his jaw-click most pronounced on the "K".

Takayuki was watching the faces. So many of them, more than

at any time before. He was surrounded by dead people—his people. Karen was back. The dead were allowed back in the schools; dozens "lived" in Oakvale.

Tayshawn's screams dropped back to a steady low groan. When the opossum, the raccoon crawls off the road and into the brush, what is the right thing to do? When the horse falls lame, what is required of the rider?

The dead were everywhere, now. Takayuki never felt more alone.

"Tak?" Clicking on the hard "k."

"Let's… find him," Tak said.

"I think he… wants some space," Popeye said, lifting his bony arms. The sleeves of his leather jacket slid down so that Tak could see more bodification, the top of the forearm just above the wrist where Popeye had removed a lengthy strip of skin so that one could see muscles and tendons working beneath. "He dragged himself… out… here… broken leg and… all… so he could… be alone."

"I know," Tak said. "But no one… really wants… to be… alone. Not… really."

Maybe Popeye just looked surprised because one did, without eyelids—or maybe he really was surprised because of what he'd heard Tak say. Either way, he followed him into the woods, following the sound of Tayshawn's agony.

Father Fitzgerald had been celebrating mass when a ghostly wail cut through the heavy silence of the processional. The communion song had just ended, the organist moving to the end with a slow moving flourish. There were two more communicants in the line; John McKenna, his deacon, and Mrs. Calabrese, an elderly widow who crossed herself—twice—as the wail warped around the church. Father Fitzgerald was almost as startled as she was and nearly dropped the chalice.

Dear God, he thought. *Melissa.*

Except… Melissa couldn't even speak, much less scream like a tormented soul. Melissa's vocal cords, along with her face and much of her body had been ravaged by fire. The fire that killed her; Melissa was dead.

Father Fitzgerald completed the sacrament of communion, managing to keep his hands from shaking as he wiped the chalice. Melissa—he was certain it was her, somehow—screamed again. He completed the benediction and soon was following the crucifix out of the church, though he did not pause on the steps to talk to the exiting parishioners, but instead hurried down and across the parking lot to the rectory, pausing only long enough to tell Mr. McKenna and Jalen his altar boy to make certain not to encourage anyone to follow him.

It wasn't that the members of his church were unaware that Father Fitzgerald was harboring a dead girl—his church had rallied around the priest after police had fired upon differently biotic people on the church's front lawn, save for a few members who dropped out entirely for the "real" religion offered by Reverend Mathers—most were accepting of the arrangement, and thought Fitzgerald's interactions with the dead were a form of ministry. That said, whatever Melissa was going through, Father Fitzgerald was fairly certain than she would not want it made public.

He threw open the door, shouting her name.

The wailing had stopped as suddenly as it had begun, and for the first time Father Fitzgerald began to feel frightened.

They found Tayshawn wedged up in the corner made by the intersection of two of the low moss covered stone walls that crisscrossed the forest. He wasn't hard to find; they just followed the noise.

"Tayshawn," Tak said. Tayshawn looked up and locked eyes with him, but only for a moment before a new wave of pain wracked him and his eyes went back up in his head.

"Dude," Popeye said. "I think… you are… sitting in poison… ivy."

Tak ignored him; Tayshawn rolled onto his side, pounding the ground with his fist.

"It hurts, Tak," he said. "How does it… hurt?"

Tayshawn was not normally an expressive zombie, but he looked as if every muscle in his face was bunched up in hard knots with the pain. In the brief pauses between his groaning, Tak heard crackling sound. At first he thought that Tayshawn was grinding his teeth, but then Tak realized that something else was going on. He reached down and gently touched Tayshawn's leg, the one that had been shattered when the ambulance had struck him on the night they rescued Karen.

"Do you… hear that?" Popeye said, catching on. His hearing didn't seem to be as good after his beating. "Sounds like… knuckles cracking."

Tak's touched Tayshawn's knee through a hole in his jeans. He didn't have much sensitivity in his fingers but he could feel a strange movement, like worms swimming beneath the skin.

Worms, he thought, drawing his hand back.

"Get… Karen," he said, just as Tayshawn unleashed a terrible cry.

"Ugh," Popeye said, ignoring Tayshawn. "Why me? Why… do I always… have to be… the errand boy?"

"Popeye."

"Every time… we get with… Karen… one of us… gets shot… or run over… or…"

"Just get her," Tak said, cutting him off. Tayshawn thrashed, legs twitching, his scrabbling hands clutching his head and then his stomach. His eyes leaked at the corners, as though his tear ducts had reopened.

Karen would know what to do, Tak said, watching him. What would Karen do?

Popeye forced out at a sigh, squeezing his lungs as hard as he could.

"Where… is she?" he said. "If she's with those… bleeders, forget it… I…"

"She's with… Mal," Tak said. He walked over to Tayshawn, where he lay writhing against the stones.

"Mal. Great," Popeye said. "Fine."

"Thank you," Tak said, crouching, propping himself against the stone wall and reaching for Tayshawn.

"What are you… doing?" Popeye said.

"I'm… holding him," Tak said. "Go get… Karen."

Popeye looked down at them for a moment, as though he couldn't make sense of what he was seeing. Tayshawn leaned into him, clutching him as though for dear life. Tak, his arms around Tayshawn's shoulders, held him as a fresh wave of pain caused him to grimace and cry out.

Popeye watched for a moment before turning and walking off in the dark, making his own path to Lake Oxoboxo.

"Popeye, go get Karen," he thought, trudging heavily through the brush. "Hey Popeye, go sweep the front porch. Popeye, go blah and blah and blah."

He wished he could spit. Always getting ordered around, always being told what to do. Karen, Karen, Karen, he thought. I'm sick of Karen, I'm sick of doing everyone's bidding. We should be figuring out how to spring George out of the Foundation; those bastards were probably doing weird experiments on him like they'd done with that girl Sylvia. She was back, but she sure didn't seem right. Augmentation, my lidless eye.

There was a moment, just a moment, where he thought that

Tak was reaching for Tayshawn for some reason other than to comfort him. Or, more accurately, to end his torment through a different means than providing comfort.

The fat moon reflected off the flat surface of the Oxoboxo. Popeye walked to the edge of the water, still cursing.

"Hey, Karen!" he yelled, startling a large heron that flapped with ungainly wings like a prehistoric beast up and away from him. "Karen! Earth to Dairy Queen, let's go!"

He saw nary a ripple on the water. Karen's bloodbag friends, Phoebe and Margi, were fond of telling everyone they thought Karen had, to use their term, "telepathetic powers". He'd always taken that to mean that she could only read stupid minds—which was probably why she hadn't sensed him coming and been waiting on the shore. He thought the whole thing was bullshit, anyway.

"Karen!" he called again through cupped hands. No reaction.

"Damn it," he said, grabbing a large rock, big enough that he needed both hands, and wading out into the lake. He swung his arms back and then hurled the rock as far as he could toward the center of the lake.

The couple months that he and the rest of the Haunted House crew had spent hiding under the frozen lake were, in his mind, the worst days of both his life and his unlife. He hated it down there. No art, no music, no conversation—although considering the verbal skills and intelligence of many of the newlydeads that had joined them recently, that may have been a blessing. Karen's big friend Mal loved it, though. He'd been down there longer than anyone else.

Popeye waded in further. He'd never been much of a swimmer in life, nor did he enjoy being in the sun. or outside, period. Being dead, he didn't register the temperature of the water—it could be freezing or boiling, it was all the same to him. It could be slimy, it could be brackish, he didn't know. He wasn't like one of those hypersensitive dead kids like the Dairy Queen or Tommy, both of whom claimed to be able to discern certain scents, taste, or feel things. Maybe they could—they had no reason to lie other than to try and look cool and he supposed it didn't follow logically that he could see and hear but not smell, taste, or touch, did it?

Not that anything about death made sense, he thought.

He was out up to his waist now and about to holler again when he saw her head and then her shoulders break the surface of the water, the moonlight making her look gilt-edged. She didn't seem to be swimming but gliding, her shoulders squared and her head held at an angle he thought regal and haughty. Soon she was visible up to her waist, which was strange because she was still twenty feet away from him and he remembered that the Oxoboxo sloped sharply from its shores. Was she levitating in the water? Her arms were held rigidly at her sides and he couldn't help but see that she was wearing an oversized white t-shirt or a shift that clung to her pale body, a body that seemed to soak up the moonlight until it shone from her.

Any of the hetero pervs from Oakvale, living or dead, would have been thrilled, but Popeye was disgusted, even before her forward movement revealed that the hem of the t-shirt ended halfway down her thighs.

"Arrrgh," he groaned, his crooked jaw rattling. "I've never… regretted… removing my eyelids… more."

"Hello, Popeye," she said, after a bemused giggle. "What brings you to the pond?"

Just when he was about to ask her how she'd acquired even more magical powers a square head broke the surface of the water between her delicate calves, and he realized that she'd been standing atop Mal the entire trip in, surfing on his broad shoulders. Mal must have been a big-time gym rat when he'd been alive; he was bigger than Adam, bigger than George—bigger than any zombie he knew.

Karen giggled again, making Popeye wonder—and not for the first time—if she really did have "telepathetic" powers. Her weird eyes—her irises looked like crystal, death having somehow drained them of color—twinkled like the stars in the sky behind her head as he looked up at her. Mal continued forward in his steady, implacable way, his own clinging clothing blotchy with algae and torn in places. Popeye turned and headed back to the shore.

"Social call?" she said.

"Tak," he replied, looking over his shoulder and projecting so that they could hear him. "Tayshawn. They… need you."

"Is everything… all right?" she said, dropping lithely off of Mal's back into the water.

"No," he said, and before he could try and explain a scream, shrill and full of pain, cleaved through the darkness.

Miles away, the screaming had stopped in the rectory at St. Jude's. Melissa had slid from her bed onto the thin beige carpet remnant some kind soul had donated to furnish her "room", formerly an extra pantry for the kitchen upstairs. She'd curled into a fetal position, the blank white mask she wore tilted at a slight angle so that the holes were no longer even with her eyes. He coppery red wig was askew. Father Fitzgerald rushed to her side, picking up the white board that she used to communicate with, but she couldn't seem to get a grip, her crabbed fingers flexing and fluttering. Her posture and the sharp, almost insectile twitching of her hands and feet he thought that she must be in pain, but the mask she wore to cover her disfiguring burns revealed nothing. He considered removing the mask, but Melissa had never allowed him to see her face without it.

Then even the twitching ceased and she lay still, her body a rigid coil of limbs on the old beige carpet.

Father Fitzgerald was praying. He'd been praying the moment he heard the first scream. No answers, as yet. He leaned in close to the fallen girl, trying to see her eyes through the narrow slits of her mask.

Was she dead? Actually dead?

"Melissa?" he said, close enough to see one open eye through the eyehole, a glint of green.

Her intake of breath was so sharp, sudden and loud that the noise momentarily robbed him of his own air, and he tumbled back, bumping his head on the edge of the wooden rocking chair behind him. Her inhalation went on for too long, as though she were trying to draw all of the air in the room into her lung, but it was also a choking, constricted breath, a desperate breath, the breath of a person who'd nearly drowned. The breath of a girl whose lungs had been singed by breathing fire. Melissa didn't breathe anymore.

He slumped against the chair, pressing his back against the hard wooden seat. After that first massive inhalation, he heard her hyperventilating, each rapid breath making the outline of her ribs rise and fall, straining and then relaxing against the fabric of her dress. Each individual breath had a rasping quality, a pronounced asthmatic wheeze.

Father Fitzgerald didn't know what to do. There was no doctor to call, and as much as he wanted for dignity's and comforts sake to lift her from the floor and return her to her bed, he was afraid to move her. Afraid, even, to touch her, not being sure if her posture, her breathing, the sudden operation of her scorched lungs was indicative of some biological change—a *differently* biological change. He felt like he was bearing witness to some new pathology or evolutionary shift. Was this how the dead died?

He didn't know what to do, and so he continued to pray.

Takayuki held Tawshawn the entire time until Popeye brought Karen and Mal to where they sat. Tayshawn's fingers were gripping him so tightly Tak thought he could feel them biting into the meat of his arm. But that was ridiculous, he knew, because Tak didn't feel anything.

Once you were dead, Tak thought, time was supposed to have relinquished its hold on you. No more schedules, no more ticking clocks—the end had already been reached. That was the only "benefit" zombies were supposed to realize, the release from time's tyranny. The gift of eternal patience should settle on your shoulders like a favorite comforter once you know longer had to worry that every breath you took might be your last. You were free to do whatever you wanted, even if what you wanted was to sink like a stone to the bottom of Lake Oxoboxo like Mal had done. Mal stayed down there for weeks or months at a time, contemplating… what? Tak didn't know, and Mal didn't say.

Dying had done nothing to blunt the edges of Tak's impatience, whatever the "benefits" he was supposed to receive in his condition, and the moments that he spent alone in the woods with Tayshawn felts like eons.

But then she was there, a girl made of moonlight with diamonds for eyes, and in her presence even deathless eons would not be enough time.

"Karen," he said, but Tayshawn chose that moment to scream, drowning his greeting out in a wail of pain.

Karen knelt beside them. She was wearing a damp white t-shirt and dry black sweatpants. Her feet were bare.

"I don't know… what is happening," he told her, in the spaces between Tayshawn's cries.

"I do," she said, her expression as sympathetic for him as it was for their pain-wracked friend. She laid one hand against Tayshawn's cheek and the other she placed on Tak's shoulder. Tayshawn quieted down almost immediately; Tak tried to convince himself that he felt differently as well—but that would require him feeling something. Popeye and Mal stood behind her, Mal's hulking presence blocking out the moon before he took a ponderous step to the side.

"You do?" he said.

She nodded, her platinum hair damp against her cheek. "He's… coming back."

"Back?"

She smiled at him, gripped his shoulder more tightly.

"To life. Only being alive hurts that much."

"You've… got to be… kidding me," Popeye said. "How can… that… happen?"

"I don't know."

"You… ," Tak began. "You're alive?" He'd suspected as much since she'd returned from Idaho. Karen had always been the most "animated" of the Oakvale zombies, able to speak and move with near traditionally biotic fluency, but since she'd come back she'd seemed even more so, although he could not be around her for very long without feeling like long serrated knives were stabbing him in the heart.

No, he thought. You do not feel; you feel nothing.

"Well," Karen said, her eyes searching his as she tried to read his thoughts. "I'm not quite dead."

"Why does… he sound… like he's got… worms… crawling and gnawing… in him?" Popeye said.

"He's healing," she told him. "His bones and cartilage… his cells. Look at his leg."

They looked, and Tak realized that she was right. Tayshawn' leg had been twisted terribly after being struck by the ambulance, and there'd been a deep and bloodless gash on his thigh visible through a rent in his pants. Tak peeled the edges of his jeans back so that they could see better; the wound clearly was not as long or deep, and the edges of the wound now looked gummy and wet as though the injury happened moments and not months ago. His knee looked straight.

"He's in pain," Tak said.

She nodded. She removed her hand from Tayshawn's cheek and placed her palm flat against the tear in his own.

"Healing his often painful," she said.

"This is… bullshit," Popeye said. "So death… is just a joke? Are we… all… coming back?"

"I don't know," Karen said.

"There must… be a reason… for this," Tak said, but even as he said it he doubted that there was a reason; nothing seemed to have real reasons. He didn't understand either why he was filled with a sudden urge to shove Tayshawn away from him like he was contagious with a disease that Tak was in danger of being infected with. Whatever "Back to Life" virus his friend had, he didn't want it.

He tried also to shrink away from Karen's caressing hand, his movement made more awkward by Tayshawn's clinging weight. She seemed to understand, and withdrew.

"If we're going to solve that mystery," she said. "Maybe what we should be asking is, why Tayshawn? Why now?"

Cooper Wilson visited Melissa nearly every day, and Father Fitzgerald felt his own spirits lift when he saw the ungainly dead boy crossing the basement. He stopped short at the doorway of Melissa's room, agape, watching her breathe, until the priest invited him to help him.

Together they lifted Melissa up and placed her on the bed after Father Fitzgerald tried to explain what had happened. As he got his hands under her shoulders, Father Fitzgerald thought that she must have every muscle in her body clenched.

"She's… breathing," Cooper said. He looked and sounded terrified, as much as a dead boy can look and sound terrified.

"And she screams, too," Father said, drawing the blankets up to her shoulders once she was settled on the bed. "Like a banshee."

"You don't… understand," Cooper said. "She breathed… fire… when she… died. She… burned from… the inside. There's no way… her face…" He trailed off, looking down at his friend. He reached out and straightened her mask with as gentle a touch as he could manage.

"I do understand," Father Fitzgerald said. "But she's breathing now. Or approximating breathing, I'm not sure."

"I don't… get it."

"I don't either, Cooper," he said, frowning. He thought that her breathing was becoming more labored, that she was working harder to make her lungs work. He could hear each exhalation puffing against the hard plastic of her mask, which had two tiny holes at the nostrils but the mouth was solid, the lips sculpted and impassive.

He sighed, a small sound in contrast with the heavy, rapid rhythm of her breathing.

"Cooper," he said. "We have to take her mask off."

Cooper looked up at him. "Father… she doesn't want… anyone… to see."

"I know."

He knew why she didn't want anyone to see—because he *had* seen. He'd gone downstairs to ask her help in distributing the new missalettes in the pews, and when he'd gotten to her room she was sitting with her back to him. He said her name in the moment that she lifted the hand mirror that she'd been looking into, a mirror he didn't even know that she owned. Their eyes met in the glass and he saw, only for the briefest of moments, what the fire had done to her. He'd seen the charred, lipless face, the flesh melted and then fused like cooled candlewax, her features mottled and blurred. She brought the mirror down swiftly, and he'd managed not to gasp, but for days afterward all he could think is that if he was standing at the very gates of hell that the face staring back at him would look just like hers.

"We shouldn't…"

"I know, Cooper," he said. "But she's breathing, or trying to, and the mask is in the way. Whatever is happening to her, I think we should try and help her breathe."

Cooper touched his sleeve.

"Father," he said. "She's… *melted.*"

"I know, Cooper."

"I… I should do… it," the dead boy said. "You… shouldn't see."

Father Fitzgerald felt a hitch at the back of his throat. Cooper, in his own way, was trying to be brave in the face of his oldest friend's—maybe his only friend's—mysterious trauma, and he was trying to spare him the shock of Melissa's disfigurement. He gripped the boy's shoulder.

"I've seen, Cooper. Let's do it together."

They leaned over Melissa. Her short, raspy breaths seemed to accelerate.

"Melissa," Father Fitzgerald said, "we're going to remove your wig."

He looked at Cooper, who was silent as he gently cradled his friend's head, lifting it slightly off the pillow. Father got one of his hands in the bushy, copper hair, his fingers locating the seam of the wig and then slowly peeling it back.

"Father!" Cooper said. Instead of a scarred, ruined scalp they instead saw smooth white skin covered by a light cover of downy copper stubble. "She has… hair!"

The dead boy in his excitement ran his fingertips over her scalp.

"Cooper, a little respect," he said, gently. He found the black elastic ribbon that secured her mask to her face.

"Melissa," he said. "We're going to remove your mask. I hope you will understand and forgive us for this invasion of your privacy. We don't understand what is happening to you, and we care about you. We love you. We think that you are trying to breathe and we are afraid the mask is making things more difficult for you."

He looked at Cooper, as though to invite him to share any additional words of wisdom or reassurance.

"Don't worry," he started. "I'll always… be uglier… than you."

Father Fitzgerald had to laugh. "Lift her head a little higher," he said, feeling the increased tension of the elastic band as he lifted the mask gently away from her face with his other hand. He could feel the mask gradually breaking contact with her skin. With a final tug the mask came away in his hand.

This time, Father Fitzgerald couldn't help but gasp.

The sun rose. Sometime in the pit of the moonlit morning Tayshawn had stopped screaming, and Popeye was getting bored watching him just lie there in the brambles. He walked around Mal, who hadn't moved a muscle since catching up with them. Popeye scrutinized him like he was studying a statue, making note of the puckered outline of two bullet holes in his broad, muscular back and of the precise shades of slime and algae staining his shirt. He couldn't understand why everyone was so interested in Karen when Mal was with them. Mal ignored him—Mal ignored everything but Karen.

Tayshawn finally spoke. He was sitting up unassisted beside Takayuki, both leaning against the stone wall. Popeye was glad that they'd broken their awkward embrace because it triggered inside of him a different type of pain than what Tayshawn had been feeling.

"This is crazy," Tayshawn was saying. "I can bend… my arm."

He demonstrated, bending his arm, rotating his forearm, flexing his hand. Popeye knew it had been broken; up until that morning it had been dangling uselessly at his side.

"Are you still in pain?" Karen asked him.

"I hurt… all over," he said, with just a little hitch in his voice. "Like I've been… tumble dried."

He grinned, and his smile was only a little lopsided.

"I feel great."

Karen put her hand flat on his chest. She was always touching people, Popeye thought, his own mouth curling up in a forced sneer that was sure to be considerably less natural than the expression Tayshawn wore.

"I can feel your heart beating," she said.

Tayshawn's grin faltered as he placed his own hand beside hers.

"It's a little slow," she said. "A little quiet. But it is definitely beating."

His eyes widened, and then he blinked. Actually blinked.

"I'm… alive," he whispered. "Holy shit. I'm… alive."

"Congratulations," Tak said, giving him a hard slap on the shoulder. Karen giggled. Mal remained motionless.

Popeye couldn't understand why he felt so uneasy.

I should be happy, he thought. Wasn't this a happy occasion?

Father Fitzgerald couldn't sleep, and Cooper had no need to, so they sat at Melissa's bedside listening to her breathe throughout the night, he in the rocker, Cooper in one of those crippling folding chairs that the parishioners used for bingo nights and socials.

His tears had dried on his cheeks but threatened to begin flowing again at any moment.

A miracle, he thought. I have witnessed a miracle.

He'd gasped after removing the mask, not because of her horrific "melted candlewax" appearance, because the skin beneath the mask was smooth and creamy white-pink, like that of a newborn. The ravages of the fire had been smoothed away, the putty nose remolded, the ruined lips regrown soft and full.

She was beautiful.

"I want… to cry," Cooper had whispered, as he'd lowered her head back to the pillow. "I can't cry."

They'd stepped back, taking their seats.

"I'll cry for both of us," Father Fitzgerald had said, for he was already welling up. "For all of us."

They sat, waiting patiently for the day, the hour, the very second that their sleeping princess would awaken.

"I'm… walking," Tayshawn said. "walking!"

On cue he stumbled, stubbing the toe of his sneaker on an exposed root, nearly taking a pratfall on the grassy trail.

"Ow!" he said. "That… hurt!"

"You'll have to… be careful now," Tak said. "No more games of… switchblade catch… for you."

"Is this… is this what it is like… for you, Karen?" he said.

"Hard to say," she said. "Is anyone's experience of life the same? Or even similar?"

Popeye dropped back, stifling yet another groan of disgust and slowing enough that ponderous Mal could almost catch up. He was so sick of Karen's faux cryptic Zen platitudes that he could roll his eyes right out of his head if he could.

He was still unsettled, and Tayshawn's obvious enthusiasm wasn't helping him feel any differently. It wasn't jealousy at the core, at least not jealousy at having symptoms of life. He liked being dead and no living person could modify their body to the extent that he modified his—his was a unique art. Maybe it had more to do with the emotions—those slippery, indefinable things—that he saw on display. Tayshawn's elation, Karen's empathy, the devotion that Tak and Mal had for her. Was it was the combination of seeing so many things that he could never participate in, thrust right in his dead face?

Or maybe, he thought, furtively scanning the perimeter of the trees just as they entered the clearing that bordered the backyard of the Haunted House, he could feel the eye of the God that he no longer believed in glancing in his direction.

He'd stopped walking, he realized. Tayshawn was practically skipping, looking back over his shoulder at Tak, his smile wide, full of—dare Popeye say it—life. Beside him, Karen said something Popeye didn't catch but whatever it was it made Tak shake his head in disagreement. Even Mal had plowed ahead, muscles in his broad back tensing as he lifted his arm to wave to an old friend peering down at them from an upstairs window in the Haunted House.

Then the first of many shots rang out, and with he and his friends so close to the relative safety of their home.

PASSING SWIFTLY

A BREAK MY HEART 1,000 TIMES STORY

"WE'RE GOING TO see the ghost," Gina said. She leaned in the doorframe of their dorm room with her hands stuffed down the front pockets of her sweats. "You should come with us."

Darvina looked up from her well-worn copy of *To the Lighthouse*. She had decided twenty pages ago that this was a book that all English majors were required to read but none wanted to keep. Regardless, her paper was due on Friday.

"You're joking, right?"

Gina laughed, pleased by her own unpredictability. "Serious. We're talking authentic haunting, Darvy."

Darvina ran her tongue over her front teeth and tapped her long fingers on the battered cover of her book. Gina was difficult to room with sometimes. She was from a small town far outside the ground zero of the Event so that ghosts were still as much of a novelty to her as they were to Darvina. Darvina herself was from a city even further away and light years away culturally, and their school was also on the outer edges of the "ectoplasmic radius" of the Event, so campus ghosts were a rarity. Gina liked her Physical

Therapy class and she liked to have fun. Darvina also liked to have fun but her definition of what constituted fun differed greatly.

She deflected most of Gina's invitations to the various social gatherings of collegiate life—the rallies, the games, the keggers, the multiform atrocities of Greek Week—with a shield of thesis-length papers and escarpments of thick trade paperback books stacked at the corners of her desk. Two semesters was a long stretch in a young life and she wanted to get along with Gina, but she found the parade of invitations—and her refusal to accept any of them—very tiring.

Darvina tried to bridge the gap by inviting Gina to independent film screenings at the student union and to her poetry professors' reading at The Sad Café. Gina declined with raised eyebrows and pursed lips. Those pursed lips made Darvina realize it wasn't just their definition of fun that differed, but really their definition of what college, and therefore life, was all about.

Gina picked a long auburn hair off the front of her sweatshirt. "Come on, Darvy," she said. She waved with flickering fingers at someone down the hall. "The White Lady of Sprague Hall only comes once a year, don't miss your chance."

Darvina stopped tapping to listen to the spooky moans Gina closed her pitch with. She and Gina needed to get along this year and Gina, at least, was trying. Even if she never became the lifelong friend that Darvina secretly longed for, they had to at least get by until second semester when students began to wash out and some vacancies began to open up in the overcrowded dorms.

"The White Lady of Sprague, huh?" she said. "I guess Virginia can wait."

"Great!" Gina said, with real feeling.

They left with two girls from down the hall, a quiet yet giggly redhead Darvina knew only as Colleen and Colleen's roommate Grace McDonough. Grace was in Darvina's English 101 class. The three girls wore either jeans or sweatpants and all three had sweatshirts that featured the school's canine mascot in different action poses. Darvina wore black slacks and a light royal blue jacket over her blouse as proof against the slight October chill. She tried not to feel self-conscious about the way she was dressed, wondering why American students with money wanted to dress like they didn't have any. She didn't own any clothing bearing the school's mascot.

Grace's sweater was large and hooded, and when the girls were outside and walking along the trim green fields of campus she withdrew a pint bottle of Peppermint schnapps from the wide pocket beneath the fiercely grinning mascot embossed in white across her chest. She opened the bottle, which was half empty, and took a mouthful.

Darvina's heart was pounding when Colleen handed her the bottle. She tilted it back and allowed a tiny sip to pass her tight lips, her dark eyes scanning the horizon for authority figures itching to expel her and her friends. The schnapps wasn't her first taste of alcohol, but it was pretty close. It was like a burning candy at the back of her throat, a taste at once sticky, sweet, and warm. She muffled a cough with the back of her hand as she handed the bottle over to Gina to complete the cycle.

"Yay, Darvvy!" Gina said.

Colleen and Grace joined in the applause and Darvina felt her cheeks flush, either from the schnapps or the attention or an alchemical mix of both. She watched, with something like wonder, as Gina's throat moved in a long swallow, and when the bottle returned to her for a second trip she almost dared a full mouthful.

Darvina waited until Gina was drinking again to ask the other girls when the ghost began appearing.

"Estelle jumped thirty-one years ago," Grace replied.

"She killed herself?

Grace seemed not to hear her. She took another bracer before continuing.

"Estelle Marie Johnston jumped to her death forty-nine years ago today. And she has been jumping every year on this day, the anniversary of her death. Even before the Event, supposedly."

"Poor Estelle," Colleen added, giggling. She stumbled over an invisible root.

"Why did she jump?"

Gina tried to hand the bottle back to Darvina, who shook her head. Gina didn't seem to mind, so Darvina assumed that she had passed whatever unspoken initiation that her roommate had been testing her with.

"It was over a boy," Gina said, taking a second sip.

Grace nodded, her long hair swaying before her eyes. "They say he was killed in Vietnam."

Colleen was having difficulty keeping up with the long-legged, purposeful pace that Grace was setting.

"And I heard she was pregnant with his child."

"Really? I hadn't heard that."

"It's true, Grace," she said, skipping to catch up. "Her unborn child died with her."

"I thought she was on LSD."

"She was pregnant and on LSD," Colleen replied, "and her boyfriend died in Vietnam."

Darvina had a dozen questions she wanted to ask as they began crossing the mall in front of the student union. The mall was criss-crossed with narrow concrete walkways, and Darvina imagined a long parade of ghosts ambling along the paths. Sad lovers, hopeless failures, young people doomed to breathe their last on foreign soil or in twisted car wrecks. They would cross the miles and end up here, either the place of their greatest joys or most dismal sadness. She could almost see them, flickering like candles in the light autumnal wind.

The buildings on this side of campus were older than where she lived, devoid of the curves, flourishes, and aluminum railings that typified the architecture there. They were stately brick and shaped concrete, and sat like the last sentinels in a forgotten outpost, guarding against the swift but less substantial era approaching. Darvina zippered her jacket as the chill began to seep to her skin.

Most of her class time was spent in these older structures, and she much preferred them to the newer buildings. There was a weight and solidity to the old buildings that she felt she could rely on. The new buildings always seemed to be in need of some sudden and major renovation, but if her father had his way she would be spending her time there, where math and sciences held sway. Daddy wanted her to be a doctor like his brother Ravi, but Darvina did not have the interest. Some people were children of the future and others, like herself, were children of the past.

She caught the lingering traces of cigarette smoke, etched onto the wind perhaps by some wayward philosophy student pondering some insoluble conundrum of the human condition. Why has man fallen? How can there be a God in a world wracked with pain? Why does someone always take the last piece of cherry pie right after I decide I want it?

There were other students crossing the mall in twos and threes, making the pilgrimage towards Sprague Hall as though following the light of the brightest nighttime star. Grace dropped the empty bottle of schnapps in a metal trash bin where it landed with a heavy, final thud.

"I hope someone brought beer," she said, the suggestion of a slur in her speech.

She needn't have worried. There were about fifty people on

the lawn in front of Sprague Hall. A good portion of their number was clustered around a keg sitting on a lawn chair. Someone had thrown a dark gray wool blanket over the apparatus in some half-hearted and unsuccessful attempt at camouflage.

"Nine fifty three," Grace said, looking at the time displayed in luminous blue on her cell phone. "Exactly a half hour to go until show time."

"Good," Colleen said, "enough time for some drinks."

She skipped over to the keg, stepping lithely between two big and bleary looking young men standing watch beside on either side.

Darvina watched her smile, taking a cup offered by one of them, who then set himself to vigorously priming the pump. She was amazed at how few sips of alcohol it took for Colleen to transform from shy giggler to gregarious giggler. Darvina still felt the swallow she had taken burning in her stomach and throat and she wondered why she wasn't experiencing the same magical transformation. Watching Colleen lean forward towards the boy she wondered if she would ever feel transformed in such a way.

Another boy walked over and hugged Gina from behind, lifting her up bodily and balancing her on his chest.

Gina shrieked. Once back on Earth, she gave her attacker a playful slap, introducing him as "Cole, one of the many jerks in my Stats class." She introduced Darvina as "Darvy" and when their eyes met Darvina felt the lingering weight of his stare.

"Hi there, Darvy," he said, offering her a sober handshake, which Darvina guessed was probably the only sober thing about him. "You here to see poor Stella jump?"

The question threw her, for in the festive social whirl she had forgotten that she had crossed campus with the intention of seeing a ghost. A haunt, a specter, a banshee, a revenant. The White Lady of Sprague. Her eyes moved from his to take in Sprague Hall, a long, proper brick building whose only visible fault was its proximity to the street. Like many of the buildings she attended classes in, as well as the many shaded stone buildings depicted within the stanzas and square paragraphs of her Oxford Introduction to Romantic Literature, it was easy to imagine Sprague Hall as being haunted.

"I guess so," she said.

Cole's friends shouldered in around them. They carried extra cups of beer which they quickly dispersed to Gina and Grace and any other girl that looked their way.

"Poor Stella," Cole said, "such a tragic end."

The way he looked at her activated the schnapps inside her belly, and when one of Cole's excitable friends pressed a cup of cold beer into her hand she took a quick sip. Cole's brown eyes were warm and friendly beneath the brim of his baseball cap.

Darvina took another sip. "Where did she—Stella—jump from?"

Cole pointed towards the third floor window above the west entrance door.

Sprague Hall's third story was shaded by a crenellated roof of slate shingles that slanted down in varying shades of gray and green. Darvina had desperately wanted to live on this side of campus, favoring Sprague and the other east campus dormitories over their more modern counterparts where she ended up, but it was a banner year for admissions and she counted herself lucky to have reserved a room at all.

Sprague sprawled before the main street like a tired cat. The light traffic moved along at a fair clip but seemed to slow on passing the building. There was a large arched doorway in the center of the building, one flanked by two short Doric columns and a low stone overhang. Two smaller entrances faced the street, though neither of these had columns or an overhang. The growing crowd spread in a scatter plot around the west entrance.

"She jumped from there," he said. "The third floor window."

"Oh."

The window was closed, the hallway beyond dark. The whole floor looked dark, although lamps were blazing on the lower floors, their light passing through windows left open a crack to cool the steam heated rooms.

"A few years ago some bright eyes left Estelle's window open," he said. "That was the only year she didn't come."

"That window doesn't look very high up."

"Doesn't need to be," he said. "You'll see. Can I get you another beer?"

She looked into her plastic cup, which had a thin foamy layer of amber fluid lining the bottom.

"I guess so."

"Great," he said, taking her by the arm. "Let's go."

Darvy risked a look over her shoulder. Gina, sandwiched between two of Cole's cronies vying for her attention, removed Darvy's guilt by flashing a thumbs' up and smile. Darvy wasn't sure which made her happier—Cole's interest or Gina's approval.

She stood with Cole in the beer line, which had grown in the five minutes or so they had been getting acquainted. He asked her where she was from and they shared a laugh as her answer was drowned out by a passing car full of blaring music and frat guys.

"Stella!" one bellowed, Brando-esque, leaning out the window so that he was nearly parallel with the street.

"There must be a hundred people here," she said after the diversion passed. She didn't want to talk about herself and the beer and Cole's eyes were working on her in some mysterious way that she didn't trust. *I'm Darvy, and I like horses and Victorian poetry. I am learning what constitutes fun.*

"They've had it on the news before," Cole said, "but she never shows up on tape or film."

"You know a lot about it," she said, noticing video recorders circulating through the crowd. One was held steadily aloft by the philosophy student of her imagination, an Ichabod thin young man with pale gray skin and a mound of unkempt curly black hair.

"I saw it when I was a freshman, and again last year," he said. "I've never seen anything like it. It's amazing. I can't imagine living in one of those places where they are everywhere."

"It." She'd been thinking of this ghost, this poor pregnant drug suicide Estelle, or Stella, as "she". Sometime during her talk with Cole, Estelle became "it". Darvina sipped her beer.

A festival atmosphere settled over the ghost watchers, who laughed and huddled under the dull glow thrown from the building and the yellow disc of moon above. Colleen was having a difficult time standing, or standing still, at least. She leaned on the boy beside her, a boy who was diligent about making sure her cup was never empty. Gina and Grace could be heard laughing shrill laughter from within the center of a ring of fraternity pledges. There were even a number of older people mixed in with the students, most of whom also had drinks in their hands. Darvina thought she spotted Dr. Lynch, her sociology professor, hovering around the perimeter that formed about five feet from the worn stone steps leading to the west entrance.

The atmosphere had a buoyancy and energy all its own, humming and throbbing with a kinetic vibration that made Darvina feel that just about anything could happen. She could drink a couple beers. She could have a conversation with a boy, maybe do a little dance and buy a big hooded sweatshirt with a doggy on the front. Maybe then the night would end with a kiss, her first kiss since Jeff Steinman kissed her at the eighth grade dance. Anything could happen. Anything but a ghost.

"I'm planning on entering the school of business," Cole was

saying, "I think my GPA is good enough. I'll probably go for an MBA in finance or management, I'm not sure."

Darvina nodded and smiled. She looked up at the darkened window.

One of Cole's friends, a chubby bald kid who was the dark horse in the competition for Gina's favor, slumped against Cole, spilling his drink and calling him names that brought the warm flush back to Darvina's cheeks.

"You drunk," Cole said, giving his friend a gentle shove which sent him pinballing back into the crowd. Cole shook his head and drained his beer in one smooth motion. Darvina thought he was so much more self-assured than the rest of the boys attempting to garner attention with loud voices, pratfalls and other displays of gross physicality. Cole's warm brown eyes projected a focus and composure she found intriguing despite the glossy redness that crept in at the corners and deepened with each swallow he took from his cup.

The crowd's laughter trailed off like a balloon from a child's hand and the people began to flow and tighten near the perimeter. All turned towards the window.

"Is it that time already?" he whispered. "I completely lost track."

Darvina nodded. She too had forgotten why she had come.

All eyes were watching the third floor window. Some wag called out for Stella but was quickly silenced by hisses and a hard slap.

"That window is at the end of the third floor hallway," Cole told her, leaning close so that she could feel his warm, beery breath on her ear. "She shows up better with the lights out."

Darvina waited for a punch line but no one in the crowd provided one. She expected some lame stunt, some pathetic initiation carried out year to year by the pledges seeking entrance into one of the college's many fraternities.

He stared intently at the window. He put his arm around her shoulders and for the first moment since Gina had first presented the idea, Darvina felt a small thrill of fearful excitement at the pit of her stomach.

A ghost, she thought.

A pale white figure appeared at the window, all at once. It wasn't there and then it was. The crowd breathed in as one, and despite their reaction Darvina still wanted to believe it was all a hoax, that the Event had never happened and the figure would be a flung effigy wearing the colors and logos of some hated conference rival and not an actual White Lady. She wanted the pale figure above to be a lie, and in realizing this she knew she wasn't at all prepared for what she was about to see, because what the white figure did next erased all thoughts of hoaxes and pranks, beer and kisses, boys and girls.

The girl—and now that she was visible and staring through the closed window, it was clear that she was a girl—had long black hair and a baggy white nightdress. The white of her dress matched the white of her skin and the white of her lips. All was white; only her hair and the equally black sockets where eyes should have been stood out against her softly luminescent aura.

She held her hands out, palms up, and her long white fingers curled. She raised her arms as though lifting the window but the window did not move. Her hooked fingers slid through the frame and then the glass as easily as trailing through water, but there was no ripple.

Darvina held her breath and Cole drew her closer. She was frightened; the seed of fear that drifted in her stomach took root and blossomed into a palpable adrenal terror. She watched the ghost withdraw her hands from the window, seeming to draw a sharp breath as her hair nightdress billowed behind her, born aloft not by wind but by the memory of wind. Tonight's breeze was light but whatever portal the ghost opened had held back a gale, one that whipped back her spectral dress and pressed it against her body.

The ghost looked down, her hair blowing back from her anguished face. At them, Darvina thought. At her. The downward curl of thin white lips and the absence of eyes gave the ghost an expression so forlorn, so full of sorrow, that Darvina felt her heart crack and break. She could only conceptualize that expression as one of utter desolation, and in staring into those bottomless sockets she knew that she would never escape the insistent tug they exerted. The message they conveyed was clear: *Look at me. Look upon my pain.*

That was when the chanting began.

Cole was the one who began the chant, and he was soon joined by his friend, the drunken bald one. Those manning the keg joined in, shouting. The chant grew in depth and volume from the moment it began until all but two—Darvina and the ghost herself—were chanting.

"Jump! Jump! Jump!"

Darvina took her eyes off the ghost. Gina and Grace and their new friends were shouting up at the window, their faces red and their fists pumping, their cries taking shape in puffs of vapor from their mouths and adding to the noise that hit like a hammer blow to Darvina's ears.

The figure in the window leaned forward and she—Estelle—passed through the pane so that she stood out in bas relief from the glass. The darkness where her eyes had been was like exploded stars as she gazed down at the crowd with bottomless sadness.

"Jump! Jump! Jump!"

Cole was shouting for the ghost to recommit suicide with a fervor that frightened Darvina. He thrust his half empty cup at the window as spit flew from his mouth. The arm he'd flung around her shoulders tightened.

The ghost climbed up on the windowsill, her softly glowing body passing easily through the metal and brick. She looked at Darvina and then she jumped, her arms drawn to her sides and her head down. The crowd went wild.

Darvina caught the impressions of her descent in glimpses through the sudden violent surging of the crowd. The images came in slow motion, looping and repeating in Darvina's eyes as the ghost fell. The stillness of the ice white body as it fell perpendicular to the ground, like a sculpture cast out of heaven and hurled to the waiting earth below. A vision of skinny white legs and tiny bare feet, the gossamer dress catching like tissue in the wind, jet black hair trailing like the tail of a dark comet.

The mob's alcohol-fueled mayhem reached a crescendo as Estelle struck the stone steps head first, her gauzy body flying apart and away in a rolling white fog that dissipated in the soft wind. Then there was nothing left of Estelle save her name being chanted by the crowd calling for her to repeat her death.

Darvina shrugged off Cole's arm, which he'd looped around her neck like a yoke. His wide red mouth was flecked with foam as he grabbed at her. Recoiling, she pushed her way through the crowd, ignoring Gina's shrieking laughter, ignoring Colleen and the drunken boy whose hand was groping down the front of her sweatpants. She squeezed through the frenzied mob, the chant ringing in her ears disintegrating into an insane cacophony of random shouts and screams, even as Estelle herself disintegrated into indiscriminate misty atoms.

Darvina wanted to scream. She wanted to scrub the sights and sounds from her eyes, ears and mind. *A difference in what college, and therefore life, was all about.* And death; so many of their definitions were different than hers. She wanted to scream and the mob around Sprague Hall *was* screaming; they were screaming *burn witch burn* and *jump Darvy jump* and she could never be a doctor and she would go this way as well no matter how square and solid the buildings and books she hid inside appeared.

She broke away from the crowd and ran into the street where the cars were passing swiftly, like soulless celestial bodies moving through an empty nighttime sky.

ACKNOWLEDGEMENTS

Al Zuckerman, everyone on the Wall, all of the readers who engaged with Tommy & the gang at Mysocalledundeath.com, the team at Damonza for formatting and the great covers, Dr. Bill Hughes, Dr. Sam George, Christian and the Rosedales, Catherine Onder, Mark Vanase for the gift of my first e-reader, Douglas Clegg and Matt Schwartz for their insights and advice on electronic publishing, Mathew Dow Smith, and to Kim, Kayleigh and Cormac.

www.ingramcontent.com/pod-product-compliance
Lightning Source LLC
Chambersburg PA
CBHW030532270626
47155CB00024B/2801
9780997294262